Theo

AMANDA PROWSE is the author of seventeen novels including the number 1 bestsellers *What Have I Done?*, *Perfect Daughter* and *My Husband's Wife*. Her books have sold millions of copies worldwide, and she is published in dozens of languages.

Amanda lives in the West Country with her husband and two sons.

www.amandaprowse.org

ALSO BY AMANDA PROWSE

Novels

Poppy Day
What Have I Done?
Clover's Child
A Little Love
Will You Remember Me?
Christmas For One
A Mother's Story
Perfect Daughter
Three and a Half Heartbeats
The Second Chance Café
Another Love
My Husband's Wife
The Food of Love
The Idea of You
The Art of Hiding
Anna

Short Stories

Something Quite Beautiful
The Game
A Christmas Wish
Ten Pound Ticket
Imogen's Baby
Miss Potterton's Birthday Tea

One Love,
Two Stories

Theo

Amanda Prowse

First published in the UK in 2018 by Head of Zeus Ltd

This is a work of fiction. All characters, organizations,
and events portrayed in this novel are either products of
the author's imagination or are used fictitiously.

9 7 5 3 1 2 4 6 8

A catalogue record for this book is available from
the British Library.

ISBN (FTPB): 9781788542104
ISBN (E): 9781788542050

Typeset by Adrian McLaughlin

Printed and bound in Great Britain by
CPI Group (UK) Ltd, Croydon CRO 4YY

Head of Zeus Ltd
First Floor East
5–8 Hardwick Street
London EC1R 4RG

WWW.HEADOFZEUS.COM

I would like to dedicate both *Anna* and *Theo* to Mr Tim Binding. Without Tim's words of encouragement and advice these books would not have seen the light of day. There are times when everyone needs someone to take them by the shoulders and gently steer them back on course.

Thank you Tim.

Thank you.

Anna and *Theo* are for you.

I did it.

X

One

1974

Theo felt the swirl of nausea in the pit of his stomach. He swallowed and looked to his right, along the length of the lower playing field, calculating how long it would take to run back to the safety of the building should the need arise. He knew that Mr Beckett, his housemaster, would be watching from his study, peering through the wide bow window and rocking on his heels with his hands behind his back. He pictured him staring, stern faced, monitoring his every move. 'You go immediately!' he'd said angrily. 'And you undertake the task assigned to you. And I want you to think, boy, think about what you have done! Yours is not the behaviour of a Theobald's boy! And I won't tolerate it, do you hear?'

And Theo had gone immediately, trying to ignore the fear that was making him shake and the sting of tears that threatened, knowing that neither would help the situation. He stared at the dark, weatherworn patina of the wooden door in front of him. Even the thought of making contact with the infamous man in the crooked cottage made his heart race fit to burst through his ribs. He'd heard terrible stories about the cranky ogre that lived within. Theo could only take small breaths now and his skin pulsed over his breastbone. Raising his pale hand into a tight fist, he held it in front of his face and closed his eyes before bringing it to the oak front door, tapping once, twice and immediately taking a step back. The wind licked the nervous sweat on his top lip. It was cold.

There was an unnerving silence while his mind raced at what he should do if there was no reply. He knew Mr Beckett wouldn't believe him and the prospect of further punishment made his stomach churn.

Finally, a head of wiry grey hair bobbed into view through the dusty little glass security pane.

Theo swallowed.

'Who are you?' the man asked sternly as he yanked open the door and looked down at him.

'I'm… I'm Theodore Montgomery, sir.' He spoke with difficulty. His tongue seemed glued to the dry roof of his mouth. His voice was barely more than a squeak.

'Theodore Montgomery?'

'Yes, sir.' Theo gulped, noting the man's soft Dorset accent and the fact that he was not an ogre, certainly not in stature. But he did look cranky. His mouth was unsmiling and he had piercing blue eyes and a steady stare.

'Now there's a name if ever I heard one. And how old are you?'

'I'm… I'm seven, sir.'

'Seven. I see. What house are you in – is that a Theobald's tie?' The man narrowed his eyes.

'Theobald's, yes, sir.'

'So you are Theodore from Theobald's?'

'Yes, sir.'

'Well, that's some coincidence.'

Theo stared at the man, not sure if it would be the right thing to correct him and tell him that, actually, it was no coincidence.

The man nodded, looking briefly into the middle distance, as if this might mean something. 'And you are here for MEDS?'

'Yes, sir.' He tried to keep the warble from his voice; it was his first time in 'Marshall's Extra Duties', a punishment that fell somewhere between detention and corporal punishment. He was grateful to have avoided the sting of his housemaster's cane, at least.

'Is this your first time?'

The man, who smelt of earth and chemicals, lifted his chin and seemed to be looking at him through his large, hairy nostrils. They reminded Theo of a gun barrel, but one with grey sprigs sprouting from it. The man was old and looked more like a farmer than a master, the kind of person he'd seen up in Scotland when his father had taken him grouse shooting on the glorious twelfth. He shuddered at the memory of that weekend, having found nothing glorious about it. He hadn't liked it, not at all, and was still ashamed of how he'd cried at the sight of the birds' beautiful mottled plumage lying limply in the gundog's mouth. His father had been less than impressed, banning him from the shoot the next day. Instead, he'd had to sit in the car for eight hours with just a tartan-patterned flask of tea and a single stale bun. There'd been no facilities, so he had to tinkle on the grass verge. It was a chilly day and his shaky aim had meant he'd sprinkled his own shoes. Thankfully, they'd dried out by the time his father returned.

'Yes, sir.' He nodded, sniffing to halt the coming tears.

'Well, for a start, you can stop calling me "sir". I'm not a teacher. I'm part groundsman and part gamekeeper. My name is Mr Porter. Got it?'

'Yes, sir. Mr Porter, sir.'

Mr Porter placed his knuckles on the waist of his worn tweed jacket and looked Theo up and down. 'You're a skinny thing, reckon you're up to picking litter?'

Theo nodded vigorously. 'Yes, sir. I... I think so, sir. I've never done it before.'

'Don't you worry about that, it's as simple as falling off a log. You ever fallen off a log, Mr Montgomery?'

'No, sir.'

'It's Mr Porter.'

'Yes! Sorry...' Theo blinked. 'Mr Porter, sir.'

Mr Porter shook his head in a way that was familiar to Theo, a gesture that managed to convey both disappointment and irritation. Again, an image of his father flashed into his head. Theo offered up a silent plea that Peregrine James Montgomery the Third, Perry to his friends, would not get to hear about this latest misdemeanour. Theo had been a Vaizey College boy for a little over three weeks. His father had been not only head of Theobald's House, but also captain of the cricket and rugby teams, earning his colours in his first term. His were big shoes to fill. '*Don't you let me down, boy!*' His father's words rang in his ears like rolling thunder.

Mr Porter broke his chain of thought, emerging from the house with a large black bin bag and a pair of gardening gloves.

'Here, put these on.' He tossed the gloves in Theo's direction. They landed on the ground. Theo cursed his inability to catch and scrabbled for them on the path before shoving them on. They were miles too big, sitting comically askew on his tiny hands.

'Follow me.' Mr Porter marched ahead, striding with purpose. Theo noted that his feet seemed disproportionately large for his small build, though that might have been because of his sturdy green gumboots. He wore a flat cap in a different tweed to his jacket, and a burgundy muffler fastened around his neck.

'Keep up!' he called over his shoulder and Theo broke into a trot, his knees knocking beneath his long grey shorts.

They continued in silence for ten minutes, long enough for Theo's body to have warmed up and for his cheeks to have taken on a flush. It was only four in the afternoon, but dusk was already nudging the sunshine out of the way. Theo liked this time of year, when the air smelt of bonfires and at home an extra eiderdown was placed on the foot of his bed against the chill of his room.

'Here we are then,' Mr Porter barked as they neared the edge of the field and the narrow lane that led to the older girls' boarding houses.

'The wind blows a stiff northwesterly…' He used his chunky fist to draw the shape of the wind in the air. 'And the litter gets picked up like a mini tornado and carried along until it meets this hedgerow, and this is where it gets stuck.' They both stared at the hedge. Mr Porter took a breath. 'I suppose you're wondering why it matters that the odd rogue crisp packet or strip of newspaper gets lodged in the hawthorn?'

Theo hadn't been wondering any such thing. His primary concern was in fact whether or not his fingers would get snagged on the spiky branches. But he nodded anyway, because it sounded like a question.

'Well…' Mr Porter bent down and placed his gnarled hand

on the top of the hedgerow. 'Come nesting time, this rather sorry-looking tangle will be home to birds. I've seen blackbirds, dunnocks and wrens all making nests here, nice and cosy for their eggs. They need to do all they can to get the environment right for their little families to flourish. Do you think they want to get their heads caught in a crisp packet? Or read what's happening in the *News of the World*?'

'No, sir.'

'Mr Porter.'

'Sorry. No, Mr Porter, sir.'

Mr Porter blinked. 'So we have a responsibility to pick up the litter and discard it sensibly and safely. And the headmaster and Mr Beckett both see this as a good way to punish boys who break the rules.'

At the mention of Mr Beckett, his housemaster and the man responsible for school discipline, Theo's bowels shrank.

'Why are you here, Mr Montgomery? What *odious* crime did you commit?'

Theo looked down at the damp grass and his cheeks flamed with embarrassment. He didn't know what odious meant, but he could guess that it wasn't good.

'Someone, erm, someone did a pee in my pyjama bottoms.'

'Oh.' Mr Porter stopped dead and pulled his head back on his shoulders. Clearly this was not the response he'd been expecting. He looked at Theo. 'Why would someone do that?'

'I… I don't know.' Theo blinked. 'Maybe they didn't do it on purpose. Maybe they were too scared to get up in the night in the dark and so they went back to sleep even though they knew they needed the bathroom and when they woke up in the morning it was too late, it had just happened.'

'I see.' Mr Porter sighed and gave a small nod. 'How did they try and dispose of the evidence?'

'They stuffed them down the back of the big radiator in Matron's study and when the radiator came on, it was a really bad stink.'

'I bet it was.' Mr Porter sniffed the air, as if considering this. 'How did they know they were your pyjama bottoms?'

'They had my name sewn in.' Theo kept his eyes on the grass.

'Of course they did.' Mr Porter rubbed his chin sagely.

Theo kicked at the soft mud with the toe of his black shoes and scrunched up the plastic bag in his hand.

'Well,' Mr Porter began, 'if you ever find out who did it, you can tell them two things. Firstly, if they're ever going to commit another crime, best be sure not to leave any items of clothing with their nametape sewn in at the scene.'

Theo nodded. This seemed like good advice.

'And secondly,' Mr Porter said slowly and kindly, 'you can tell them from me that there is never any reason to be afraid of the dark. Everything is just as it is during the day, like a room without the light switched on, and any talk of ghosties or ghouls is poppycock. Those things don't exist. They're just the stories some boys use to frighten others.'

Theo looked up at the man with the crinkly eyes, red cheeks and hairy nostrils.

'Don't you forget that now,' he said.

'I won't, sir.'

'Mr Porter.'

'Yes. Sorry, sir.'

*

Theo made his way across the quadrangle with something of a spring in his step. He wasn't quite sure if it was down to relief that the o-d-i-o-u-s chore was now over or the fact he'd enjoyed litter-picking far more than he'd expected. There was something about Mr Porter that he liked – the man was far from scary once you got used to him. Granted, he looked a little odd with his wild hair and peculiar smell, but Theo had found his company to be the most pleasant he had experienced so far at Vaizey College. He tried to remember what the man had said about ghosts, that they didn't exist.

'Poppycock!' he said out loud, liking the word.

'What was that, Montgomery?' It was Magnus Wilson, also a Theobald's boy, two years older and a whole head taller, who called across the walkway.

'I... I'm...' Theo knew what he wanted to say, but nerves again rendered his tongue useless.

'"I'm a faggot" – it's quite easy to get out,' Wilson yelled, and the two friends either side of him, Helmsley and Dinesh, laughed. 'Where have you been? You weren't at tea,' Wilson asked in a manner that told Theo he expected an answer.

Theo felt anger and fear ball in his gut like a physical thing. He wanted to shout back, but he didn't have the confidence or the words. 'I've been doing MEDS,' he whispered.

'Ha!' Wilson laughed. 'With Porter, the old homo? Where did he take you? Up the back alley?'

His friends snickered.

Theo shook his head. 'No, but near the back alley, to... to the hedge.'

The boys' roar of laughter was deafening. Theo had no idea what was so funny and now he was embarrassed as well as frightened. He wanted to cry but knew that was the worst thing he could do. Instead, he bit the inside of his cheek until it hurt. The taste of iron and the seep of blood into his mouth was the distraction he needed.

'Heard you pissed the bed, is that right?' Wilson said.

'No! It wasn't me!' Theo kept his eyes down and willed his heart to not beat quite so loudly, for fear of them hearing it. His legs swayed, as if they belonged to someone else.

'Good afternoon, gentlemen,' Mr Beckett offered crisply as he swept by with his hands clasped behind him and the cape of his black robe billowing, bat-like, as he moved.

'Good afternoon, sir,' all four boys said with their heads lowered.

'Prep should be your main focus at this time of day, not loitering in the quadrangle. So off you go!'

The three bigger boys jostled each other as they ran off towards the dorms.

I want to go home. I just want to go home. Theo closed his eyes and concentrated on not saying the words out loud. If he did, he'd probably land himself in more trouble than he could cope with.

It was now Thursday, the day Theo longed for. This was the day each week when just before bedtime he was allowed to call home. Having waited all day in eager anticipation, he lined up outside his housemaster's study along with the other boys in his year. One by one they were called in and handed the telephone. It was, as ever, ringing by the time it was deposited in his hand, giving him less opportunity to plan what he wanted to say.

Actually, this was a lie, he knew exactly what he wanted to say, but he was more concerned about what he *could* say while under the watchful eye of Mr Beckett, or Twitcher, as he was known among the boys on account of his left eyelid, which blinked rapidly and seemingly with a will of its own.

'Perry Montgomery.'

The booming sound of his father's voice answering the call sent a stutter to Theo's throat. He wanted to be brave, wanted so badly to make his father proud, but it was hard when he was fighting back tears and what he really wanted to say was, 'Please, Daddy, let me come home! I hate it here and if you let me come back, I promise I'll be good. I'll try harder not to cry on the grouse shoot. I miss you so much! Let me come home!'

But of course he would never do this, especially not with Twitcher sitting only three feet away.

'Daddy, it's me, Theo.'

'Ah, Theo old boy!' His father sounded pleased to hear from him and this alone was enough to lift Theo's spirits while at the same time causing more annoying tears to gather. 'One second. I'll fetch your mother.'

And just like that, his father was gone.

Theo wanted to talk to him; he always wanted to talk to him. The trouble was he never had anything of interest to say, and even if he had, his father didn't have the time to hear it. He remembered summoning up his courage before walking out to the garage in the summer, determined to talk to his dad. The sight of him holding a chamois leather in his big hand, preoccupied as he buffed the paintwork on his pride and joy had left Theo flustered. 'I… I…'

'For God's sake, spit it out!' his father had yelled, and Theo had turned on his heel, embarrassed, and hotfooted it back up to the safety of his bedroom. He'd sat on his bed and stared at his tiny, sausage-like fingers, wishing that he could be grown-up with big hands like his father's, certain that when that time came, when he had hands like his dad's, he would know exactly what to say.

Today was no different. In fact, trying to think of 'chitchat', as his mother called it, was even harder with an audience. He pushed the earpiece close to his head and could hear his father's voice. He pictured him standing in the lamplit hallway as he called into the dark recesses of their grand Edwardian house. 'Stella! It's the boy on the phone!'

Theo knew his call was being timed and he cursed the silent seconds while his mother made her way to the phone. *Hurry up! Hurry up!*

Finally, he heard the rattle of her charm bracelet.

'Mummy?'

'Hello, my darling!' she breathed. 'How lovely to hear from you!' She sounded surprised and he swallowed the urge to remind her that it was Thursday, of course she was going to hear from him! But he knew that it would be a waste of time as well as a waste of words. 'What did you have for supper?' She always asked this.

'Erm, we had steak-and-kidney pie, but I picked the kidney out, although one bit got through and it was yucky.'

'Oh, Rollo, that's Daddy's favourite! Don't tell him or he'll be very jealous!' she trilled, before screaming loudly, 'Waaaagh! Oh my good God – I called you Rollo!' This was followed by a series of great gulping guffaws that lasted many seconds.

Theo waited until it passed, then whispered, 'Yes, you did.'

'Oh good Lord above!' she shrieked. 'How could I possibly have called you Rollo? I am a terror! Although that's quite funny in itself, if you think about it, as Rollo is a terrier!' She howled loudly once again.

And Theo had to admit that if time were not of the essence and if there hadn't been so much he needed to say and reassurances he needed to hear, being called by the dog's name would indeed be very funny.

Help me, Mummy! Please help me! Read my thoughts: I want to come home, I am so sad here. Please, please let me come home! Theo screwed his eyes shut and hoped that his pleas might float through the ether and reach her. He liked to think they had this psychic link that stretched all the way from his school in Dorset to the family home in Barnes.

'Darling, I'm still chuckling! I only made the slip because Rollo is on my mind. He's been a bit of a scamp, let me tell you. He got out of the garden and caused absolute havoc in Mrs Merriton's rabbit run. Created quite a stir. He was only playing, of course, but the poor rabbit looked fit to have a heart attack. I told him, "No sausages for you, naughty Rollo", and do you know, he looked at me as if he knew he'd been a bad boy. So of course that *melted* my heart and I gave him some sausage anyway, but don't tell Daddy! He says I spoil him.' She whispered the last bit.

'I won't tell Daddy.' He felt a small flicker of joy at this shared confidence.

'Anyway, very much looking forward to seeing you for exeat, only a few weeks now.'

Twitcher stood up and tapped his watch face. Time was up. Theo felt the pressure to say something, to get something across, anything! 'I saw a hedge…' He took a breath. 'Where… Where birds lay their eggs and it's very important that we don't let crisp packets gather in it or they might get their heads stuck.'

'Theo, you're such a funny little thing!'

He thought about his mum's parting words as he lay under the taut white sheets on his bed later that night. *I am a funny little thing, but I don't want to be.* He turned his face into the pillow. Unseen in the dark dorm, he was finally able to give in to the tears he'd kept at bay all day.

* * *

Theo regularly hid during lunchbreak. Not literally – there was no climbing into small spaces or standing still behind cupboard doors, although he'd considered both. No, his hiding was subtler than that. He became adept at loitering and looking purposeful, reading and rereading noticeboards slowly, as if engrossed, stooping to painstakingly tie and retie his shoelaces, or sitting endlessly in a toilet cubicle while killing precious time, willing the clock to go faster. And if he had to move on, he walked with a resoluteness to his step and an expression that suggested he had a mission on his mind. This was all very exhausting, but it was unavoidable because he had no one to talk to and nowhere to sit. Try as he might, he couldn't understand how all the boys in his house and all the girls in his form had friends who they could talk to, sit with and eat with, or even just read next to in silence. How come he didn't have one single friend?

What's wrong with me? It was this question that haunted him.

Walking across the quad, he spied Wilson and his cronies, Helmsley and Dinesh. All three were in their games kit, coming from the squash courts to the right. His heart jumped and his palms began to sweat at the prospect of an encounter. Averting his eyes, he broke into a light jog, pretending he hadn't seen them as he made his way along the field. He carried on jogging until he found himself outside the crooked cottage where Mr Porter lived. The man himself was sitting on a bench attached to a slatted table similar to the ones he'd seen in the garden of the Red Lion pub, where his parents took him sometimes for Sunday lunch when he was at home.

Theo stared at Mr Porter and hesitated, trying desperately to think of a reason for being there, uninvited, in front of his path during lunchtime.

Mr Porter looked up briefly before returning his gaze to the fiddly task that seemed to be occupying him fully. 'How good is your eyesight, Mr Montgomery?' he called out.

'It's good.' Theo glanced up the field to see if Wilson had followed and breathed a huge sigh of relief that he hadn't. His gut muscles unbunched.

'In that case, you can help me with this.'

Theo clenched and unclenched his hands, unsure whether it was okay to enter Mr Porter's garden.

'Well, come on then, lad, you can't help me from all the way down there now, can you?'

He didn't need telling twice. He walked up the short path and stopped at the table, on top of which he saw piles of small, brightly coloured feathers, shiny glass beads and thin strips of wire.

'What... What are you doing?' he asked softly, wanting to know but not wanting to be a nuisance.

'I'm making fishing flies. Do you know what they are?'

Theo shook his head and took a step closer.

'You can sit down.' Mr Porter nodded at the bench on the opposite side of the table.

Theo sat on the edge, feeling the rough texture of the untreated wood against the underside of his legs. He watched, fascinated, as Mr Porter took feathers into his nimble fingers and bound the ends with an almost invisible twine. He worked slowly and carefully, wrapping them into little bundles.

'That looks like an insect.'

Mr Porter sat back and shook his head. His expression this time was one of surprise. 'Well, I didn't realise you were so smart.'

Theo's face split into a smile. He let the compliment slip under his skin, ready to warm him on a cold night at the end of a bad day.

'That's exactly what it's meant to look like – an insect! This "fly", as we call it, bobs on top of the water and will help me catch game fish, like salmon or trout. It tricks the fish into thinking they're getting a tasty bug.'

'But really they're getting this fake bug!'

'Exactly.' Mr Porter winked.

'I've never been fishing. Apart from with a net in a rock pool, but I don't know if that counts,' Theo mumbled, wary of saying the wrong thing. 'I caught a starfish once, well, half a starfish. It was dead.'

Mr Porter shook his head sympathetically. 'Sure it counts. But what I do is very different to rock-pooling. I like nothing more than to stand on a riverbank, or in the river itself, feeling the flow of the water, and watch the sun dappling the surface with light, birds fluttering overhead – and with a flask of tea and a sandwich or two in my pack. That's where my happiness lies.' Mr Porter smiled and closed his eyes briefly, as if picturing just that.

'Do you catch many fish?' Theo found it easy to think of what to say because he was interested.

'Nope. I hardly ever catch a fish. Truth be told, I'm not as keen on the catching bit as much as the standing bit.'

'It... It...'

'Spit it out, lad!' Unlike his father, Mr Porter issued this familiar instruction in an encouraging voice and with a crinkle-eyed smile. This had the opposite effect to normal and instead of clamming up, Theo continued calmly.

'It seems like a lot of trouble to go to if you don't catch any fish – couldn't you just buy some from the shop?'

Mr Porter leant back and laughed. Slipping his fingers up under his tweed cap, he scratched at a bald patch on his head and Theo saw that the skin there was a shade or two lighter than his face. 'Well, yes, I'm sure I could buy some, but shall I let you into a little secret?'

Theo nodded.

Mr Porter looked at him and spoke levelly. 'The best thing about fishing is the stillness, the quiet. And the one thing I have learnt, possibly the most important lesson of all, is that when you're still and quiet, that's when your thoughts get ordered, when your mind sorts out all of its problems and when you're able to see most clearly. Don't ever underestimate the value of stillness.'

Theo digested his words.

Mr Porter placed his hands on his greasy lapel and turned it over to reveal a delicate turquoise-and-gold-feathered fly with a blue glass bead attached to a safety pin. He ran his fingertip over it. 'I wear this here to remind me of just that. If ever my head is too busy or the world feels like too big a place for me to find my corner in it, I run my fingers over this and it reminds me to seek out the stillness.' He looked directly at Theo. 'Do you understand what I mean by that, lad?'

Theo nodded, even though he only half understood.

'Now, if you want to help, sort these feathers into piles for me. Group them by colour.' He tapped the tabletop with his square finger.

Eager for a job, Theo swung his legs over the bench and began pulling the little feathers apart, grouping them into colour-coordinated piles. It was fiddly work.

'When did you learn to do this?' he asked in his high voice.

'In the war. I fought some of my war in Italy and that's where I learnt to fish.'

'Did you fire a gun?'

'No, we just used rods and bait same as everyone else.' Mr Porter chuckled.

'I didn't mean to fish – I meant to get the baddies.' He blinked, unsure of whether the topic was off limits, as it was with Grandpa, who'd been in a place called Burma and had, according to his parents 'had a terrible war'. This phrase intrigued him, as he couldn't picture a war that was anything but terrible.

Mr Porter paused what he was doing and stared at him. 'That's the thing, Mr Montgomery. I did my duty for King and country and would gladly do so again.' He straightened his back and tilted his chin. 'But as for "baddies", as you call them... I only saw people. People in all shapes and sizes, but people just the same. War is a terrible thing and sometimes you might think you've got home scot-free, might think you've got away with things, but you haven't. You never know what's waiting for you around the next corner or even at home. There is always a price to pay. It's as if fate waits in the wings to rip the heart out of you and it's then you realise your war will never be over.'

Mr Porter took a big breath. It was only when he continued making his fly that Theo took his cue to continue chatting.

'How did you know who the baddies were then? How did… How did you know who to shoot?' He looked up, wary of entering unchartered territory.

'As I said, I didn't do much shooting, but the enemy, if you will, were pointed out to me by my commanding officer long before I ever set foot on foreign soil and before I met a single one of them. I was told to identify them by the uniform they wore. But therein lay the problem.' Mr Porter leant in, and Theo was thrilled at the possibility that he might be sharing a secret. 'I considered my commanding officer to be a baddy. I was unsure of his judgement – he was no more than a boy himself, just a few months free of his mother's apron strings and a bit of a bully, and yet he held my fate and the fate of many others in the palm of his young hand. That made it hard for me to trust him. Whereas some of the fellas who wore a different colour uniform to me, baddies if you will, well, close up, they had similar faces to those of my mates. We were all as scared and desperate as each other.' He let this hang. 'And let me tell you this, Mr Montgomery, those that didn't make it home were mourned by their families just the same, goodies and baddies alike.'

Mr Porter gave an odd little cough and his eyes looked misty, so Theo knew it was time for quiet. And that was all right with him. He was happy to have somewhere to sit and someone to sit with, though he would have found it hard to fully explain how or why Mr Porter's garden felt like a refuge from loneliness.

The two worked in silence until the sound of the school bell echoed along the field.

'That'll be the end of lunch then,' Mr Porter muttered without lifting his eyes from his fishing flies.

Theo gave an involuntary sigh. 'I'd better go back up to school.'

'Here.' Mr Porter pulled a slim navy tube from his jacket pocket and handed it to Theo.

'What is it?'

'What does it look like?'

Theo scrutinised the object in his palm. 'A pen!'

'Ah, appearances can be deceptive! Look.' Mr Porter took the fake pen from him and twisted the lid until a beam of light shone from the nib. 'It's a torch. I thought you might be able to give it to that boy you know. The one who you thought might be afraid of the dark. You see, with this in his possession, he can get up in the night and go to the bathroom without fear and that might stop him pissing in your pyjamas.' He gave a small chuckle.

'We're... We're not allowed torches.' Theo ran his fingers over the gift. He felt torn, desperately wanting to keep it but painfully conscious that it would be contraband.

'Of course not – that's a rule I'm perfectly aware of. But that's not a torch, is it? It's a pen!' He smiled.

Theo rolled the marvellous gift in his hand. 'Yes! It's a pen.' He beamed. 'Thank you.'

'You are most welcome.'

Theo swung his legs out from under the bench and started to walk up the path. Turning back, he called over his shoulder, 'Mr Porter?'

'Yes, Mr Montgomery?

'It... It was me.'

'What was you?'

'It was me that pissed in my pyjamas and hid them behind Matron's radiator.'

Mr Porter looked startled. 'Well, I never did! But here's the thing: you never have to lie to me, and I will never lie to you, how about that? Deal?'

'Deal.' Theo twisted the pen cap and smiled at the thin stream of light that shone into his palm.

Two

Theo had just finished another unsatisfactory Thursday phone call with his mother and was making his way from Mr Beckett's study. He was in a world of his own, struggling with the latest wave of homesickness and desperate for his first exeat, when quite unexpectedly Twitcher grabbed the top of his arm, pulling him back into the room.

His housemaster bent low and spoke directly into his ear. Theo could smell his piquant breath; he tucked in his lips to avoid inhaling it.

'I have to say, I find it quite troubling that you can never think of anything informative to share with your parents, Montgomery. Listening to your weekly call is painful. Your father was head of house here! He's a good man, paying a small fortune to turn you into a Vaizey boy, and yet you don't have the courtesy to let him know how the 1st XV are doing or that the quadrangle race record was broken by Danvers only last week? These things *matter*, especially to an OVB.'

At the mention of the Old Vaizey Boys, Theo's insides curdled. His father held regular and horribly loud dinner parties for other members of this esteemed club and the deafening noise of their reunions always floated up the stairs to his room. He had spied on them through the keyhole once. They were all dressed in dinner jackets and bow ties in their old house colours, and they were banging their palms on the white tablecloth and belting out a tuneless song about port and knickers, taking it in turns to swig the dark red wine from a silver cup.

'But I think that's the problem in a nutshell.' His housemaster's booming voice pulled him back to the present. 'I don't think these things *matter* to you.'

'I... I...' Theo's mouth was having trouble catching up with his brain. This happened sometimes.

'Tell me...' Mr Beckett let go of his arm and walked towards the study window, which had an unusually good view along the field and all the way down to the crooked cottage. 'Why do you hang around with the ground staff?' His eyelid twitched as he clasped his hands behind his back.

Theo shrugged. 'I don't know, sir.'

'Let me put it another way. What is the nature of your relationship with Porter, the groundsman?'

'He... He's my friend. Sir.'

'Your friend!' Twitcher guffawed. 'Good God, man, don't you have any friends your own age?'

'No, sir.' He felt his cheeks colour at the admission.

Mr Beckett stopped dead and turned, an expression of disbelief and disdain on his face. 'None at all? Not one?'

'No, sir.' Theo's shame wrapped around him like a heavy cloak, dragging him down.

Twitcher took a deep breath and spoke over Theo's head, as if he were invisible. 'Do you know what I think when I see a boy who, in a school of over six hundred pupils, in an environment where friendships flourish on and off the sports field, and where connections are made that can last a lifetime, still finds himself on his own?'

'No, sir.'

'I think it can't possibly be the other five hundred and ninety-nine or so who are at fault. The odds are simply too high. I believe there has to be a reason for your isolation, and do you know what that reason is?' He lowered his eyes to meet Theo's.

'No, sir.'

'Weirdness.'

Mr Beckett was silent for a second, letting the horrible word with all its negative connotations sink in. 'I've seen it before and will no doubt see it again. You have a weirdness about you, Montgomery, and weirdness is something that the other pupils, in fact all humans, fear more than anything. It's like a disease and, believe me, it's contagious. That's why weirdos stick together in toxic little huddles, backs to the wall, eyes wide, waiting to see who might be picked off next.'

Theo wanted badly to cry, but doing so in front of Mr Beckett would be asking for trouble. Twitcher did not like weakness. On or off the field.

'Do you want some advice?'

'Yes, sir.' Despite his housemaster's hurtful words, Theo looked up with genuine hope, feeling a flash of excitement that there might be a cure for his toxic condition. Because what Theodore Montgomery wanted more than anything in the whole wide world was not to be weird!

He wanted a friend, a proper friend of his own age.

Mr Beckett leant in closer. Theo cocked his head so he could take in every detail of the advice that just might prove invaluable.

'Stay quiet and stay out of sight. Become invisible. Go to ground and try not to take root.'

It was a strange thing, but as Theo turned his face into his pillow that night and waited, he was surprised to find that there were no tears. It was almost as if this wounding was so deep, so visceral, that he was hurt in a place beyond tears.

I'm weird. Weird. The word tumbled around his head until sleep claimed him.

* * *

There was a burble of excitement all through the school: everyone got to go home for three whole days and they weren't due back at school until Monday. Theo had packed a day ago and now sat by his bed with his tan leather suitcase at his feet and his eyes glued to his watch, waiting for the minute hand to tick again, each cycle taking him closer to the comfort of his father's car and escape. His leg jumped and his heart raced; the moment could not come soon enough.

And then, like a vision, there she was, standing in the doorway – his mother. Her floral scent permeated the air, red lipstick shone from her pale face and her impossibly long dark eyelashes fluttered upwards. She looked… She looked beautiful. Soft, pretty and familiar in an environment that was none of those things.

'Theodore!' She giggled in her high-pitched way, which sounded to him like the tinkle of glass.

At the sight of her, his reserve disappeared and he ran into her, gripping her tightly about her waist, inhaling her smell with his head buried against her chest.

'Darling! Now that's quite a welcome. How lovely.' She patted his head before easing him away by his shoulders, turning the whole embrace into something a little embarrassing. 'Come on, Daddy's in the car. We don't want to keep him waiting, do we?'

Theo lifted his small suitcase off the ground, letting it bang against his skinny leg with every step.

'If it isn't Mrs Montgomery!' Twitcher called from his open study door in a loud, happy voice.

'Well, hello you!' she shouted back.

Theo shrank, not sure if his mother or indeed anyone was allowed to talk to his housemaster in such a fashion. Apparently she was forgiven, as Mr Beckett trotted out from behind his desk and held her in a tight hug, smiling in a way Theo hadn't seen before. He noted with a twinge of envy that their hug lasted at least twice as long as his had.

'So good to see you!' Mr Beckett beamed.

'You too, darling.' His mother gripped Twitcher's forearms with her dainty hands and stared into his face.

She called him "darling"! Theo looked over his shoulder with trepidation, checking no other boys were around to witness this. But he was the last to be collected, so he was quite safe.

'So are we seeing you at Le Mans? Tiffany has had the house redecorated apparently and is very keen for us all to go and admire it. I've been assured that the plumbing actually works now!' His mother spoke with her hand resting on Twitcher's chest; it was a gesture so intimate, it made Theo's heart race and his stomach flip. He thought he might be sick.

He wanted to hurl his suitcase to the floor and shout out, 'He's mean to me, Mummy! Don't be happy to see him! He says I'm weird, and I hate it here! I hate it! Please don't be his friend.

Be on my side!' But of course he didn't, because he was seven and he had neither the confidence nor the wisdom to know when to shout.

'Do you remember the great bathroom fiasco?' his mother continued. 'Poor Gerry, he's still mortified, by all accounts. I have this image of him running onto the veranda starkers and with a scalded bottom! I shouldn't laugh really.' She hid her mouth with her hand and laughed anyway.

'God, don't remind me. I still haven't recovered from last year!' Mr Beckett bellowed and the two laughed like old friends.

'Oh, please don't be boring, Becks, I'm counting on you. No one, but no one makes a Manhattan like you do.' His mother dipped her head and spoke with lowered lashes.

'Stella, you know that where you are concerned, flattery will get you everywhere.' He winked. The phone rang on his desk. 'Duty calls,' he shouted as he made his way back into his study. 'Love to Perry!'

'Of course. Come on, Theo.' She walked ahead and clicked her fingers.

As he skipped to heel, he wondered if once again she might have got him confused with Rollo the terrier.

He waved at his father, who'd parked the shiny dark blue Aston Martin V8 across two parking spots reserved for staff. This was another reason for Theo to feel anxious.

'Mind the paintwork!' His father winced as he approached with his suitcase. He sprang from the car, placed his lit cigarette in his mouth, popped the boot and lifted the luggage with such ease that Theo's arms seemed to weaken in protest.

His father ruffled his hair as Theo climbed into the back seat. He liked the weight of his dad's palm against his scalp and could feel its heat for a while after. The car smelt of leather, cologne and cigarettes and Theo hoped he wasn't going to be sick.

'All set?' his father asked, looking at him in the rearview mirror. His mother buckled up in the front and twisted the chunky green glass bangle on her wrist.

Theo nodded.

'God, I bloody love this building!' His father beeped the horn and whooped as they drove out onto the lane. 'Spent the best years of my life here, and when I come back, it's like coming home! I don't want to wish your life away, Theo old son, but I can't wait for you to feel like this!' He beeped the horn again.

His mother turned round and pulled a face at Theo. It made him smile, but it was a fake smile. He knew he was never going to feel anything other than hatred for the whole place.

His mother ran her arm along the back of the leather driver's seat and toyed with the lick of dark hair that curled at his father's neck. 'I saw Becks. He's moaning about last year's Le Mans hangover, sounded like he might be wimping out of the trip. Can you believe it?' she drawled, reaching into her clutch bag for her cigarettes.

'Tell him to man up! For God's sake.'

'I did, more or less. He's such a darling. He won't miss it, of course. I think he's teasing, fishing for compliments.' She lit her cigarette and in a well-practised motion flipped the gold Zippo lighter. It closed with a loud thunk.

Theo stared out of the window, watching the hedgerows whiz past. He pictured the wrens, blackbirds and dunnocks that would make them their home when the time came and hoped they wouldn't get their heads stuck in an old crisp packet or a strip of newspaper. He patted his pocket to make sure his trusty pen torch was where he could find it.

As they left Muckleford and continued along twisty Dorset lanes, heading towards London, Theo listened to his parents chatting and laughing and playfully slapping each other's hands away from the radio dial. He liked being in their company but he wondered if he should cough, remind them that he was there. Just as he was considering this, his mother turned to him.

'Have you had supper?'

Ignoring the growl of hunger in his gut, he smiled at her, not wanting to be any more trouble than he already was, interrupting their busy lives to travel down to Dorset and bring him home. 'I'm fine,' he lied.

'Thank God for that!' She giggled, resting her hand on her husband's thigh. 'I'm not sure what we have in?'

'You are a crap wife! The crappest!' his father yelled in jest.

'Don't listen to your father, Theo. I am an exceptional wife! I can't help it if cooking and food shopping and all that stuff bores me rigid.' They both laughed. 'Ooh!' She raised her index finger to indicate that an idea had occurred. 'I think I have some cheese in the fridge and a tin of crackers in the larder – that'll do. We'll make a meal of it, bottle of plonk, none for you, Theo, but some of Edith's chutney… We could even eat by candlelight!' She laughed, turning to him briefly before reaching for another cigarette.

It felt like an age before the car pulled into the gated driveway of their grand red-brick home in Barnes. No longer laughing, the three had travelled for the last hour in silence, his father gripping the steering wheel with white knuckles.

Now his father tutted as he alighted from the car. His face

was thunderous, his anger coming off him in waves. 'Out you jump,' he instructed, his tone curt and his eyes blazing.

Theo clambered out on wobbly legs. The fresh air was a welcome tonic.

'I'm very sorry, Daddy.'

'So you said, and it's not your fault, but a bit of notice would have been nice and no amount of sorrys is going to get rid of that bloody smell.'

Theo looked at the dark stain on the pale brown leather where his vomit had splashed. 'Shall I wash it for you?'

'No!' his father barked. 'For God's sake don't take a scourer, or detergent or in fact anything to the leather, you'll only make it worse.' He ran his hand through his hair.

'He's only trying to help!' his mother called across the wide bonnet.

His father pinched the bridge of his nose and Theo knew he was angry with him. The whole horrible journey home had burst the happy bubble that had filled him up all day. He'd been so excited about coming home, but now he felt nothing but awkward and embarrassed, and rather than enjoying his exeat, he was already dreading the drive back to school, knowing that the combination of cigarette smoke and winding roads might have the exact same effect on the return journey. The only thing he was dreading more than the drive back to school was arriving there.

His mother climbed the steps to the front door and as she put the key in the door he heard Rollo's bark.

'There he is! There's my baby boy!' she said in a baby voice that sent a tingle of envy through him. 'Look! It's your brother! Theo's home!' She lifted the lithe Jack Russell and waved a paw in Theo's direction.

His father jogged up the steps in his brogues, bent forward, kissed Rollo's nose and muttered something to his mum. The occasional word floated down to Theo and made his tummy hurt. 'Fucking smell... vomit!... bloody expensive... idiot!... what the fuck is wrong with him?'

Theo went inside and climbed the stairs. Ignoring the stabs of hunger, which seemed almost insignificant now, he sat on the end of his bed. The pale green and pink floral carpet he'd always hated had been vacuumed ahead of his visit, but the place was still thick with dust. The room had been decluttered. Gone was his collection of Matchbox cars, which had once filled an entire bookshelf, and his *Rupert the Bear* annuals were missing too. There was a new reading lamp, a mahogany sideboard and a flowery chair that he hadn't seen before. These items had probably been brought up from the basement, where his grandpa's furniture was stored.

He unbuckled his suitcase and pulled out his pyjamas, red-striped and edged with white piping. They smelt of school and because of that he was loath to put them on. He'd forgotten that his bedroom could be quite noisy with the traffic on the road between their house and the river and the shouts of people returning home from the pub. It would take a bit of getting used to after the quiet of Vaizey College and all that countryside.

He slipped between the cold sheets and laid his head on the flannelette pillowcase. He liked its soft bobbles; they comforted him and reminded him he was home. Curling his feet up under his bottom to try and get warm, he reached into his discarded blazer for his pen torch and, twisting it on, fired shafts of light up towards the ceiling. A thousand million particles of dust danced in the beam; he disturbed them with his fingers before settling into the dip in the mattress where the springs had gone a little slack.

'What's that you've got?' his mother asked from the doorway.

'It's my pen torch. My friend gave it to me.'

'Oh, Theo, I'm so pleased you have a friend! Well done you. Is he nice?'

'Yes,' he whispered.

'What's his name?'

'I... I don't know.'

His mother snorted her laughter. 'You don't know his name? You are a funny little thing.'

You don't need to keep saying that to me. I already know!

'I don't want to go back to school, Mummy.' He switched off his torch and toyed with the silky edge of the wool blanket.

'Yes, you do! It's a wonderful school, with wonderful opportunities for you.'

He stared at her and for the first time her full smile had the opposite effect to the one intended. Instead of reassuring him that things were okay, he knew that even though she might be listening, she didn't actually hear him, and that made him feel invisible.

'I hate it there.'

'No, you don't, not really. Everyone feels like that when they first start – ask Daddy or Uncle Maxim. Even Grandpa felt like that in his junior years! And they grew to love it, all of them. They would all say their time at Vaizey was the best time in their whole life and look at some of the amazing things they've done. And you are a Vaizey boy – it's in your blood! Goodness me, you're even named after Daddy's house.'

'I wish I wasn't named after Daddy's house. I wish I was called

John. And I don't have any real friends,' he whispered, carefully placing his torch on the bedside table.

'Well, making friends takes two, you know! You have to make the effort, put yourself out there a bit, chat!'

'What should I chat about?'

'Oh, for goodness' sake, Theo! You're being a wee bit silly! You *know* what to talk about!' She sounded irritated now. 'Sport? School subjects? Good God, the weather? Anything!' She threw her hands in the air before sweeping across the room to his bed and kissing him firmly on the forehead.

He fought the temptation to reach out and pull her to him, clinging on as if his life depended on it. Instinct told him that she might think that was a wee bit silly too.

'You're probably just tired. Things will iron out, you'll see, they always do. Now then, I need to go and let Rollo out for his night-time tinkle. Sleep well, John.' And with her delicate laugh floating in the air, she closed the door.

Theo did his best over the weekend to keep quiet and stay out of his father's sight. Every time he thought about being sick in the car, he felt like crying. This was not how he had envisaged his time at home, not at all. His parents had got their weekends in a muddle and had invited the Drewitt-Smiths over to dinner, even though it was his special Saturday night at home. While the adults squawked laughter from the dining room and popped in periodically for bottles of wine from the fridge, he sat in the kitchen with the portable TV for company. He watched *Dad's Army* when the picture wasn't too fuzzy and ate chicken pie with mashed potatoes and green beans while Rollo sat on the seat next to him. Theo petted him and fed him tiny morsels of chicken.

'You can stay here with me if you promise not to make a noise,' he whispered. Rollo laid his head on Theo's leg. 'Do you ever think about running away, Rollo? I do, but I don't know where to go. And I don't like the dark.'

It was as he lay in his bed, wide awake and staring at the ceiling while the adults screamed their laughter below, that a sad realisation came to him. He didn't want to be anywhere, not at school, not in the back of his father's car, where cigarette smoke and fast corners had made him sick, not in the cold kitchen with the fuzzy TV, where there was no one to talk to, and certainly not in this bedroom filled with antiques from his grandpa's house. And that left only one question: if he didn't feel comfortable anywhere, then where was he supposed to be?

Relieved that he'd made it back to school without vomiting, Theo knew he had to be brave. He felt sick at the prospect of not seeing his parents for another six weeks and even sicker at the thought that he'd been looking forward to the exeat for so long and now it was over. In truth, it hadn't gone as he'd hoped. He tried to quash the ache of disappointment.

As they left, his mother kissed him warmly on the forehead and hugged him too tightly; his father ruffled his hair briefly, before looking at his watch and clapping his hands together.

Theo watched the car drive away, waving until they were completely out of sight, in case they could see through the scratchy hawthorn hedge.

'Who are you waving at, homo?'

And there they were, the torturous words that marked his return. He'd been praying for a gentle easing back in, but no.

Theo whipped round to see Wilson standing with muddied knees in his hockey kit, twirling his stick in the air and catching it with one hand. He felt torn, knowing that to leave the question unanswered might invite further attacks and yet to answer without knowing fully what a homo was would leave him wide open to ridicule.

'I was waving at my... my parents.' He cursed the wobble to his bottom lip.

'My parents! Boohoo! But at least I've got old Porter the homo to keep me warm!' Wilson mimicked Theo's voice and pretended to cry.

Theo dug deep, ignoring the taunt. Recalling his mother's advice, he plucked a desperate piece of small-talk from the swirl of nerves in his stomach. 'I... I quite like hockey!'

'You *quite* like hockey? Well you'll never make a team, because you can't run with a stick and your hand–eye coordination is shit – you can't even catch a bloody ball!' Wilson jeered.

While Theo tried to remember what had come next on his mother's list of suggestions – was is the weather? – Wilson walked towards him and raised his hockey stick, making as if to strike him at close range. Theo flinched and covered his eyes, awaiting the full force of the blow. His reaction sent Wilson into fits of laughter.

'You, boy!' The bellowed words echoed off the old walls.

Theo looked up to see Mr Porter pushing a wheelbarrow full of compost along the path.

'You! Mr Wilson!' Mr Porter barked, his finger extended in Wilson's direction.

Theo's blood ran cold as Wilson slowly turned on his heel and walked back to where Mr Porter stood in his plaid shirt and corduroy trousers held up by leather braces. His sleeves were rolled above the elbow, revealing his brawny arms.

'Did I see you with a hockey stick in this area? Because that's against the rules. It should have been put away at the end of the session and I would hate to have to recommend you for a detention.'

'Then don't,' suggested Wilson calmly.

Theo didn't recognise the voice Mr Porter used. If his usual voice was like warm, soft toffee, this one was like cold, sharp glass.

'Here's the thing, Mr Wilson. You need to be very careful that you respect everyone in your path, as you never know where they'll pop up again. And, trust me, the path we walk is long and winding.'

Wilson smirked. 'Got it – long and winding.' He nodded and turned back to walk across the quad.

'Did he hurt you?'

Theo shook his head.

'Did you have a good exeat?'

Theo shook his head again.

'Want a cup of cocoa?'

This time he nodded and fell in step beside Mr Porter.

Mr Porter heated some milk in the green enamel kettle that sat on the stove top and with mugs of hot cocoa in their hands they sat side by side on the bench, looking out over the cottage garden and the field beyond. Their breath sent plumes of vapour up into the air. Mr Porter liked to be outside in all weathers, as if he was most at home there, surrounded by nature.

'What's a homo? I think I know, but I'm not sure,' Theo asked as he sipped the warm froth from his drink.

Mr Porter placed his mug on the table and twisted a little so he could look Theo in the eye. 'It's a horrible word, and like all horrible words, if used enough it will make the person who says it ugly on the outside as well as on the inside.'

Theo nodded.

'What do you think it is?' Mr Porter eventually asked.

Theo looked up at him, kicking his legs back and forth. 'Um, I think it's a boy who loves other boys.' He scratched his nose.

'Yep, that'll do. And if a boy loves another boy, that's just fine.'

'They call you "homo".' This Theo offered in the spirit of their pact that they would never lie to each.

'I know.' Mr Porter picked up his cocoa and slurped it.

'Are you a homo?'

'No, I am not and if I were, as I said already, that would be absolutely fine. Let that be the last time you use that word.'

'I'm sorry.' Theo looked into his mug.

'It's okay, you weren't to know, but now you do, do not say it again.' This was said in the voice that was more sharp glass than soft toffee.

'I won't.'

There was a moment of quiet. Then Mr Porter said, 'I love girls, if you must know. Well, one girl, to be exact.'

'What's her name?'

'Her name was Mrs Porter, or Merry to me, and she *was* merry and beautiful.' Mr Porter twisted the worn gold band on his finger.

'Did she die?'

Mr Porter coughed, nodded and pulled his white handkerchief from his top pocket. He blew his nose and dabbed at his eyes. 'Something in that compost must have got to me.'

And there it was again, the quiet.

'I told my mother about you and she asked me what your name was and I didn't know. Apart from Mr Porter, I mean.'

'My name is Cyrus.'

'Cyrus,' Theo repeated, trying it out. 'Doesn't it make you angry when they call you a name like the one I'm not allowed to say any more?'

'No, it doesn't.' Mr Porter rubbed at his stubbly chin.

'Why not? It makes me angry when they call me names.'

'It doesn't make me angry. It makes me sad. Because, like you, they're only children and they do that because they're afraid and I don't like the idea of anyone being afraid. In fact I fought a war so that no one would be afraid.'

Theo pictured his pen torch. 'What are they afraid of?'

'Who knows, Mr Montgomery? Not being heard, having their own secrets discovered... But it's best to learn to rise above the things they say and the things they do, otherwise a man can spend his whole life fighting, and I reckon we've all had enough of fighting.'

Theo nodded to show that he understood, even if he didn't.

'Having said that, are you familiar with Gandhi? He was a fine man and he said something similar to this: "Where there is only a choice between cowardice and violence, I would advise violence."'

Theo shook his head. 'No, I haven't heard of him.'

Mr Porter took a deep breath. 'Well, I'm beginning to think it might be time you did.'

'Why did Mrs Porter die?'

'Oh, now there's a question I ask myself every hour of every day.'

Theo and Mr Porter stared ahead and sipped their cocoa. That wasn't even close to a satisfactory answer, but Theo could tell by the set of his friend's face, and the silence, that it was the only one he was going to get.

Three

Theo sat in the hundred-year-old library, where the smell of old books danced up his nose. Hunched over his geography textbook, he folded his slim, toned arms and became engrossed, keen to learn about how the earth's crust, its shell, was divided into tectonic plates and how they'd shifted over the last two hundred and fifty million years to form continents and mountains. It was incredible, a reminder that his place in the world was as nothing by comparison.

'Two hundred and fifty million years…' he whispered.

He ran his finger over a map showing the edges of the shifting plates and realised it made sense that this was where there were more volcanoes.

A scream of laughter came from behind him, breaking the silence of the library. He looked round quickly to see Wilson, now in the fifth form, with his cronies Helmsley and Dinesh on either side, chatting to the fourth-form girls. It appeared to be the same interaction, as ever, Wilson leading the pack and the girls flicking their long hair over their shoulders and gently thumping him, a chance for contact. Theo hated the way Wilson had grown his fringe, trying to look like Simon Le Bon, he hated his cockiness, and he hated his friends; in fact he hated most things about him. This had been the case now for the last seven years, ever since Wilson had singled him out in his first weeks at Vaizey College. Theo had learnt to ignore him and continued doing his best to remain invisible, as instructed all that time ago by Mr Beckett, but it wasn't always easy.

Mr Porter reminded him regularly that people who were mean like Wilson had something dark growing inside them and were to be pitied. Theo tried, he really did, but he couldn't help wishing the dark thing growing inside Wilson would just get on with it and suffocate him, anything to get him out of his life and ease his torment. At the start of each new school year, Theo prayed that Wilson might back off, get bored or, shamefully, find a new victim. His bullying was relentless, and Theo had to be permanently on guard. It was exhausting and distracting.

At fourteen, Theo had lost his gangliness. He was tall, slim rather than skinny, and muscular thanks to his running and gym regimes. Everything about him was well proportioned, and with his square jaw and thick hair it was clear he was on the way to becoming a handsome young man. Not that he saw this. He avoided mirrors and kept himself to himself, preferring a quiet life. He was a loner and could only see himself as the weedy boy with the nervous stutter and pallid complexion. Outside of studying, his sole preoccupation was to try and keep his weirdness at bay.

'What are you looking at, Montgonorrhea?' Wilson fired this latest moniker in Theo's direction, before looking at his group to make sure his comment had been properly appreciated.

Theo hadn't realised he was still looking in their direction. He redirected his gaze back to his book, his pulse racing. Closing his eyes, he offered up a silent prayer that they would leave him alone. This he did without conviction; if prayers were all it took, his torment would have abated long ago.

'Quiet, please!' The elderly librarian looked up from her desk and put down her mug commemorating the engagement of Prince Charles and Lady Diana.

'Sorry, miss, it wasn't us, it was Mr Homo here.' Theo glanced up as Wilson stood and pointed in his direction. 'He's making a proper racket and we're trying really hard to study.'

Theo felt the burn of several pairs of eyes fixed on him and a hot prickle spread across his skin.

The girls placed their hands over their mouths to stifle their giggles.

The librarian stood up. 'Right, Mr Homo, gather your books and leave!' She seemed oblivious to the snickers that rippled around the room. 'I will not have disruption in my library. There are people trying to work. Off you go!' She made a shooing sign towards the door.

Theo knew there was no point protesting and, besides, he wanted to be as far away from Wilson as possible. He gathered his books, as instructed, and made his way along the corridor, walking slowly down the wide stone stairs, trying to kill time, practising the art of hiding in plain sight. Even so, despite his best efforts at purposeful dawdling, he arrived at his English class ten minutes early.

He hovered in the classroom doorway and leant his palm on the frame, content to stand and stare. For sitting in the seat next to his was the most beautiful girl he had ever seen. She seemed to be whispering to herself as she ran her hands over her skirt. Her thick flame-red hair hung around her face and her peachy skin was dotted with adorable freckles. Her eyes were green and her nose was tiny and snub. He looked around the classroom to see if it was a set-up, another joke at his expense, but she was alone.

Theo walked slowly forward, mindful that he had only minutes before his classmates arrived and introduced him as the school weirdo.

He pulled out his chair and tried to order the jumble of words flying around inside his head. But before he'd had the chance to construct a comprehensible sentence, she spoke to him.

'Hi there, I'm Kitty.' She smiled warmly and waved at him, even though they were close enough to speak, and he liked it. It was the nicest welcome he'd received in a long time.

'I'm Theo.' He sat down and stared at her face.

'Well, you're going to have to help me out here, Theo. You know when a girl is a million miles from home and is smiling as though she has it all figured out but is actually just very scared, wondering how to fit in at a new school this late in the term?' She dipped her eyes, her tone sincere, her Scottish lilt most attractive.

'Uh-huh.'

'Well, I am that girl.' She laughed softly and leant in closer, laying her fingers briefly on his arm, with the lightest of touches.

Theo's limbs jumped and a jolt of pleasure fired through him. He wouldn't have been surprised to find that her fingers had burnt right through his flesh.

Kitty continued, whispering now. 'Actually, that's not strictly true. I'm a warrior like my mum and that means I can get through just about anything.' She sat back in the chair and rested her hand on the desktop. Theo had a strong desire to place his on top of it. Kitty the warrior carried on. 'Mr Reeves told me to sit here and then left me all alone. He seemed a bit odd.'

'I guess.' Theo nodded. 'And people fear people who are odd, weird. They think they're toxic, contagious.' He blinked.

'I suppose we do.' She gave a small laugh and it was abundantly clear that this beautiful, confident girl was not one of life's weirdos. 'I was going to give it five more minutes and then run and hide somewhere, but then you turned up. You just might be my knight in shining armour.'

He liked this idea very much. 'I'm not usually this early. I was working in the library...' He let this trail, not wanting to recount or even recall what had happened only minutes earlier. 'It's a coincidence, really. Out of all the people that might have turned up early... I'm a Montgomery, so you must be...?'

'Oh! Oh, I see!' She smiled when she caught his thread. 'I'm a Montrose. So that explains the seating.'

Theo loved that she was smart.

'I think I can get through this, Mr Montgomery, with you by my side. What was your first name again?' She was so close now that tendrils of her thick hair were brushing his shoulder, vivid orange against the navy of his V-necked school jersey. It took all of his strength not to reach out and touch them.

'My name's Theodore, but everyone calls me Theo.' *Not that they call me anything really, as no one talks to me, but I don't want you to know that and right now you don't and I feel like someone else and that's brilliant.*

She twisted her head to look at him. 'Theodore? Let me guess... after Mr Roosevelt? I must confess, I can't think of any other Theodores right now!'

'Actually, no.' His face broke into a wry smile, but he made sure his lips covered his teeth, which he had neglected to clean that morning. 'I was named after Theobald's House. My father was a Theobald's boy and my grandfather too, in fact all the men in our family came here, but I think my mother drew the line at Theobald and so Theodore was the compromise.'

'That's crazy!' She put her hand to her cheek and he noticed a kink in her left forearm, a slight bend that meant her hand curved ever so slightly to the left. Imperfect and therefore, to him, perfect.

She continued, either unaware or uninterested in his scrutiny. 'So your family are, like, Vaizey College through and through?'

'I guess.' He shrugged, pleased to have impressed her a little and sad that it was based on a lie. It might have been true that in the past the Montgomery men were Vaizey to the core, but his hatred of the place meant that line ended with him. It felt to Theo as if his awkwardness at the school was like a loose thread and that each time it got pulled it left another little hole in his father's reputation as well as his own. It was a huge weight to carry. 'I sometimes wish I was named after Roosevelt instead.' This was as close as he could come to admitting how he felt about the school. 'It would be easier and quicker to explain.'

'And is that a Rudyard Kipling novel I see in your bag?' she asked in her soft voice as she peered at the green cloth spine.

'His poetry actually. For prep.' Not that he'd started it yet. He was, in truth, dreading it. *I mean… poetry? What's the point?*

'We have a lot of it in the library at home, you must know some of it already?' Her eyes blazed with enthusiasm.

He looked at her and in that moment wished beyond everything that instead of maths equations, tectonic plates and the properties of light, all the things that had held his attention over the last term, it had been the poetry of Mr Rudyard Kipling that he had studied. To have been able to recite just a single line from one of his poems would, he knew, have made the greatest impression on Miss Kitty Montrose. And he wanted to impress her. He wanted that very much. Instead, he hesitated and confessed with a flush of embarrassment to his cheeks. 'I'm afraid not. I haven't really read any yet.'

Her smile faded a little and her brows knitted. But she quickly regained her equanimity. 'Well of course, why would you? My boyfriend is the same. He only reads comics, if you can believe that!' She shook her head and reached for her textbook.

Theo felt his stomach bunch as if he'd been punched. This was the very worst news imaginable – not that Kitty's boyfriend only read comics, but that she had a boyfriend at all. A surge of something thick seemed to clog his veins, making his limbs feel leaden and his head light. He hated the boy, even if he had no idea who he was.

'You have a boyfriend?' he mumbled weakly.

'Yes.' She nodded. 'My cousins are already here at Vaizey – Ruraigh and Hamish Montrose...'

Theo nodded. He knew them of course and with this information came a sickness in his gut. Her cousins would no doubt fill her in on all of his quirks, laughing, probably, as they did so. And, just like that, the crackle of confidence that had flickered into life when Kitty had considered him her knight in shining armour, was now extinguished. He watched her beautiful mouth move and half listened to the words that came out.

'They always bring their friends home for the holidays, and he's one of their gang, so we kind of met a while ago. He's a fifth former,' she said with pride. 'Angus Thompson, do you know him?'

Theo could only nod as he pictured the confident, athletic Thompson, a full two years older than him, good-looking in a New Romantic kind of way, and captain of the 1st XI. His heart sank. He stared ahead, almost unable to look at Kitty. *I wish I was Angus Thompson. I wish I was anyone other than Theodore Montgomery.*

'Are you sporty?' she asked, as if she'd read his thoughts.

He shook his head. 'Not really. Are you?'

'Swimming, that's my thing. I love to swim. My dad always says that one day I'm going to develop gills behind my ears!'

Theo watched, fascinated, as, at the mention of her dad, her eyes narrowed and for a split second there was a look of longing on her pretty face. Could it be that she too came from a home where she felt like a guest and with parents who made her feel like an encumbrance? Oh, to have someone to discuss this with – it would make things so much easier to bear.

'I'm finding being here harder than I can say,' she said.

Theo's heart lifted. 'I understand that.' And he truly did.

She sighed. 'My mum and dad are my best friends really. God, I know how naff that sounds, but they are. We do so much together and I would rather be with them than do anything else. Do you know what I mean?'

He nodded vacantly. *Of course she's not like you, idiot.* He cursed the very idea. *Look at her, she's perfect.*

The moment the bell rang at the end of class, Theo gathered up his books and headed off to find Mr Porter. He knew the man's routine as well as his own and figured that he'd be up at the cricket pitch on this sunny day.

'Now what's that face for?' Mr Porter placed his hands on his lower back and stood up slowly from where he'd been crouching. He made his way to the other side of the crease, where he bent down again and with his little white dabbing stick filled in the gaps in the line.

Theo sighed and began stripping the bark from a twig he'd found on the path. 'Do you know any of Rudyard Kipling's poetry?' He thought it might be easier to learn a poem off Mr Porter than try and find an appropriate one in the book he had in his bag.

'Can't say as I do.'

'Dammit.' Theo tutted.

'I see someone's got a cob on today.' Mr Porter laughed. 'Poetry's not really my thing. I might have recited the odd ditty to my comrades during the war, but none that's fit for your tender ears, Mr Montgomery.'

For the umpteenth time that afternoon, the name and image of Angus Thompson came into his head. A fine name for a fine scholar and sportsman. 'I wish I wasn't named after Theobald's House, a place I hate. It annoys me.'

'Well, don't let it,' Mr Porter said, keeping his eyes on the white line as he continued dabbing it with paint.

Theo huffed. As if it was that easy.

'When you met Mrs Porter, did you like her the first time you saw her?'

'Ah, so that explains the face.' Mr Porter rocked back on his haunches and looked away to the horizon. 'Yes, I did. I liked her the very second I saw her and I loved her until the very last.' His eyes crinkled in a smile.

'Did you tell her you liked her?'

'Oh no. Not at first. That's not how it's done. You have to be subtle, get to know a lady and win her over.'

Theo snorted. He had never won anything in his life, let alone a prize like Kitty Montrose. 'I just wish…' He kicked at the ground.

'You just wish what?'

'I wish I could be someone else.'

'And who would you like to be, might I ask?' Mr Porter's knees creaked as he stood up. He looked Theo in the eye, easy now they were of a similar height.

'Anyone,' he said quietly.

'Here's the thing, Mr Montgomery. There isn't a single pupil in this school, or any other, come to think of it, who hasn't wished for the same at some point. Everyone wants to be taller, thinner, smarter, funnier, faster, less afraid, you name it! I've known you for a very long time and I can tell you that you are one of the best people I know. You have heart!' He placed his fist on his chest. 'And if you can find the confidence to follow your heart, which one day you will, you will be happy and that's the greatest gift you can give yourself.'

'How do I win a girl over?' he asked. These life lessons were all well and good, but time was of the essence.

Mr Porter reached up under his cap and scratched his head. 'Well, it depends on the kind of girl she is. You might be able to impress her with gifts and expensive treats, but therein lies a problem, because if she's the kind of girl that's *impressed* by gifts and expensive treats, the kind of girl who won't pay her own way, then I would say she isn't the girl you want, even if you think you do. But if you can make her laugh and she can make you laugh in return, oh boy, that's the nicest way to live.' He gave a small chuckle.

'Did you and Mrs Porter make each other laugh?'

'Every day, Mr Montgomery, every day. Spending time with her…' He looked into the middle distance, his expression wistful. 'It was like the sun was out, even when it was raining. She was my sunshine.' He chuckled. 'It's important, those little things that bind you, and they're often found in the mundane. There are some men, Mr Montgomery, who are like a glass of champagne – exciting, glamorous – but you don't want to be a glass of champagne.'

'I don't?'

'No. You want to be a cup of tea.'

Theo stared at Mr Porter. 'I think I might like to be a glass of champagne!'

Mr Porter shook his head. 'No, you don't. Champagne is for high days and holidays – people don't always have a fancy for it. But a good cup of tea? There isn't a day in the year when it isn't the best thing to have first thing in the morning. A cup of tea warms your bones on a cold day and can bring you close together as you sit and chat. You want to be a cup of tea.'

Theo smiled at him. 'You sound mad. Going on about tea and champagne when all I want to know is how to make a girl like me!'

'Aye, maybe so, but love makes you mad, that's a fact, and when it comes to affairs of the heart, I know what I'm talking about. Merry was…' He paused. 'She was perfect and yet she picked me.'

'Because you were a cup of tea.'

'Exactly.' He winked. 'I was a cup of tea.'

A burst of laughter filtered across the grass. It came from behind the wide oak tree, where a gaggle of his peers were sitting chatting, flirting and studying, enjoying the freedom of being fourteen and with only a couple of weeks left on the school calendar.

'Why don't you go and sit with them?' Mr Porter asked.

'Are you joking? They hate me!'

'They don't hate you! And if they do, then it's because they don't know you. You should give them the chance to get to know you and you can only do that by going and saying hello.'

'Mr Porter, I've been in their classes for seven years and they haven't once shown any sign of wanting to get to know me. And I know why – it's because I'm weird.' He held the twig in both hands and pushed on the middle with his thumbs until it snapped.

Four

The end of term arrived quickly and Theo was in his dorm packing his case for the summer break. He worked slowly, distracted as ever by thoughts of Kitty, the girl whose face sat behind his eyelids and pulled him from sleep in the early hours. He now longed for his English class, previously his least favourite subject, just for the chance to sit with arms touching and her scent filling his space with a cloud of sweetness. Under the ruse of reading the set texts and with his head propped on his arm, he was able to stare at her unnoticed, fascinated, while his heart ached with longing and regret that it was Angus Thompson whose name she wrote in a circle of hearts on her folder. He knew that if it had been his name so artistically inscribed, he would want for nothing else ever again.

'Get a move on, Montgomery. No one wants to be hanging around here after the bell, especially not for you!' The prefect, Xander Beaufort, hovered in the hallway, shouting his commands through the open door of Theo's dorm.

Theo got it. Being held up when everyone was keen to get their summer started would be bad enough, but being held up by him would be doubly annoying. For the good-looking and popular boys there was always some leeway, but for him there was no softening of the rules and no kindness.

Toxic...

Having tossed his belongings into his case, he buckled it up, then sat on the end of his bed and waited.

And waited.

And waited.

Once or twice he walked to the deep-set mullioned windows and watched boys and girls being swept into hugs by parents who seemed to be just as excited as their offspring, clapping and skipping as they herded them onto the leather backseats of Bentleys, Jaguars and a snazzy new Audi Quattro. But the cars had stopped coming a little while ago, and it was now painfully quiet. Theo looked up along the lane and over the hedge, where he knew the birds would have been hiding from the earlier cacophony.

'You still here?'

Theo stood up and faced Mr Beckett, as was the custom when addressed by a master. 'Yes, sir.'

'Parents collecting you?'

'Yes, sir.'

He felt the familiar rush of heat to his face that came whenever he sensed he was inadvertently doing or saying something wrong. His housemaster snorted his irritation and swept from the room. Theo again walked to the window and prayed they might come soon. *Please, Mum. Please hurry up.*

It was evident after a further hour that his parents had been horribly delayed. Mr Beckett reappeared, in worse humour than before and with two high spots of colour on his cheeks. Theo's spirits sank.

'Come with me. Bring your bag.' His housemaster pointed at the suitcase, his eye twitching furiously.

Theo knew it could only be bad news and wondered if his parents had crashed the car in the lanes. He pictured it: his mother slapping his father's hand away from the radio dial through the fug of cigarette smoke and then quite suddenly the car swerving sideways...

He followed Mr Beckett into his study with his stomach bubbling, prepared to hear the worst. To his surprise, he was handed the telephone. He held it to his ear and heard the echo of a voice far, far away, along with the squawk of birds and the shouts of a crowd in the background. It sounded a bit like a party.

'For fuck's sake!' His mother was roaring with laughter, carrying on a conversation with someone at her end, presumably. 'It's *not* funny!' Her raucous giggles suggested the exact opposite.

'H... hello, Mum?' he interrupted.

'Darling!' She shouted this loudly, as if surprised to hear his voice on the end of the phone. There was a slight delay on the line. He could hear the sound of water splashing and it seemed like there were a lot of people around; mixed-up chatter floated down the line. Her words carried the slight slur they usually had after she'd drunk alcohol. 'Darling, I am a terrible mother! Just terrible! Oh my goodness, Theo, what is there to say?'

'You bloody are!' he heard his father call out in the background. This was followed by another roar of communal laughter.

'Okay, so this is what's happened.' There was a pause and then the unmistakeable sound of his mother drinking from a glass with ice in it. 'Daddy and I got our dates in a muddle.'

'Don't fucking blame me!' Again, his father's voice called out, and again it was followed by a collective burst of laughter.

'Sssshhh! I'm on the bloody phone! Keep it down!' she yelled.

Theo felt his cheeks flame, not only because his mother sounded inebriated and was swearing, but also because he was in Twitcher's study, and because the call felt a lot like eavesdropping on her and her friends. He pushed the earpiece closer to his head, hoping this might muffle the sound.

'As I said, we got our dates in a muddle and didn't realise that it was *today* that you broke up and, well, there's no easy way of saying this, but we're in St-Tropez!' she squealed, as if the whole thing was uproariously amusing.

And maybe it was. For them.

'I... I don't...' Theo struggled to find the words that would smooth the situation. 'I don't know where that is,' he managed.

'The French Riviera, darling! And you are going to love it here!'

'How am I going to get there?' he whispered, gripping the phone in both hands.

'Now, we've been giving it some thought and plans are afoot! Fret not! We're sending a girl and a car to collect you from school tomorrow, she'll have your passport and she will drive you to the airport, where tickets will be waiting. Simply hop on a plane and Daddy and I will meet you at Nice airport.'

'What girl? And what should I do today? Everyone else has left.'

'Theo, listen to me, darling, you're a wonderful boy and we are all very much looking forward to seeing you tomorrow! Tata for now!'

The line went dead and Theo was engulfed in silence.

Twitcher broke the quiet, firing a question that indicated he had heard the whole exchange, and this made Theo's face even redder.

'So the problem is, where are you going to spend the night? School is effectively closed and I'm heading off any minute. Are you friends with any of the day boys who live locally?'

Theo shook his head.

Mr Beckett gave a deep sigh and Theo wished he could drop through the floor and disappear. He hated this feeling of being unwanted, a nuisance, even though he was well used to it.

'I do have one friend, I suppose.' He paused and blinked at his housemaster.

'There's no need to look so fed up. You shouldn't write off a place before you even get there. It might be wonderful – sea, sun, sand.' Mr Porter spoke as he pottered in the tiny cottage kitchen, reaching behind the faded floral fabric that hung in lieu of cupboard doors and delving into the creaky, bulbous refrigerator as he packed the khaki knapsack with slabs of pound cake and freshly made cheese-and-pickle sandwiches. 'There are many who've never left England's shores and would give their right arm to travel to the south of France—'

'They can have my ticket,' Theo interrupted. 'I hate sand.'

'Well, aren't you a ball of fun. And if you hate sand that much, my best advice would be, don't joint the Foreign Legion!' Mr Porter chuckled.

Theo didn't get the joke and ignored it. 'I just don't like going on holiday. Well, I do and I don't. I'll be glad to be away from here.' He jerked his head in the direction of the main school building.

'Speaking for myself, I'm looking forward to the break. It's a hell of a lot easier keeping the grass in tiptop condition and the place litter-free when there's only the summer-school kids to contend with.'

'You don't know what it's like. You don't know what they're like!' Theo said, recalling his mother's slightly sloshed voice and the raucous background noise.

'You're right, I don't. But the fact is, you have to go tomorrow and the way I see it is you have two choices: you either jump into it and make the most of it, or you sulk and make yourself and everyone around you miserable.' He fastened the buckles on the bag and slung it over his shoulder. 'Come on then, let's get walking while we've still got the light!'

The two set off in the late afternoon with the sun still warm and the birds singing overhead. Theo knew it was Mr Porter's favourite time of day, in his favourite time of year.

'Can you help me with my English assignment?' he asked. 'I have to do this writing thing and it's really hard. I'm rubbish at that stuff. I just can't do it.'

'No such thing as can't.' Mr Porter stopped and turned to face him. 'I will, however, help you because I know that otherwise it will prey on your mind and stop you having fun when you're away, and that would be a rotten waste of a good summer.'

Theo felt a surge of affection for his friend, who was always so considerate. 'Thank you.'

'What's it meant to be about then, this assignment?'

'Oh…' Theo tried to recall the title. 'We have to write as if we're an animal and describe how we see the world. So a dog in a car, or a rabbit in a hutch or something like that.'

'Okay, I think I can manage that. Not a word to anyone, mind. They'd have my guts for garters if they knew I'd helped with your homework.'

'I won't tell anyone!'

'In that case I'll do a rough copy and post it to your room, then you can improve on it, use it as your template and make it your own.'

'Thank you.' Theo grinned. That was one less thing to worry about.

Mr Porter opened the kissing gate and set off down the bridleway. Theo followed in his wake, inhaling the scent of freshly mown grass and dry, sun-scorched earth. They trudged on, across hard, dusty ground that was littered with stones and uphill via sloping fields, until with sweat on their brows and a shortness to their breath, they reached Jackman's Cross an hour or so later. Mr Porter came to a stop and sat himself down on a patch of lush green grass. Theo sat next to him and the two, now so comfortable in each other's company, were happy to stay there in silence for a bit.

'This is some view, eh?' Mr Porter said appreciatively.

Theo let his eyes sweep the broad fields of the Dorset countryside from left to right. Full hedgerows formed the boundaries and deer frolicked on the lower slopes in the pink haze of the evening sun. It was when their breath had steadied and their muscles were rested that he spoke.

'They… They forgot to pick me up,' he whispered, running his hand over the grass and cursing the thickening in his throat.

'So I believe.' Mr Porter rested his elbows on his raised knees.

Theo pulled at clumps of grass and threw them into the air. 'Kitty told me her mum and dad are her best friends.' He paused. 'I can't imagine that.'

Mr Porter considered this. 'It's my belief that there are many types of parent, each probably doing what they think is best.

My dad was raised under the philosophy "spare the rod, spoil the child" and because of his experience he never raised so much as a finger to me.'

'I don't think…' Theo swallowed. 'I don't think my mum and dad like me very much. Whenever I'm with them, I always feel as if they're just waiting for me to go back to school.'

Mr Porter glanced at him and gave a wry smile. 'Well, I'm sorry you feel that way. Have you ever considered that maybe they like you very much but don't know how to behave any differently? I mean, there's no handbook that arrives with a new baby – I don't know how we'd have fared.'

Theo looked at him. *You'd have fared brilliantly.* 'I wish I had arrived with a handbook,' he said, 'although I'm fairly sure my parents would have been too busy to read it.' He smiled at the laugh this raised in his friend. 'I do know that if I had a son, I would never forget to pick him up at the end of term. I wouldn't get in a muddle over exeat dates and invite friends over instead of cooking supper just for him. And I'd try to remember that he needs to eat more than cheese! And on phone-call night, I'd sit by the phone so that no time was wasted. In fact I'd never send him to a school like Vaizey College. I'd let him choose where he went to school. I'd let him be happy.'

Mr Porter waited until Theo had calmed before he answered. 'I understand why you're aggrieved…' He nodded. 'But here's the thing: everyone is different and some people can only repeat the choices their parents made because they're too scared to do anything else. I'm sure your parents meant no ill. They're probably just very busy people.'

Theo stared at him and shook his head, remembering their honesty pact. 'I just don't think it's good enough.'

Mr Porter sniffed and returned his gaze. 'Okay, I agree.' He wiped his hands on his trousers. 'You're right. If I had a son, I too would never forget to pick him up from school and I too would sit by the phone if I knew he was going to call. Happy now?'

'Happier,' Theo admitted. 'It's funny, the date of the start of the summer holidays has been in my mind for weeks and weeks, but I guess it just isn't important to them.'

'Well, as I said, they're very busy people, and—'

'Can't you just admit that it's shit?'

Mr Porter harrumphed his laughter and sighed. 'You're right. It's shit.'

Theo felt the twitch of a smile at the shared swearword, as well as relief that his anger was not misplaced.

A light evening breeze brushed over the hill.

'I've got you something.' Mr Porter reached into the breast pocket of his checked shirt and handed Theo a little gold safety pin. Attached to it was a delicate fishing fly of green and blue feathers, with a square red bead at the end.

Theo turned it over in his hand and stared at it.

'Now, I don't want to hear no more talk of being someone else. Be proud to be you, Mr Montgomery. Wear this somewhere discreet and use it like I do, as a reminder to seek out the stillness. That's where you'll find peace.'

Theo cursed the tears that spilled down his cheeks. He was fourteen now and there were lots of things that he didn't know, but he did know that big boys weren't supposed to cry.

'There, there.' Mr Porter patted him on the shoulder. 'No need for tears, not today, especially not with this view in front of us. This landscape should do many things, inspire you, calm you even, but it shouldn't make you sad.'

'Th... thank you.' Theo wrapped his fingers around the fishing fly and sniffed as he looked out over the magnificent vista.

'You're quite welcome, son. You're quite welcome.'

Theo stood in the front courtyard next morning as instructed and waited to be collected. His pulse raced at the prospect of what might happen if the girl failed to show up. He was certain they wouldn't let him go back to Barnes on his own, and another night on the camp bed at Mr Porter's was probably out of the question.

At a little after nine o'clock a red Mini pulled sharply through the gates as its horn let out a tinny beep. A blonde girl in jeans, black espadrilles and a worn, black, cap-sleeved T-shirt jumped out of the driver's seat.

'Theodore?' she asked, pointing at him, chewing gum and smiling at the same time.

'Yes. Theo.'

'I guessed it might be you – as you're the only person stood here with a suitcase and a face like a smacked arse!' She laughed loudly and bent double. 'Get in the car. That's such a cool name – Theo,' she wheezed. 'Are you all set?'

'Yes.' He placed his case on the back seat and climbed in after it.

'What are you doing? You think I'm a cab? Hell no! Get in the front!' she yelled as she slammed the driver's door and clipped in her seatbelt.

Theo reluctantly left the safety of the rear seat and settled himself in the front. No sooner had he shut the door than the girl drove back out through the gates at speed.

'What the fuck? That's actually your school? I've never seen anything like it! My school looked like a crappy old office block. I mean, seriously? It looks like something out of a Hammer horror movie.'

'It *feels* like something out of a Hammer horror movie.' He felt his muscles unknotting with every yard they put between themselves and his school.

'Ha! You're funny. I like that.' She twisted her head to the left to get a glimpse of him.

Theo smiled. He'd never been told that before and it felt nice.

'I'm Freddie, by the way, short for Frederica – named after my dad, the bastard, who did a runner when my mum was up the duff.'

'I...' Nervous of saying the wrong thing, Theo didn't know whether to apologise, sympathise or laugh, so he said nothing more. This girl was unlike any other he'd met.

'So how old are you? Twelve?'

'No.' Her guess both irritated and embarrassed him. 'I'm fourteen.'

'Christ, okay... Fourteen! I'm nineteen and you look a million years younger than me.'

Again, he decided that silence might be the best policy.

'So what's the deal here? Your parents *actually* forgot to pick you up? How whacked is that? I nearly pissed myself laughing! I guess it's lucky you're fourteen or whatever and not a baby. You could easily have been one of those kids whose parents leave them outside the supermarket and when they go back for them, they've been nicked.'

Theo stared at her, not sure which kids she was referring to but feeling a wave of concern for them nonetheless.

'Have they left you anywhere before?' she asked.

'I don't think so.'

'You don't *think* so? Jesus, what kind of people do that? It's hilarious! Completely off the scale!'

Theo didn't think there was anything funny about it. He stared out of the window.

Undeterred by his silence, Freddie continued. 'I have seriously never heard anything like it – how could they just forget to pick you up?'

'I don't know,' he admitted. 'They're very busy people.'

'I should cocoa, but that doesn't really cut it – how busy do you have to be to forget you have a kid?' She wrinkled her nose.

Far from taking offence, he was a little reassured by her being so shocked, feeling, as with Mr Porter's reaction, that it legitimised his own response. It made her seem like an ally of sorts.

'But I guess shit happens. So what music do you like?' Freddie rattled on without giving him time to reply. 'I love ABC. Do you know their stuff? They're brilliant. I'll let you borrow my tape if you like.'

'Thank you.' He found it hard to keep up. Freddie spoke so quickly and changed the subject without warning, not bothering to pause for breath.

'Have you got a girlfriend?' she asked suddenly.

His face coloured as he had just that second been thinking about Kitty. He shook his head. 'No.'

'What? You are kidding me? A good-looking boy like you? I would have thought you'd be beating them off with a stick!'

He shook his head again, wishing they could go back to talking about ABC.

'My boyfriend and I just finished. His loss. Cheating arsehole!'

She yelled this out of the window, as if the message might carry on the wind and land in the boyfriend's cheating arsehole ear. 'It's good though, in a way,' she continued, using brute force to crunch the gearstick through the sequence at every corner. 'I mean, if we'd still been going out, I wouldn't be here today.' She smiled at him. 'And this is an adventure!'

He wished she didn't feel the need to yell everything.

'Thank you very much for driving me to the airport.'

'No worries.' She grinned at him, still chewing her gum.

'I think my ticket is waiting for me, I'm not sure where, but I know I'm flying to Nice.'

'Yes, you wally, and I'm coming with you!'

'You're coming with me to Nice?' He twisted in the seat. 'Why?'

'Why?' she yelled. 'Because why not? And because it's the best fucking job in the world! I get to hire a car, pick you up, fly first class, sit by a pool for weeks on end and then fly you home! Hell, yeah!' She banged the steering wheel. 'The Riviera here we come!'

He wondered how this had been arranged. 'Do you know my parents?'

'Not exactly, but I used to nanny for the Mendelsohns?'

Theo shook his head. That name meant nothing to him.

'Charlie Mendelsohn used to work with your dad and then moved to Hong Kong a couple of years ago, and I looked after his kids when they were in London.'

'You're not my *nanny*?' Theo asked. That would be too much to bear.

'No, you dick!' She tutted. 'You're fourteen. I'm your companion.'

He looked out of the window and felt a familiar ball of rage and embarrassment growing in his stomach.

'Don't look like that! You seem mightily pissed off and I am far from the worst companion in the world.'

Theo ignored her, closed his eyes and rested his head on the juddering window. He decided to feign sleep.

Getting through to the departure area had left him flustered, but with his suitcase and Freddie's holdall whisked off on a conveyor belt, they now had two hours to kill. As they were debating whether to go and eat or find a place to nap, Theo spied Helmsley and his younger brother making their way through the banks of seats and heading in their direction.

'Oh shit!'

He didn't realise he'd spoken aloud until Freddie placed her hand on his arm.

'What's the matter? You look like you've seen a ghost.'

'Nothing, it's just a boy from school who… who…' He didn't know where to begin, how to phrase exactly just how miserable Helmsley and his best mate made his life.

'That guy?' She thumbed in Helmsley's direction.

Theo nodded quickly, hoping that he wouldn't be seen. 'Please don't speak to him! Please! He'll only tell Wilson!'

'Who's Wilson? Jesus, are you afraid of them?'

'I…' Theo still couldn't find the words. He sat down on a vacant chair and shrank back in the seat, wishing he was invisible, which made a pleasant change from wishing he was Angus Thompson.

Freddie, however, had other ideas. She sat down next to him

and began laughing loudly, so loudly that several people looked in their direction. Theo didn't know what to do.

It had the desired effect. Helmsley glanced across and grinned. Then he jabbed his brother in the ribs and the two made their way over. Freddie laughed again and placed her hand on Theo's chest. Theo's skin jumped beneath her touch. 'You are hilarious!' she shouted.

'Montgomery!' Helmsley called. 'We're off to Florida, where are you going?'

'Who the fuck are you?' Freddie turned suddenly to face Helmsley, who opened his mouth and faltered.

'I'm... a friend of Montgomery's.'

'Don't lie! If you were a friend of his you'd know not to call him Montgomery! Plus, if you were a friend of my boyfriend's, he'd have told me about you and he hasn't.' With that, she lifted her legs, stretched them out over both of Theo's and placed her hand in his hair.

Helmsley's eyes widened. 'I just wanted to...'

'Just wanted to what? Sod off!' she fired back.

Helmsley grabbed his brother by the shoulder and they walked off briskly in the direction they'd come from.

Astonished, Theo looked at Freddie. To his even greater surprise, she kissed him sweetly on the cheek.

'He looks like a right stuck-up prick.' Again, she made no attempt to lower her voice.

'He is.' Theo smiled at her, changing his mind about her in an instant. She was right, she certainly wasn't the worst companion in the world.

*

The drive from Nice to St-Tropez was fantastic. His mother kissed Freddie warmly on the cheek in the arrivals hall, like they knew each other, and thanked her profusely for bringing her son safely to her. Theo rolled his eyes at his new fake girlfriend. The way his mother spoke made it sound as if they had climbed mountains and trekked through the wilderness instead of sitting in first class and overdosing on cold lemonade and over-chilled chicken sandwiches. He put on the sunglasses that someone had left in the glove box of the black and burgundy Deux Chevaux and they drove along the winding coastal road with the top down and the warm wind blowing away the cobwebs. With no cigarette smoke to breathe in, his travel sickness was kept at bay. Theo felt good, in fact he felt *great*! He was away from school and, better than that, Helmsley thought that Freddie was his girlfriend!

'What are you looking so smug about?' His mother patted his thigh.

'Life!' he called out with his arms over his head.

'How marvellous!' His mother beamed. 'Does this mean I'm forgiven for getting in a muddle over the dates?'

'Of course you are. Shit happens!' He smiled, happy to get away with swearing in front of Freddie.

The three of them laughed out loud and Theo knew that how he felt at that exact second with the sun on his face and holding the attention of these two women was a moment to treasure, a moment when all good things felt possible. He liked feeling this way. He liked it very much.

La Grande Belle, the house his parents had rented for the summer, was both vast and beautiful. Its pale stone seemed to change colour depending on the time of day and bright pink bougainvillea clung to the walls, twisting round the ironwork of the Juliet balconies at the shuttered first-floor windows. These had the most beautiful views over the little village of Gassin. Theo stared out from his twin room at the sparkling azure swimming pool, the ancient olive grove and the sea beyond.

They had arrived during naptime and the rest of the party – various friends of his parents – had retreated for a postprandial siesta behind the carved wooden doors of their bedrooms. He was standing by his bed, trying to decide between unpacking and exploring, when he heard a loud splash. Running to the window, he saw that Freddie was already in the pool. Her blonde hair floated behind her, on top of the water, then she twisted and dived under again and everything but the pale soles of her feet disappeared. She bobbed up again, this time further along the pool. The water clung to her sodden T-shirt and black bikini bottoms. He watched, fascinated, as she pulled herself out of the water and lay cruciform and panting on the marble slabs. He ducked down out of sight, his heart beating very fast, and wondered what Kitty, the swimmer, would look like in her bikini.

Wary of discovery and unable to take his eyes from Freddie's slender form and the droplets of water shimmering on her skin, he sat by the window and tried to control his breathing. He wiped the slick of sweat from the dark, fuzzy down above his top lip and recalled the wonderful weight of her legs resting over his at the airport, and that sweet kiss on the cheek…

'There you are, boy!'

His father's booming voice made him jump. He hurriedly stood up and raced over to the bed, where he fiddled with the buckles on his suitcase – anything to occupy his shaking hands and distract his roving gaze, busy with the image of a semi-dressed Freddie.

'Sorry about the mix-up, but no harm done, eh?' His father

laughed, strode forward and patted his back, as if they had simply ordered the wrong milk or inadvertently jumped a queue. 'We had planned to pop back and collect you, but time kind of ran away with us. You know how it is. The days and nights merge into each other out here.'

Actually, Theo didn't know 'how it was', but he smiled anyway, wanting to get the holiday off to the best possible start. 'It's okay, Dad.'

'Good. Good.' His father beamed and wandered across to the window. 'Well, well, well.' He locked his fingertips together behind him and rocked back and forth as he stared down at the pool. 'Is that the little hottie that chaperoned you?' He turned to nod at his son. 'Goodness me, Theodore, no wonder you're transfixed by the view! I tell you what, if that's the welcome committee you get, I bet you want us to leave you behind every time.' He laughed. 'I have to say, I wouldn't mind where or when I was left if it meant I got to spend hours with that. Good Lord above, will you look at her?'

Theo stared not at the pool but at his father's expression. It sent bile rising into his throat. His father's eyes bulged and his mouth was slack.

'I'll let you get on.' He winked and left the room with a spring in his step.

Theo wasn't sure what bothered him most about his father's behaviour: the fact that his ogling of Freddie made him feel uncomfortable, jealous, even, or how it sent a tremor of sadness through him on behalf of his mother. It was a hard thing to explain. He continued to slowly unpack and, even though he had only just arrived, already saw the shiny veneer peeling from this beautiful day.

Having deliberated long and hard over what might be appropriate to wear, he decided eventually on tennis shorts and his gym shirt and then made his way downstairs. By now, at least half a dozen couples were sitting around the vast wooden outdoor table, which was illuminated by large pillar candles burning in glass lanterns. Some were sipping cold flutes of champagne, others enjoyed long cocktails, and all had the sun-kissed tans that came from spending days lounging by the pool.

'Here he is!' his mother called out and he felt the familiar awkwardness descend. 'For those of you who don't know, this is our son, Theodore – Theo to friends!'

'Ah, Theo, I hear they left you at bloody school? Unforgiveable, if you ask me! What kind of parent does that?'

'Oh do shut up, Pepe! Stop stirring!' His mother laughed and threw a cork at the man, who ducked and winked at him, to show it had all been spoken in jest.

'Darling, this is Pepe and Jemima, and then Leopold and Nancy...' She continued pointing out each couple as Theo nodded and mumbled 'How do you do?' knowing he would never remember who was who. 'Saskia and Konrad, Marcus and Pauly, Jennifer and Duncs – and Daddy and me you know!' She laughed and gave a small clap.

'Or does he? I mean, the poor sod hardly ever sees you, and don't forget, you did leave him in school!' Pepe shouted this loudly, and the whole group chuckled their laughter.

Theo pictured them sitting exactly like this during the phone call yesterday. How they must have laughed while he stood in Twitcher's study, waiting.

'Evening, everyone!' Freddie appeared, looking lovely in a

white strappy summer dress and with her hair wet around her shoulders.

'Ah yes, do come and join us, darling!' his mother called. 'This is Frederica, our guardian angel who gathered up Theo and brought him safely to my side.'

'I wouldn't mind being gathered up by Frederica!' Pepe yelled.

'Oh for God's sake, Pepe! Poor girl!' the group chorused, as Jemima, his wife, covered her eyes in mock shame.

The whole conversation made Theo's stomach flip with unease. He looked at his father, noting the way his eyes ran the length of Freddie's dress from over the rim of his champagne glass. Freddie, however, seemed unflustered and reached for her own glass of champagne before taking a seat next to his mother.

'What would you like to do, darling?' his mother asked loudly. It took him a second to realise it was him she was speaking to. He stared at her, not having the confidence to mention that he had thought he might like to sit at the table and join in. 'You could go and watch a bit of TV, might help your French?' She smiled. 'Or there's a whole stack of videos. There are snacks in the kitchen. Or you could have a play in the pool, it's still lovely and warm!'

Theo felt reduced. Dismissed. It bothered him that she didn't realise that not only was he too old to play in the pool but that there was no one to play with. He looked at the people seated around the table and wondered how it was that no matter where he was in the world or who he was with, he always felt like an intruder, a late arrival for whom no place had been set. And it felt horrible.

*

It was four days into the holiday and close to midnight when Theo was woken by shouts in the hallway. It took a beat for him to remember where he was. He heard his mother's voice and recognised the slight slur to her speech that meant she'd been drinking.

'Don't you give me that bollocks! I fucking saw you!'

His heart hammered at her words. He sat up in the bed, aware that his parents' fight would be heard by all of their friends. He closed his eyes at the thought, feeling the hot prickle of shame on her behalf.

'She's a kid, for God's sake!' his father barked. 'Give me some bloody credit!'

Theo hugged the white bolster to his chest.

'Give you credit? You make me laugh! I don't forget, Perry. I wish I could, but I don't bloody forget!' she yelled. 'You know what they say, that the clearest conscience is held by those who have the shortest memory! And that's you. You are like a fucking goldfish! But I'm not! I don't forget, ever!'

He heard his father make 'sssshhh' sounds, trying to contain his mum's outburst. Theo sensed the enforced silence in all the other rooms, as if, like him, everyone was listening with bated breath and ears cocked to see what would come next. And what came next tore at his heart: it was the sound of his mother weeping and howling with raw, animal-like distress, followed by the closing of their bedroom door.

And then nothing.

He lay awake, looking up at the dark, starry sky through the open balcony window and trying to quiet the nagging voice in his head that told him things were only going to get worse. Hopping out of bed, he grabbed his pen torch. It had gone through numerous batteries over the years and now sported a hairline crack, having been dropped onto the flagstones of the school bathroom in the dead of night. Mr Porter had fixed it with a well-placed spot of glue. Theo thought of him now, as he shone the beam up onto the ceiling of his grand bedroom. He pictured him asleep under the rafters of the cosy crooked cottage. 'Night, night, Mr Porter,' he whispered as he turned onto his side.

The days at La Grande Belle were bearable, pleasant even. Theo spent a lot of time alone, but unlike in Barnes, the weather was glorious and there was always plenty of food in the house. Fresh bread and croissants arrived every morning, pots of jam and chutneys lined the larder walls, and the fridge was packed with fragrant cheeses, cold cuts of ham and roasted chicken wings. He liked to eat his breakfast with the gang, listening to their chatter before setting himself swimming challenges throughout the day, seeing how far he could swim underwater and then how fast. He was a good swimmer and he enjoyed it. The solitude suited him and he liked the feeling of his body growing stronger every day. He noted new definition to his stomach and a broadening of his shoulders.

Freddie sometimes joined him, throwing coins or objects to the bottom of the pool, which they would race to retrieve. Occasionally she took him in the Deux Chevaux down to the harbourside for ice cream, or to the market, where they bought punnets of fat, soft peaches and brown paper bags full of fresh, sweet cherries. She was quieter in his company now than she had been on that first day; she kept her sunglasses on and smoked angrily, throwing the butts out of the car window, acting more like she had when she'd mentioned her arsehole boyfriend. He didn't blame her. Now that she'd got to know him, she probably realised what everyone else knew: that he was weird, and not funny after all.

The nights, however, were very different. When darkness fell, the tension rose as the wine flowed and the candles flickered. The air tasted the same as it did at school in the seconds before a fight and Theo didn't like it one bit, unable to fully explain the hostility he sensed lurking behind the humour. He spent most nights in his room with the balcony doors open, listening to the raucous chat and salacious gossip that was bandied back and forth across the table. At least he hadn't heard his mother crying again, and for that he was grateful.

That was until the night before he left for England. That night, all hell broke loose.

Theo had been in a deep sleep but woke to the sound of smashing glass. He sat up in the bed, fearing a break-in, but then realised he was at La Grande Belle and not at home in Barnes. The smash was followed by the deafening wail of his mother's sobbing, and then her loud shouts in a voice he hardly recognised.

'You fucking pig! This is it! This is it! I have put up with Shawna or whatever the hell her name was from the office and the horse woman from Crewe, and the bloody air hostess, all of them bitches! But this! This is the last straw, Peregrine. This is worse even than you cheating on me just after we got married, worse than you fathering that bastard boy, Alexander, worse than all of it!'

Theo's heart jumped into his throat and a massive roaring filled his ears. It was so loud that for a minute or so he couldn't hear anything else but his own blood pumping through his head. A bastard boy? His dad had another son? This fact ripped his heart, as tears began streaming down his face.

'I can't stand it!' His mum was shouting now. 'You're destroying me! We're here with our friends and she is just a kid!'

'Darling, you're overreacting. Keep your voice down, please!'

'Why should I? I will *not* keep my voice down! And don't you dare smile! Don't you dare! I will stop payments to Alexander, I will take the house and I will take your beloved cars and I will take Rollo and you will be out on your ear. I mean it. This is it. You can fuck off. I am done! It's over! It is really over, Perry.'

With his heart still hammering and his thoughts racing, Theo jumped up and watched from behind the shutter as his mother grabbed another bottle of champagne and threw it onto the marble by the side of the pool. It shattered. The green glass scattered like irregularly shaped marbles and the foaming liquid slithered into the pool. Looking to the left, he spied Freddie lying on a lounger, wearing her pants and what looked to be his father's dinner jacket. His mother continued her rant, lunging in Freddie's direction.

'And you – you little whore! You can guess again if you think I am flying you home. You are stuck here, but not in this house! Get out! Grab your nasty clothes and get out!' She was screaming now. 'I don't give a fuck if you have to *walk* home!' And she lunged forward again, seemingly intent on lynching Freddie.

Theo watched, horrified, as his father grabbed his mother roughly around the waist and manhandled her back inside. She shrieked and clawed at him, her hair falling over her face and her arms outstretched. Just before they disappeared into the house, she shouted, 'There are only two types of people, Perry:

those who cheat and those who don't. The number of times is irrelevant! The tenth time cuts just like the first.'

Theo sat on his bed and listened to the sound of his parents stumbling into their bedroom. He waited until silence fell and the night took on a new shade of darkness, the quiet broken only by the cicadas chirruping in the trees. It was hard to think straight. He had a brother, a half-brother who his mum hated. Alexander! That was a proper name, not like Theo. Why did his mum pay for him? What did she buy him? Did they take him home for weekends while Theo was safely away at school? There were kids at Theo's school who had complicated home lives, whose parents had gone off and had children with other people. But they didn't make a secret of it. What was he supposed to do with this information? His dislike for his father flared. What a horrible thing to do to his mum.

And suddenly it was as if a fog lifted. It was obvious! This was his chance to change his life! Theo now knew with certainty that his mum was unhappy. And so was he. The prospect of going back to school brought nothing but dread. He tightened the rope of his dressing gown over his pyjamas, took a deep breath and crept down the hallway and into his parents' bedroom.

His father was snoring lightly. His feet were sticking out of one end of the sheet and he was clasping the other end to the chest of his coffee-coloured silk pyjamas. Theo crouched down quietly and gently tapped his mother on the shoulder. She sat up and narrowed her eyes at him.

'What is it?' she whispered, looking to her right at her husband's slumbering form.

'I need to talk to you, Mum.' He reached for her arm and guided her from the bed and out onto the landing.

'What is it, Theo?' she asked again. Her gait was unsteady and her breath putrid with the odour of stale cigarettes and booze.

Theo gazed into her red, puffy eyes. His heart swelled with sadness that she had been made to feel this way. It took every ounce of his confidence and courage, but he looked her in the eye and in a lowered voice he told her, 'It's okay, I agree you should send Dad away, and you and I can stay in the house in Barnes and I can go to a local school and I will look after you, Mum. I will always look after you.' Theo had never meant anything more sincerely than these words, whispered on the landing of La Grande Belle.

His mother looked over the galleried landing and towards the great window. Moonlight streamed through it. She screwed up her face and he waited for the tears he expected would follow. But instead of crying, she burst out laughing. And once she began laughing, she couldn't stop. With her face all scrunched up, she tittered as if Theo's suggestion was the most bizarre, ridiculous and abhorrent idea she had ever heard. She looked at her son with a shake of her head and delivered the words that would lodge in his consciousness for the rest of his life. 'I love Peregrine! He is my heart, my soul, my life! And there is no one on this planet I would rather spend my days with!'

'But... But what about Alexander?' he managed.

With whip-like crispness his mother made herself abundantly clear. 'Do not ever, ever mention that name to me or anyone else again. Is that understood?'

Theo stepped backwards as if he'd been physically struck. Her words confirmed what he'd always dreaded: that he had no place there, not with her and not with them, not really. He realised then that no matter how bad things got between his parents or what foul infidelities his father committed, they were a couple, bound together through good and bad, and he was... He was alone and adrift. He swallowed and was overtaken by a great wave of sadness. He was nothing more than an inconvenience, a burden, so forgettable that they hadn't even registered when his school holidays had started.

He left his mother on the landing and shuffled back to his room, weighed down by embarrassment and tears. Walking over to the window he saw that Freddie was now sitting up on the sun lounger crying. Two long snakes of black make-up streaked her face. She looked up and they locked eyes. He stared at her and realised that his first hunch had been right after all: she was the worst companion in the world.

Five

Theo walked across the quadrangle with his suitcase under his arm. His trousers were a little high on his ankle and his blazer was tight across his back. A month of vigorous daily swimming at La Grande Belle had been good for his physique.

It had been a relief to travel back to the UK alone, leaving his parents to wallow in the unpleasant soup of their own making. He had said his goodbyes over breakfast, watching with barely disguised astonishment as his mother, her face hidden behind oversized sunglasses, sipped coffee and laughed at a remark Nancy made, while his father bit into a hot croissant and flicked through a copy of *Le Monde*. It was as if the previous night had not occurred, as if he'd dreamt the whole thing. Whereas he'd lain awake until dawn, replaying the row in his head like a movie, his gut twisting with anxiety. His parents seemed to have forgiven and forgotten and were now simply looking forward to another fun day on the Riviera. He realised that for them this was almost routine – the booze, the row, the hurt, the forgiveness – and it changed nothing. But for Theo, everything had changed. He'd made the extraordinary discovery that he had an illegitimate brother, Alexander. And, even more shattering, he'd learnt that his mother would choose his philandering father over him every time. That was a very bitter pill to swallow.

He thought of Kitty, wondering how they could possibly chat about the summer and how he might phrase the horror of his experience. She'd be full of the pleasures of having spent her holidays with her mum and dad. He thought of Freddie, who'd disappeared completely, and wondered if she was literally walking home. He couldn't help the flicker of concern for her wellbeing, despite what she'd done. Knowing now what he did about his father and recalling the way his dad had looked at Freddie on that first day, Theo saw her as a victim; troublesome, but a victim nonetheless.

Keeping his head low, he made his way towards the dorm with dread in his stomach and a head full of the events of La Grande Belle.

'There you are, sonofabitch.'

Theo stopped at the sound of Wilson's voice over his shoulder. *Oh please, no! Not now, not today.*

'Well, look at you with your lovely tan. Been sunning yourself, have you?'

Theo ignored him, hoping, though not believing, that if he stayed still and quiet, Wilson might leave him alone.

'I know you can hear me. Not so cocky now, are you, without a mouthy little whore to stick up for you. I thought not. Told you, boys.' Wilson laughed. 'Helmsley filled us in on how you gobbed off at him in the airport. Sonofabitch, who do you think you are?'

Who do I think I am? Good question. Theo's thoughts raced with images of his bulging-eyed dad and the cruel laughter of his mum. He turned slowly, preparing to reason with Wilson.

'What's that on your mouth? A caterpillar?' Again the boys guffawed into their hands.

Theo ran his index finger over his top lip and cursed that he'd forgotten to ask his parents for a razor and find out what exactly to do with it. He would ask Mr Porter.

'Is that all the rage in the gay clubs? Is that why you've grown it? To make your boyfriend happy?'

Theo shook his head. Tears of frustration threatened, which he concentrated on holding back; letting them flow would be the very worst thing.

Wilson dropped his sports bag at the feet of his chums and sauntered over, pushing his sleeves over his elbows. Theo knew what came next, but he couldn't think what to do. Ridiculously, his mother's advice came to mind. '*Oh, for goodness' sake, Theo! You're being a wee bit silly! You* know *what to talk about! Sport? School subjects? Good God, the weather? Anything!*'

He opened his mouth to speak, to try and use his smarts to defuse the situation. But Wilson's speed denied him the chance. He was fast. His first blow glanced off Theo's cheekbone, sending a searing pain whistling from one side of his brain to the other. It hurt. Theo's fingers curled into his palms.

'What's the matter?' Wilson bounced on the balls of his feet with his fists raised, as if he was observing the Queensberry Rules rather than brawling in the schoolyard. 'Too scared to hit me, faggot?' He rocked his head from side to side and jabbed a couple of mock blows before landing the third on Theo's left eye socket.

Theo winced and held a cupped palm over his face, cursing the tears that now spilled, as much in response to the pain as in frustration.

Helmsley and Dinesh skittered about like excitable pups. They darted around the two of them, shouting their approval and whooping and hollering as they cheered their leader on. 'Poof!' Dinesh yelled for good measure.

Theo tried to stand up straight, thinking that he should now speak, try to reason... The next blow caught him on the side of the head and for a second or two his vision blurred.

'What sort of bloke doesn't fight back? What the fuck is wrong with you?' Wilson spat. 'Is it like the homo code?'

Theo would have had difficulty describing the exact order of what followed. His fogged brain, a preoccupation with his injuries and a sense of disbelief made him a less than perfect witness.

He saw Wilson's head jerk sideways as something struck him on the side of the face with force.

'What the fuck?' Wilson yelled, in a high-pitched voice that Theo hadn't heard before.

What had struck him was a palm on the end of a brawny arm, belonging to none other than Cyrus Porter.

Wilson turned to face the groundsman and laughed, his face puce. 'I see how it is. Come to defend your boyfriend! So it *is* a homo code!'

Mr Porter slapped him again. His knuckle made contact with Wilson's mouth, whose lower lip split like an overripe tomato. Blood trickled over his chin and down his shirtfront.

'Fucking hell!' Wilson yelled and dropped to his knees, dabbing at the blood and rubbing his thumb over the pads of his fingers before bringing them up to his eyes, as if he needed visible proof. He remained kneeling, shocked and subdued by Mr Porter's intervention, stunned by the flow of his blood.

'What is going on here?' Mr Beckett's voice boomed across the quad.

Dinesh and Helmsley froze. Theo staggered backwards and tried to slow his breathing, which was now the only thing he could hear, loud in his ears. He glanced over at Mr Porter. The colour had drained from his face and he looked as pale as the ghosts he lived with.

The clock on the mantelpiece ticked insistently as Theo sat on the other side of the headmaster's desk and waited. Mr Beckett hovered, straight-backed, by the door, as if ready to stop any escapees, and Mr Porter stared out of the window. It occurred to Theo that this was probably a rare opportunity for Mr Porter to see his work from this vantage point: the cut grass, the trimmed borders and the immaculate playing fields.

'Mr Porter, I—'

'Best say nothing,' Mr Porter offered in a neutral tone, his head making a slight incline towards Mr Beckett.

Theo swallowed the words of gratitude and apology he wanted to share with his friend. They would keep.

Once the adrenalin had calmed, his face, and in particular his eye, began to throb. He looked down at the red stain on his right hand and flexed his fingers. He wasn't sure if the dried blood crusting the underside of his hand was his own or Wilson's.

The headmaster entered the room in a hurry. His robe billowed behind him and Mr Beckett followed in his wake like an impatient page. The head coughed and sat down hard in his leather chair. He let out a deep sigh, as if the whole thing was an inconvenience, before resting his elbows on the inlaid desktop and touching his fingertips in front of him to form a pyramid.

'I must say that I am at a loss, Montgomery.'

There was another pause. The sound of the clock was now quite deafening.

Mr Porter coughed, as if clearing his throat to speak.

'I will address you presently,' the headmaster snapped in his direction.

For Theo, despite everything he'd already gone through, this was the worst part of his day, hearing his friend Mr Porter spoken to with such disdain. He glanced at Mr Porter, who seemed to shrink. Theo felt like weeping at the reddening of the man's complexion. For him to be so humiliated when he'd only been trying to help, trying to stop Theo from getting a further beating. Mr Porter had defended him just as he'd defended his country. That was the sort of man he was.

The headmaster sighed again, his irritation apparent. Mr Beckett stood like a sentinel to his right, looking furious. Theo faced the two men and wished they would hurry up and get this over with. He wanted to be free to leave and to talk to Mr Porter out of earshot.

'I don't need to remind you that your father and your father's father both made head of house. They are Vaizey men, like myself. In fact your Uncle Maxim and I played in the 1st XV together. This fact alone is going to earn you a second chance.'

'Thank you, sir.' Theo barely hid the disappointment in his voice. He'd been half hoping for expulsion and permanent liberation.

'Not that I shall be easy on you, and nor indeed will Mr Beckett. It is obvious that you need a firm hand.' Theo looked up at them. It was laughable, the implication that until now they'd been soft on him. 'I don't need to tell you that yours is not Vaizey behaviour. Where did you think you were? A public house? The docks?'

'I don't know, sir.' He kept his eyes fixed ahead. 'It wasn't my fault.'

The headmaster exhaled loudly through his nostrils. 'In my experience, there are certain reasons why a boy might display such violent behaviour, especially when it is out of character, which I believe for you this was.' He sat forward in the chair. 'Mr Wilson, despite his injured state...' He fixed Mr Porter with a steely glare. '... was able to throw a little light on the possible cause of this scuffle.' He raised an eyebrow. 'Is there anything you would like to share with me?'

'No, I don't think so, sir.' Theo shook his head, trying to think what Wilson might have said. 'Just that it wasn't a scuffle.' That implied it had been a mutual thing, an altercation, almost playful, but Wilson's actions had been nothing of the sort. 'I would say that rather than a scuffle it was an attack. I didn't do anything wrong. I had only just arrived back and they called at me from across the quad—'

'Saying what, exactly?' Mr Beckett interjected.

'Erm...' Theo wondered whether to repeat the vile taunts, taunts that Mr Porter had taught him would make you ugly on the inside as well as the outside. 'They called me a sonofabitch. And then a faggot and then poof and homo, that kind of thing.' A blush spread across his cheeks. 'And then he called Mr Porter a homo.'

'I see.' The headmaster nodded and looked down at his hands, as if considering these words.

'And then he punched me. And he carried on punching me,' he levelled. 'I didn't punch him at all.'

'So it was an entirely unprovoked attack?'

'Yes.' Theo nodded with confidence.

'And Wilson attacked the groundsman too?'

Theo looked up at his friend and couldn't decide how best to answer. The words caught in his throat as he recalled their pact, made on a rough wooden bench many years ago. '*Here's the thing: you never have to lie to me, and I will never lie to you, how about that?*'

'Mr Porter is my friend. He… He was only—'

'It's a simple enough question,' the head interjected. 'Did Wilson attack the groundsman?'

'I…'

'Yes or no, Montgomery.' Mr Beckett joined in. 'Did Wilson hit the groundsman?'

Theo looked directly at the men, unable to hold his friend's stare. 'No,' he answered clearly. 'Wilson didn't hit him.'

The two masters exchanged a knowing glance and Mr Beckett breathed in and out through his nostrils.

'But Wilson was hitting me, he hurt me! And Mr Porter hates fighting, he says we've all fought enough, and he was only trying to—'

'Enough!' The headmaster held up his palm. 'You cannot possibly know what Mr Porter was or was not intending to do.' He took another deep breath. 'Mr Beckett, kindly escort Mr Porter to the staffroom. I would like to talk to Montgomery alone.'

Mr Beckett tilted his head in response and walked to the door. He opened it and stood back, waiting for Mr Porter. As he walked past, Theo caught the whiff of earth, petrol and real fires that he had so missed over the summer.

When the door closed behind them the head dropped his

shoulders and gave a small smile that softened his face. 'Now, Theo, is there anything else you might like to tell me about Mr Porter?'

'No.' Theo looked up, wondering what he might be getting at. He knew it was against the rules to loiter around Mr Porter's house during lunchbreak, as it was officially off school premises, but he'd been doing that for years and had never been taken to task over it. He remembered then that Mr Porter had agreed to do his English assignment for him. Had Wilson found it in the dorm? Was that what he was talking about?

'You have no secrets? Nothing that you would prefer to remain between the two of you?'

'No big secrets, only small ones…' Theo swallowed, remembering their agreement. '*They'd have my guts for garters if they knew I'd helped with your homework.*'

'Has Mr Porter ever asked you to keep anything… private?'

He turned to face Theo, who felt a flush of fear that his friend was going to get into trouble. He pictured his pen torch, given all those years ago and still serving him well. 'Nothing important, just something to help me, at night…' He swallowed.

The headmaster stood and walked around the desk slowly, before placing his hand on Theo's shoulder. 'I take the reputation of my school very seriously. Do you understand that, Montgomery?'

Theo nodded. Even though he didn't understand at all.

'Very well, you are free to go.' The head coughed again and sat back behind his desk, where he reached for his telephone.

Theo looked to his left but couldn't see Mr Porter anywhere. He walked to the dorm with the strangest of feelings; it was as if every pair of eyes in the school was on him. It wasn't until he got to his room and looked in the mirror that he saw the mess of his face. There was already a yellowy green bruise forming around his swollen eye socket and the white of his eye was scarlet. Touching the soft tissue, he wondered what Kitty Montrose would make of that.

Despite being the innocent party, Theo was gated, so it wasn't until the weekend that he was allowed to leave the confines of Theobald's House. He made an effort to order his thoughts and calm the anger bubbling inside him. Twitcher gave him a nod of acknowledgement as he walked from the dorm and for the first time Theo wondered if Mr Porter had been right about that Gandhi fellow. Had he been cowardly? Should he have fought back?

His cheekbone was no longer swollen, but the rainbow-coloured bruise left by Wilson's sharp fist had not yet disappeared. He walked purposefully along the length of the field, eager to thank Mr Porter for his intervention, keen to know what had been said and desperate to tell him about all the comings and goings at La Grande Belle. He was also hoping that Mr Porter would do what he did so well and help him make sense of what had happened, explaining Wilson's sudden violent attack and making him feel better about it all.

Jogging up the path, he knocked on the door and with his hands in his pockets called his usual greeting through the letterbox.

'Only me!'

There was no response. Theo ran through Mr Porter's schedule in his head. He should be home. He turned and knocked again, then made his way along the wall to the sitting-room window. Bringing his hand up to his forehead, he leant on the glass and squinted.

A pulse of shock rocketed through him. The room was bare! Gone were the books from the shelves and the cushions from the chairs; the mantelpiece was empty of the knick-knacks that usually sat there gathering dust. It was as if Mr Porter had never been there.

Theo raced back to the front door and barged it with his shoulder until it shifted and opened. He raced from room to room, ending up in the kitchen, where a green enamel kettle had once whistled on the stove and the radio had burbled with the gentle sound of the cricket.

As realisation dawned, Theo felt a physical pain in his chest. The knowledge that Mr Porter had gone was a sharp thing that now lodged itself in his skin. Sinking to his knees, his fists balled against his thighs, he howled a loud guttural cry that came from deep within.

'My friend! What am I supposed to do now?' he screamed as hot tears streamed down his face. 'My friend! I'm sorry! I should have said more. I should have told them to leave you alone! I'm sorry!' He yelled loud enough that the words might travel high and far, to be heard by his friend, who might or might not be sitting on the brow of a hill, letting his eyes sweep the broad fields of the Dorset countryside, where full hedgerows formed the boundaries and deer frolicked on the lower slopes in the pink haze of the evening sun.

With no Mr Porter to turn to, Theo's last four years at Vaizey College passed slowly and miserably. As he was driven out through the school gates for the final time, he swore he would never return. No way was he going to be one of those Old Vaizey Boys like his father who met up every year for reunion socials and came back for sports days and fundraisers. It would have been different if things with Kitty had been rosier. But she was still with Angus Thompson, they were still the school's golden couple, and Theo had found out to his cost that it was far better for his mental health to simply keep out of her way. On his last day at Vaizey he hadn't said goodbye to her or anyone else.

Now, though, he was determined to try and start afresh. He'd got a place at University College London, and he and his parents had just arrived at his hall of residence, not far from the British Museum. They'd helped him carry his suitcase and stereo up to his room and had been there all of five minutes when Theo noticed his father pulling his jacket sleeve up over his watch and surreptitiously checking the time. He felt the familiar flush of unease at the realisation that his parents wanted to be elsewhere. He actually wanted them to stay, though he wasn't sure why.

It wasn't as if they hadn't left him many times before, throughout his school years, but this felt different. University was a big step.

From the corridor outside his room came the sound of two blokes yelling obscenities at each other. Theo cringed and glanced at his parents. It wasn't that the swearing bothered him per se – he'd heard far worse at school, often directed at himself – but watching his parents flash their fake smiles and speak a little louder, making out they hadn't heard, caused his anxiety levels to rise. They behaved the same way on the mornings after their own rows, acting as if nothing had happened. They were so proper most of the time, but when they were drunk they dropped all their airs and graces and swore like troopers, ignoring all the rules of acceptable behaviour that they'd drummed into him his whole life. The nasty, bitter arguments he'd witnessed at La Grande Belle had recurred with depressing frequency during subsequent exeats and holidays, but no one ever mentioned them and it was clear he was expected to carry on as if everything was fine. Theo had hoped that the three of them would get closer as he got older, that he'd be treated more as an equal and would no longer feel so nervous or unwelcome in their company. But it had been many years now since he'd felt comfortable running to his mother for a hug or speaking plainly about his emotions, and here he was at eighteen feeling increasingly ill at ease in their company.

His mother squeezed past the desk in her royal blue Laura Ashley frock and stared down at the street below. 'Good job you've got this double-glazing.' She tapped a slender knuckle on the window. 'Of course it looks absolutely ghastly, but it'll keep out some of the noise.'

'Yes.'

'Quite a nice spot though, really. Handy.' She smiled.

Handy for what, Theo wasn't sure, but he nodded anyway.

His mother looked back at him as if at a loss for what to say. She sighed and clasped her hands in front of her.

'We are going to be *late*, Stella.' His father widened his eyes, as if this were code. 'Besides, Theo probably wants to dive into his books or whatever it is students do all day.'

Theo clenched his jaw. His dad would not let it rest. A year ago, when he'd been filling out the application form at the kitchen table, his father had stopped en route to the fridge. 'I don't know why you're bothering, Theodore,' he'd boomed. 'We'll have you behind a desk in Villiers House in no time, and you don't need a fancy degree to do that, not when it's the Montgomery name above the door.' He'd huffed. 'A Vaizey education has always been perfectly sufficient, as your grandfather and your great-grandfather and myself have all demonstrated.'

Theo's insides had churned. 'Actually, Dad, I have thought about it and I would really like to go to university.'

'Anything to delay a hard day's graft, is that it?'

'No. I just like the idea of getting really good at something, becoming an expert.' He was determined not to work with his dad or for the family business and he knew that the only way to ensure that was to do a degree and then follow his own path.

His dad had stopped rummaging for the bottle of tonic and looked in his direction. 'An expert, eh? Oh good God! Don't tell me your bloody mother has finally managed to bend your ear about the law or, God forbid, medicine! Ghastly profession, full of egos and long shifts. Don't listen to her, she's as thick as mince, doesn't understand the business at all!'

Theo sat up straight. 'It's nothing to do with Mum.' He felt his cheeks colour, hating his inability to stand up for his mum in the face of his dad's relentless jibes. 'It's something I've been thinking about for a while.' He took a deep breath and then blurted it out. 'I want to study social science and social policy.'

His father laughed. 'You want to study *what*?'

'Social policy. It's about looking at social movements and ways to address social problems, help society. A lot of people that study it go on to be policy makers all over the world.' He grew quieter as his confidence ebbed.

His dad pivoted and placed his hands on his waist. His chin jutted sideways, which was a sure sign he was angry. 'Social problems, eh?' He gave a cold, hollow laugh. 'And tell me, Theo, what social problems have you ever encountered?'

'I... I...'

'I can hear it now.' His father guffawed and adopted a falsetto voice that made Theo's stomach bunch. 'I want to change the world! Even though I have only ever known the bloody best education, an education offered to the top ten per cent!' He shook his head in disgust. 'They'll laugh you out of town, boy!'

Theo's mind was racing. It was precisely because he'd seen the ten per cent in action that he wanted to do something that might help the other ninety per cent, but he kept this to himself.

His father returned his attention to the fridge. 'Just remember who pays for your education, boy. Social policy, over my dead body! I want to hear no more about it.' He grabbed the bottle of tonic, slammed the door and whistled as he made his way back to the drawing room.

This encounter had been followed by a tense week during which his parents weren't speaking to each other and neither appeared to be speaking to him. The impasse had ended when his mother had called to him casually from her bedroom. He stood at the door, inhaling the cigarette smoke that encircled her in a pungent cloud, her aqua silk housecoat spread around her on the bed like a pond. She narrowed her eyes at him and placed the novel she was reading face down on the bed. 'I've had a word with your father, darling. You can go to university if you want, but you'll have to study engineering, not social work or whatever it is you were on about. That's Daddy's condition, otherwise he won't pay. He says at least engineering might be of some use to the company.'

Engineering! Theo's heart sank. But it was better than nothing. And what mattered more than anything was that his mum had stuck up for him. That meant a lot. 'Thank you, Mum.' He smiled as he backed out of the room.

The blokes outside his uni bedroom had finally moved elsewhere and there was a sudden hush. His father coughed and rocked on his heels. 'As I said, we really can't be late, Stella. And Theo doesn't want us to hang around, do you?'

'No. I'm fine. I… I don't want to make you late.'

'If you're absolutely sure, darling?' His mother quickly acquiesced, just as she always did. 'I feel like we should stay and help you unpack your clothes or put up a poster or something?' She waved her hand limply towards the ceiling.

'I don't have that many clothes and I'm good for posters, thanks.' He scanned the blank white walls of his tiny room.

'Well, look…' His mother grabbed her cream pashmina from the back of the chair by the desk, gave a nod to her husband and smiled thinly. 'You have our number of course and it's not like we are far away!' She laughed. 'Call if you need anything, anything at all.'

He nodded. If anyone were to listen in on the conversations he had with his parents, they'd probably be touched at how loving his mum and dad sounded. What they wouldn't pick up on, though, were the stolen glances, the sighs, the hurried tone and the awkward pauses. It was these that spoke loudest to Theo.

After shaking his father's hand and accepting his mother's fleeting kiss on his cheek, he waved them goodbye and flopped down onto his bed. He noted how confined his room was and how bland. Actually, though, he didn't mind that. He was almost looking forward to being on his own in the middle of London, an invisible figure among the crowds, one of many, with no one to single him out as a loner, a weirdo. Almost subconsciously, he reached inside the neck of his sweatshirt and ran his finger over the fishing fly, pinned there.

Shivering, he felt suddenly cold and rolled himself into a sausage within the coverless duvet. Finally his time was his own: no bell was going to call him to study, to go to lessons or to have supper. He lay on the bare mattress and fell sleep.

A couple of hours later he was woken by a knock on his door. Startled, he took a sharp breath and quickly disentangled his feet from the duvet. He opened the door to find a tall, skinny, dark-haired boy with a bulky rucksack over his right shoulder and a toothy grin on his face.

The boy beamed at him. 'I'm your next-door neighbour,' he said, as if this were grounds for some special connection.

Theo thought of the countless boys he'd roomed next to at Vaizey – none had ever smiled at him like this. He looked at him nervously, wondering what he wanted, then dropped his gaze, waiting for the inevitable snide comment. None came. 'Right. I'm Theo,' he eventually offered.

'Did you say Cleo?' The boy took a step forward and squinted earnestly at Theo's face.

'Cleo?' Theo sprayed his laughter. 'Do I look like a Cleo?'

'No!' The boy laughed. 'I just thought that was what you said. I'm from Wigan!'

'What's that got to do with anything?'

'I don't know, man, I'm just freaking out!' He ran his fingers through his wiry hair. 'I'm in London and this is scary shit!'

Theo laughed. 'Well, I've lived not far from here my whole life, when I wasn't away at school, and I can assure you you have nothing to be scared of.'

'Thanks, Cleo.' The boy smiled, showing his large teeth. 'I'm Spud, by the way.'

'And I'm *Theo*.' They exchanged another smile. 'Is Spud your Christian name?'

'Kind of. My surname is Edwards and it started as King Edwards when I got to secondary school and within a year it was Potato Boy, and then Spud, and that stuck – even my parents call me it!' He chuckled. 'My school friends call my mum and dad Ma and Pa Spud – it's become a bit of a joke.'

'Spud it is then.' Theo hovered in the doorway, wishing he had a similarly witty anecdote about Ma and Pa Montgomery. He was badly rehearsed in what to do next, how to chat, though he did know that neither the weather nor sport were the answer. 'Anyway, I better unpack or something.' He pointed to the suitcase on the desk.

'Do you want to go the student union and get a beer later?' Spud asked, almost casually but with a flicker to his eyelid that suggested nerves. 'I mean, only if you haven't already got anything else planned. I'm not being pushy and I'm not trying to get invited, I just thought...' He ran out of steam, clearly flustered.

Theo nodded. 'Sure. A beer would be good.' He tried to sound cool, hoping to hide the explosion of nerves and excitement.

And just like that, Theodore Montgomery made a friend. A proper friend of his own age.

Holding their warm pints, served in plastic glasses, and with Van Halen's 'Jump' playing on the jukebox, the two took seats at the edge of the union bar. The furniture was dark, cheap and tatty and the walls, painted a deep red were covered with posters.

'So what are you studying?'

'Engineering. You?'

'Economics,' Spud answered with pride. 'Have you got brothers and sisters?'

'No, just me.' In the four years since that horrible night when he'd made the shocking discovery about his half-brother, Alexander, not a word had been said about him, and Theo hadn't told a soul. It wasn't that he dwelt on it, exactly, but it came into his mind sometimes. He felt nauseous at the thought of his dad cheating and lying to his mum. 'What about you?'

'Two sisters. One older, married with three kids, and one younger, still at school.'

Theo couldn't imagine having that many people in his life.

'We're just hoping my older one stops having sprogs and my younger one doesn't start too soon. Already at Christmas my nan has to sit at the table on the laundry basket with a cushion on top, and last year my cousin ate his lunch standing up!' He laughed. 'My mum says at this rate she'll be doing two sittings.'

Theo stared at him, trying and failing to picture the world he described.

'Have you got a girlfriend?' Spud kept the questions coming.

'No!' Theo laughed, despite himself. He tried to ignore the pull of longing in his gut as his thoughts turned to Kitty. 'You?'

'Nah.' Spud sighed. 'I saw a couple of girls at school, but nowt serious.'

'I liked a girl at school, but she had a boyfriend, so...' Theo shrugged.

'Well, you need to find a girl here and erase the memory of her!' Spud laughed. 'What's her name?'

'Kitty.' He swallowed. Even saying her name out loud felt like a big deal.

Spud raised his pint. 'To erasing Kitty!'

They clinked their plastic glasses.

'So you're from London?' Spud put his pint on the table and rubbed his hands together, whether with excitement or nerves it was hard to tell.

'Yes, but I went to school in Dorset.'

'Boarding school?'

'Yes.' Theo smiled. 'It would have been one hell of a commute if I was a day boy.'

Spud laughed loudly and Theo joined in. *That was funny. I can do funny!*

'I've never met anyone that went to boarding school.'

'You have now.' Theo sipped the pint. It was horribly bitter, left a nasty aftertaste and made him feel gassy. It would take some getting used to.

'God, living without your parents and being with your mates, it sounds mint. Was it like a party every night? Girls having pillow fights, midnight snacks, smoking out of the window?' Spud sat forward eagerly.

Theo gave a dry laugh. 'Not for me. I hated it, I really did.'

'Why?'

Theo considered his response, knowing how people feared the contagion of weird. 'I didn't like a lot of the people there. Some of them were right bastards.' He liked how easily he could talk to Spud. His new friend's kindly nature and their liberal consumption of booze made it possible.

Spud nodded. 'I suppose there are always going to be bastards. The trick is to avoid the wankers.'

'Yep.' He nodded. 'So what's Wigan like?'

Spud shrugged. 'Like anywhere else, I s'pose. I've never lived anywhere else, mind you. I mean, not like London! Nothing's like this place!' He giggled. 'We've got a good football team, a canal, shit shops, great pubs and even better clubs if you know where to look. People are friendly and that's about it. It's struggled since we've started losing the mines.'

'I'd hate to go down a mine. Can't imagine it – dark and cold.' He shivered.

Spud eyed him over the rim of his second pint. 'I guess most people would hate to go down into the cold and dark, but when that's the thing that's going to put bread on the table, you'd be surprised what folk'll do. My dad's a miner – like my grandad before him.'

Theo felt his face colour. He hadn't meant to be rude.

'I've never met anyone like you, Theodore.' Spud smiled. 'Have you ever been abroad?'

'Yes.'

'Have you ever been on a plane?'

'Yes!'

'Have you ever bought a single fag from an ice-cream van?'

'No!' It was Theo's turn to laugh.

'Have your mum and dad got a car?'

'Yes.'

'What kind?'

'My dad has a vintage Aston Martin.'

Spud nearly choked on his pint. He laughed and slapped the table. 'You, Theo, are the poshest person I have ever met.'

'I don't know if that's a compliment!' Theo pulled a face.

'It is what it is, my friend. It is what it is.' Spud shook his head and prepared to return to the bar for their refills.

That beer was to be the first of countless pints Theo and Spud drank together over the coming months, in pubs, bars and clubs across London. By the end of their second term, Theo had more than got used to the taste. Tonight he and Spud had gone out together as usual, and, as sometimes happened, they'd become separated a little after midnight.

Theo grabbed the hand of the girl he'd been talking to for the last half-hour and started running. 'Come on!'

'I can't keep up!' She giggled. 'I'm wearing heels!'

'Then take them off!' he yelled through his laughter.

The girl did just that, hopping, mid run, from one foot to the other and gathering her shoes into her hand. She gripped them like a pointy bowling ball and with Theo pulling her along she zigzagged down the pavement in just her tights, her fur bomber jacket and her blue suede mini skirt.

'Why are we running?' she asked between more giggles.

'Because I'm pissed and it seemed like a good idea!'

As they rounded the top of Inverness Street and turned right into Camden High Street he slowed and bent double, laughing loudly while he tried to catch his breath.

'You are fucking insane!' She laughed loudly too, then stood on tiptoes, reached up and kissed him full on the mouth. Her hand snaked under his shirt to find his solid chest. 'Did we really just run away from my mates?'

He looked back up the street. 'It would appear so.'

'Why did we do that?' She laughed.

'Because I wanted to get you on your own.' He grinned.

'You nutcase.' She kissed him again. 'So where now?' she whispered suggestively.

'My room?'

'Sounds like a plan.' She giggled some more and gave him a coy look from beneath her heavily mascaraed lashes.

The two walked with their arms across each other's shoulders, picking their way through litter, knotted black bin bags left underneath trees, prostrate clubbers and some market traders unloading their transit vans ready for their Sunday morning stalls. It was a typical Saturday night, or had been. Theo loved this time, just before dawn broke, the transition point between a good night coming to an end and a good day just beginning. They wobbled away into the dawn, stopping to snog where and when the fancy took them.

Theo put the key into the door of his building and turned to the girl. 'Ah, I should probably mention that it's my student room and I am not strictly allowed guests, plus my half-wit mate, who might or not have made it home before me, *might* be crashed out on my bed.'

'You share a room?' she asked, clearly unimpressed.

'No, we don't share a room, but he tends to fall wherever

is closest when he's pissed. He's not… how should I say it… boundary conscious.'

'Right.' She looked at him quizzically.

Theo paused and turned back to her. 'What's your name, by the way?'

'Mitzi!' She tittered.

'And I'm Rollo.'

'Rollo!' She laughed again. Theo prayed that she was really high and not just really stupid.

His room was a mess, although this was standard. It was no longer the kind of mess that could be fixed with a quick whizz round with a duster and a vacuum cleaner – it was way past that. The room was grubby and disorganised. A poster for the movie *Halloween* hung down from the sloping ceiling, its corner displaying a strip of yellowing Sellotape. Books and takeaway containers littered every surface and his bedside table was covered with the detritus of discarded joints, Rizla packets with the corners torn off to make roaches, thin strands of tobacco and an overflowing ashtray. An abandoned cereal bowl sat on the windowsill with a ring of sour milk clinging to the insides and soggy cornflakes stuck to the rim. Empty Sol bottles with shrivelled wedges of lime were lined up like skittles on the floor around the skirting board, and the air was stale with the tang of cigarette smoke and old food.

Theo took in the expression of disgust on Mitzi's face. 'It's the maid's day off.'

'Day off?' Mitzi curled her top lip. 'I think she wants firing.'

As Theo looked at her, at the dark rings of kohl around her eyes and her vacant stare, an image of Kitty popped into his head. Beautiful, clean, sparkling Kitty. There was a moment of awkward contemplation, in which he lost enthusiasm for her company.

'Do you know what, Mitzi?' He spoke calmly, rubbing at his stubble. 'I think we should call it a night. You shouldn't want to be here in this grubby room, with someone who's dragged you from your mates. You deserve better.'

'Are you kidding me?' She glared at him. 'You march me back to this shithole and now you're *dumping* me?'

'I'm not dumping you. I don't know you! And look, please let me pay for your cab, to wherever.' He reached into his back pocket and removed his wallet, peeling off a ten-pound note.

'What the fuck? You think you can pay me off?' she shouted as she slipped her red-heeled shoes back onto her now grimy stockinged feet.

'No! I'm just trying to be gentlemanly.'

'Gentlemanly? You are weird as shit is what you are!'

'So I've been told.' He blinked, sobering a little now and wanting nothing more than for her to leave so he could go to sleep. His messy bed had never looked more inviting.

'Morning. I think.' Spud walked past Theo's open door in a striped towelling dressing gown that was open, revealing his green underpants. 'Just off to the loo.' He scratched his hairy chest and yawned. 'God, don't remember much about the night. I think I lost you after Dingwalls. Are you coming in or going out, Theo?'

'Theo?' Mitzi screeched. 'You told me your name was Rollo!' This subterfuge was apparently the final straw for Mitzi, who snatched the ten-pound note from his hand and stomped off in her red heels. She turned at the end of the corridor to flip him the bird. 'Dickhead!' she yelled, loud enough to wake anyone who might have been sleeping off the night before.

'My bad,' Theo mumbled as he sank down onto his bed and closed his eyes.

'She seemed nice,' Spud called from the doorway. 'Your parents are going to love her! Are you thinking a spring wedding?'

Theo laughed despite his tiredness and turned on to his side. He needed sleep.

With Def Leppard's 'Animal' blaring out of the stereo in his room, Theo lay in the slightly rusted bath down the corridor. It was as good a remedy as any for his post-Mitzi hangover. The cold tap dripped constantly, leaving a mottled brown residue on the old enamel, but he had perfected a manoeuvre whereby he could turn on the hot tap with his toes, allowing him to languish in the bath for hours.

Spud banged on the bathroom door, pulling him from his daydreams. 'How much longer are you going to be in there?' he yelled. 'I need a shit!'

Theo laughed. 'Getting out now!'

'Cool. Wanna come out and get pissed? Hair of the dog?'

Theo laughed at his mate's favourite and only suggestion when it came to socialising. 'Oh really, and forgo our usual seats at the opera? If you insist! Let's go via the takeaway first.'

An hour later they were both sitting on the low wall outside their nearest kebab shop. Theo bit into the kebab and simultaneously took a swig from his can of pop.

'So who was that girl night last night? Thought you were going to see the French one you met?'

Theo shook his head, 'No, lost her number, kind of on purpose.' He pulled a face.

'I can't keep up.' Spud laughed and dug a small plastic fork into his polystyrene punnet loaded with heavily salted chips. 'Seems you are doing quite well in your quest to erase Kitty.'

'I was,' Theo paused, 'and then last night, I looked at Mitzi and thought about Kitty and I just wanted to be on my own.'

'A mere setback my friend.' Spud chuckled.

'I hope so, my social life is all I have to look forward to, bloody engineering!' he bit his kebab.

'I like my lectures!'

'It's all right for you, you love your subject. I hate mine!'

'So switch! You've only done two terms. Ben on the floor below us swapped from medicine to biology, it was easy and now he's happy. I mean, you'd probably have to work hard to catch up, but you work hard anyway. It's the answer. Life is too short, Theo old son, do what makes you happy!'

'I wish it was that straightforward,' Theo said with his mouth full, 'but my dad would go crazy.' It was a miracle he was at university at all and not chained to a desk in Villiers House.

Spud made as if he was answering a phone. 'Oh hello, yes. Right, I'll tell him.' He theatrically mimed replacing the receiver. 'That was the Universe on the phone. It said, "Tell your mate that this is his life, not his dad's, and he needs to do what makes him happy!"'

'You make it sound easy.' Theo took another bite, he was famished.

'I think it's as easy or as hard as you want it to be.'

'For you maybe. What would your dad say if you changed course?' He licked his greasy fingers.

Spud held his gaze. 'My dad doesn't care what I study, he just wants me to be happy and he is beyond chuffed that his son has got a place at university. It's a big deal for us. I'm the first ever on either side of the family to go and not just to any university – UCL, in that London!' He was making fun of himself, but Theo knew his humour masked a very real truth and he envied Spud that.

Seven

Spud had been right, as he often was. Switching degrees had been a doddle and Theo had thrown himself into his new course, attending lectures with pleasure and writing essays with gusto. The hardest part had been trying to tell his parents, but after one attempt he made a decision and kept his course change to himself. They hadn't exactly taken an interest in his engineering degree anyway, so why should this be any different? It was now the autumn term of his final year and he had already started looking at the jobs pages, keen to get on with his chosen career as soon as he graduated. He was particularly interested in housing policy, which was one of his specialisms.

It was rare that he slept through his alarm, but today had been an exception. He cursed the fact. It was vital that he get in on time for this morning's tutorial. His tutor had made it quite clear from the beginning: 'A degree from UCL cannot be coasted. A degree from UCL requires investment from you in the form of hard work and commitment and if the concept of industry and reward is something you do not understand, then might I suggest that a degree course here is not for you.' His dissertation was looming and today was the day set aside for discussing it with his tutor. It was important to Theo that he be the best he could, and regardless of whether he eventually managed to get his hoped-for 2:1, a good reference from his tutor would be enormously helpful.

'God, I hate being late!' Theo muttered under his breath as he raced from the flat in Belsize Park he shared with Spud and ran down the street. Jumping back onto the kerb, he tucked his shirt into the waistband of his jeans and looked the length of the road and back again, his eyes searching for a cab. 'Come on, come on!' he pleaded. He glanced at his watch. 'Shit!'

He started to half walk, half run in the direction of the UCL campus, watching eagerly for a cab as he went. Finally one swung into view. He jumped up and down, calling out 'Taxi!' with his arm straight up in the air. The cabbie flashed his lights and pulled over. Theo scrambled in, sat back and took a deep breath. He wished he'd had time to shower properly instead of doing only a quick spritz with a can of deodorant.

As the cab trundled along Eversholt Street and idled at the lights, Theo stared distractedly out of the window, mentally rehearsing the excuses he might offer to explain his tardiness to his tutor. And suddenly, there on the pavement, waiting to cross over, dressed in high-waisted baggy jeans, a cropped baby-pink sweatshirt and with a purple file in her arms, stood none other than Kitty Montrose.

'Stop the cab!' He leant forward and banged on the dividing screen.

The cabbie tutted and pulled over.

Theo thrust a note at him. 'Sorry! Keep the change!' he managed as he jumped out, desperate not to lose sight of her.

His heart thumped as he drew closer. He hoped he wasn't

mistaken. Many had been the time during the two and a half years since leaving Vaizey that his spirits had lifted at the sight of a red-headed girl, only to be disappointed when he got near enough to see that she was a poor imitation of the real thing.

He sidled along the pavement and watched her peer into the newsagent's window. He looked to his left and felt a spike of joy through his gut. It was her! No doubt about it. His jaw tensed and his mouth went dry. He tried to calm his thoughts, didn't want her to know he'd followed her – it *had* to look casual, a coincidence.

He willed her to go into the coffee shop, giving him a legitimate excuse to follow and bump into her in the queue.

'Hey, Kitty,' he practised in his head, 'fancy seeing you here!' He experimented with the face he would pull, sucked in his stomach and wondered how he should stand, how best to show off his height and broad shoulders.

'Oh my God! Theo? Theo!'

Her yell drew him from his thoughts. He looked and did a double-take for real, no time for rehearsals, as there she was not three feet away and she was smiling at him. He needn't have worried about feigning surprise; his shock at interacting with the girl who haunted his dreams was genuine.

'Oh my God! Kitty!' He beamed. 'No way!'

She rushed forward, dropping her bag and file on the pavement, and threw her arms around his neck. For a glorious second he knew what it must have felt like to be Angus Thompson, with Kitty's body pressed against his and her floral scent enveloping him like a gossamer cloth.

It felt bloody brilliant.

'What are you doing here?' she asked as she pulled away.

He slid his hands from her waist, where his fingers briefly made contact with her silky skin, and tried to hide the tremble to his limbs. 'Just on my way to uni. Exams are coming up, so I'm looking for a few pointers on my dissertation,' he said, with none of the urgency he should have felt.

'Oh God, it's *so* great to see you! Look at you!' She bobbed her knees, and he understood, because he too felt like dancing. 'Do you want to grab a coffee? Have you got time? I don't want to keep you.' She pointed over her shoulder with her thumb, to the coffee shop along the street. It had tables outside and a chalkboard detailing the cakes on offer and the soup of the day.

'Now?' His mind raced, weighing up the consequences of missing his tutorial against the chances of seeing her again, alone like this.

'Yes, now!' She laughed.

'Yep, of course, great!'

He fell into step beside her and it was a strange thing. He was twenty, working hard for his degree, living with Spud and, emboldened by booze, had spent time with a fair few girls, yet at that precise moment, walking along the street with Kitty by his side, he felt like he was fourteen again and just as clumsy. Even his natural walking pace lost its rhythm and he feared he might stumble if he didn't concentrate. He dismissed the several topics of conversation that flared in his mind, wanting to say the right thing, wanting to sound cool and yet interesting. His thoughts raged.

'I'm at college, not far from here.' She nodded into the distance. Her soft Scottish lilt hadn't disappeared and this made him happy. It would have been difficult to supplant the voice he heard in his daydreams.

'And you're studying journalism, right?' He tried to make it sound like he didn't know exactly what she was studying, as if he might have forgotten her plans laid out excitedly during one English lesson.

'Yep.' She nodded. 'Don't know if that's what I'll do finally, finally, but I'm enjoying it, so…'

'You're a long way from the Highlands,' he said, stating the obvious.

'I know.' She looked down. 'And I miss it so much. There are days when I have to stop myself throwing everything I own into a suitcase, jumping on a train, climbing into my walking boots and racing up a mountain to gulp down lungfuls of that beautiful clean air!' She closed her eyes briefly and he glimpsed the freckles that dotted her lids, just as he had remembered.

'Racing up a mountain or going for a swim.' He smiled.

'Oh, Theo, you remembered! Yes, I still love to swim.'

I remember everything: each word, each touch, each burst of laughter.

He studied her pale complexion and that tiny nose, half listening to her chatter about her course and her flatmates but at the same time taking in every detail of her, which he knew he would replay in the early hours whenever sleep evaded him. He watched her gather her cappuccino from the counter into her dainty hand and make her way past the tables to a vacant booth along the laminate-clad wall. He paid for the two of them, then followed with his can of 7up, remembering suddenly Mr Porter's words about girls who always assumed the man would pay: '*If she's the kind of girl that is* impressed *by gifts and expensive treats, the kind of girl who won't pay her own way, then I would say she isn't the girl you want…*' He swallowed the familiar mixture of guilt and sadness that hit him whenever he remembered Mr Porter and automatically felt inside his jeans pocket for the fishing-fly pin he carried whatever he was wearing.

'It is good to see you, Theo.' She studied his face and he felt himself blushing under her scrutiny. 'You look…'

'I look what?' He was curious and self-conscious in equal measure. He watched the words form on her lips.

'You look lovely.'

'Lovely? I'd prefer something a bit more rugged,' he quipped, tensing his arms into a he-man pose before sipping from the can. He was delighted nonetheless.

'Nope.' She shook her head. 'It doesn't work like that. You don't get to choose the words in my head and that's it: you look lovely to me.'

There was a second or two of silence while he let her words settle on him like glitter. They held each other's gaze without embarrassment, as if their shared history allowed for this intimacy.

'I've often thought I might bump into you, and I've kept a lookout for you, but you never go to any of the reunion events at Vaizey, do you?' Her words robbed him of the chance to respond to her compliment.

'No. I have absolutely no desire to go back.' He sat up tall in the seat, subconsciously showing her that he was now grown-up, different.

'But you should. They're good fun and it's nice to catch up with people.'

Theo struggled with how to respond, saddened and inexplicably angry that she felt affection for the place he'd detested, and wary of sharing his true feelings about their school. He didn't want the glitter to lose its shine. 'Only hell or high water would drag me back there,' he offered finally and firmly, hoping this was enough.

'I always liked sitting next to you,' she continued, seemingly oblivious to the depth of his feelings about Vaizey. 'I liked it very much. I remember how whenever Mr Reeves said something risqué or stupid we'd look at each other – that little glance that meant we both got it!' She threw her head back and laughed her beautiful laugh.

'He was so dull.'

'He was *so* dull!' She laughed again and he joined in. It felt good to share this. '"Page forty-three of the nominated accompanying text on *Othello*, please, ladies and gentlemen!"' She mimicked their English teacher's monotone warble perfectly.

'Oh my God, don't! That's too scary!'

'Shall we get some cake? I'm starving.'

'Sure.' He stood up.

'Just one bit, we can share.' She spoke matter-of-factly and he felt his heart might burst through his ribs.

The two sat in the booth with a slab of Victoria sandwich between them and two forks, jousting for the best bits of the disappointingly dry sponge. Theo didn't care that he'd missed his tutorial. He didn't care about much. He just wished he could bottle the hour and a half they sat there together, isolated from the real world, so he could carry it around in his pocket for the rest of his life. It was one of those rare, rare moments when there was nowhere else in the world that he would rather be.

'So, Theodore,' she asked sternly, 'have you learnt any of Mr

Kipling's poetry yet?' She dipped her chin and looked at him through her strawberry-blonde lashes.

Theo carefully laid his fork on the tabletop and took a swig of his lemonade to wash away the cake crumbs. He stared up into her green eyes and began.

'This is from "The Gipsy Trail".' He coughed. 'By Rudyard Kipling.

"The wild hawk to the wind-swept sky,
The deer to the wholesome wold,
And the heart of a man to the heart of a maid,
As it was in the days of old.

"The heart of a man to the heart of a maid—
Light of my tents, be fleet.
Morning waits at the end of the world,
And the world is all at our feet!"'

He had never imagined he might say the words out loud to her. He'd memorised the poem purely to plug the gaping hole in his knowledge, exposed that first day he'd met Kitty, and because the words seemed so apt.

Kitty's eyes glazed over with emotion, and so did his. They stared at each other in silence, and like the white spaces that allow an image to stand boldly on the page it was the silence that spoke loudest to him. It was a moment to be cherished. A moment in which to do something – when would he ever get another chance?

Her eyes were searching for something and her mouth moved, as if she was ordering the thoughts that hovered on her tongue.

She looked down into her lap and her voice when it came was hushed.

'That's beautiful.'

'You are beautiful. The *most* beautiful. I have always thought so. Always.' He offered this, not knowing where the courage to speak his mind had come from; it was as if the words tumbled out of their own accord.

He watched aghast as her tears fell. He focused on a solitary tear that slipped like glass over her cheek, magnifying the freckles as it travelled. He so wanted to wipe it away with the tip of his finger.

'Please don't cry! I'm sorry if I made you sad.'

'I'm not crying because of you, I'm crying because I have so much going on that sometimes I can't think straight.' Kitty sniffed and looked up at him.

Emboldened, he placed his hand over hers. 'Oh, Kitty, I'm sorry to hear that. Do you want to go and get something to drink that isn't coffee?'

Kitty nodded and managed a smile. 'I really would like to go and get something to drink that isn't coffee.'

The pub was quiet, not that this put a dampener on their day. Their boozing was frenzied: whisky shots followed pints of beer, and by early afternoon they were more than tipsy. Theo was fearless whenever he wore his booze cloak. Reaching for her hand, he pulled her to him and kissed her firmly on the mouth. He might have been part sloshed, but that kiss was as good as any he'd dreamt about. They parted and stood inches from each other, as if no words were needed. Theo reached for his bag and coat and watched as Kitty downed the last of her drink and picked up her file. Hand in hand, with Theo leading the way, they part ran, part walked to his flat in Belsize Park. They kissed on the stairs and again in the hallway and by the time he opened his front door, Kitty was pulling at his shirt, yanking it free from the waistband of his jeans.

'If you knew the minutes, hours, days, weeks I have dreamt of this moment, Miss Montrose.' He kissed her hungrily, guiding her to the bedroom.

'You are my knight in shining armour, remember?' Kitty slurred, hooking her hands around the back of his neck.

Theo felt the swell of joy in his gut. This was happening! Kitty was in his arms, in his bedroom and she was taking off his clothes...

Propped up on his elbow, he watched Kitty sleep. He was sobering up now and totally in awe of the beautiful girl lying on the pillow next to him. His face ached from smiling. He lay down next to her, suffused with an unfamiliar serenity. In his head, he made plans. *When you wake up I'll take you for supper, and one day we'll go to the Highlands together. I'll watch you swim and then I'll wrap you in a warm towel...*

Her eyes fluttered open and she smiled, stretching her naked arm over her head with abandon. 'Oh God, Theo!' She placed her hand over her eyes, as if the lamplight offended. 'What time is it?'

He glanced at the alarm clock on the bedside table. 'Nearly seven.'

'In the evening?' She sat up straight.

'Yes, in the evening!' He laughed.

'Shit! Oh Shit!' Kitty flung back the duvet and, unabashed by her nakedness, felt around on the floor for her hastily discarded clothing.

'It's not that late – I thought we might get some supper?' He moved the pillow beneath his head to get comfy.

'Supper?' She stopped ferreting on the floor and glanced at him. She looked stricken, and though her expression was hard to read, it was clear that supper was out of the question. She was squinting now, her brow furrowed in confusion and her top lip hooked with what might have been disgust.

Theo swallowed as a gut-churning quake of nerves and inadequacy burbled inside him.

'Theo…'

She faced him now, and he knew that whatever was coming next, he didn't want to hear it. His confidence collapsed and all of a sudden he was sitting in a puddle of regret and shame.

Kitty blinked rapidly and looked mournfully into her lap, her knickers in her hand.

Theo saw her eyes jump to her bra, jeans and top, locating them on the floor in case she needed a quick exit.

'I'm getting married.'

Her words cleaved open the quiet tenderness between them, peeling the beauty from the day, leaving him raw and feeling horribly foolish. He was that same fourteen-year-old boy all over again, his hopes newly dashed, just as they had been back in the classroom that first day.

What had you honestly expected, Theo, you weirdo? She's probably never given you a second thought, not really.

'You're…?'

'I'm getting married,' she repeated, a little louder this time.

'To Angus?'

'Yes, of course to Angus!' she snapped. She sighed. 'Sorry, but who else?' She stepped into her pants and bent down to retrieve her bra.

Rather than savour the sight of Kitty naked in his room, Theo looked away, almost wishing he could go back to longing for the sight of her nude because when he'd longed for her, wished for this chance, there'd still been hope.

'Who else indeed.' He ran his palm over his stubbly chin.

'I feel...' she began. 'I feel a little... uncertain,' she mumbled as she fastened her bra.

'Well, I guess that's something for you to discuss with your... fiancé.' The word was sour on his tongue. He sat up against the wall and watched her dress, torn between wanting her to go quickly and desperately wanting her to stay.

'I have to go. I'm late.' She shook her head, flustered, angry. Finally, she slipped into her trainers and made for the door.

She looked back over her shoulder. 'Goodbye, Theo.' She bit her lip and her expression softened into that of the girl he used to know. 'Today was lovely.'

'Lovely?' He wrinkled his nose at this inadequate description.

'Well, it was for me.'

And just like that, she was gone.

* * *

It was rare for Theo to cry in this way. If he ever had. Each gulped breath seemed to provide fuel for the next bout of tears. A salty mass sat in his throat, behind his eyes and at the back of his nose. He was utterly consumed by sadness. He wiped his face on his sleeve, then used his palms to mop up what he could, until there was no point and he just let his tears run off his chin and his snot snake down his face. Now that he'd started, he couldn't stop. Between sobs he let out occasional throaty growls, almost animal-like. A pain hovered in his chest, like indigestion. His heart hurt and his head ached.

Pushing his arms into a cradle on the tabletop, he laid his head on his forearms and found some relief in closing his stinging eyes in the darkness, crying quietly now. He didn't hear the key in the door.

'Mate!' Spud rushed forward, dropped his bag and without hesitation wrapped his friend in his arms. 'It's okay. Don't cry. What's happened?'

Theo allowed himself to be embraced, taking comfort from the unfamiliar warmth of another human so close. He opened his mouth to speak, but his breath stuttered in his throat and a new wave of hot tears formed. Instead, he pushed the letter across the table and watched as Spud held it close to his face, devouring every word.

Spud pulled out the chair opposite and the two looked at each other, both now at a loss for words. Spud reread the note and only then broke the silence.

'Jesus Christ.'

Theo nodded. *Yes, Jesus Christ.*

'When did this arrive?'

'Probably this morning. I just got it from the table in the hallway.' It was the communal dumping spot for all five flats in the building, a dusty place where mail, flyers and such forth gathered.

'Have you called her?' Spud asked.

Theo shook his head. 'I don't have her number, I don't know where she lives, plus I will do as she asks.'

Spud sighed. 'Oh, mate.' He picked up the letter and read it a third time, its neat script written in blue ink on white paper.

Theo didn't need to read it again. Each word was indelibly etched on his mind.

Hello, Theo,

I hope you're still at this flat. I have thought long and hard about whether to write and what to write, so here goes.

It was an unexpectedly joyful day when I last saw you. It was a day of escape and I want you to know that I have never done anything similar before or since. I hope you believe me when I tell you that it was special for me. I know how that reads and we both know that alcohol was the catalyst, but there are very few people on earth I trust in the way I trust you, Theo.

Theo, oh, Theo…

I'm pregnant.

I can only imagine what it's like for you to read these words. Perhaps it feels the same as it did for me, when I found out.

I thought you deserved to know. It is yours. I want to keep this baby and I'm still figuring out how to make it all work. The one thing I do know is that this is not the path for us, for you and I. We are not those people. I'm marrying Angus soon, in a few weeks, and he is aware. It's been horrendously difficult for us both. For this reason, I think it only fair that we have no further contact. If our paths should ever cross, please respect my wish for us to never mention this. I beg you, Theo. This is the only way I can build a life. Please.

I say goodbye now.

Your friend,

Kitty X

'A baby.' Theo shook his head.

'And she's told her bloke?' Spud asked softly.

'It would appear so.' Theo took a deep breath and forced the wobble out of his voice. 'I realised today that I know very little about her. The real Kitty and the one that has lived inside my head for all these years are probably very different people.'

'I'd say that's true.' His friend sighed. 'I mean, I know you've always had a thing for her, but she shagged you knowing she was about to marry someone, this Angus bloke, and she treated you like shit, just upping and leaving. It's not like it was a one-night stand, a mutual thing – she knew you had history.'

'But that's just it…' Theo coughed. 'It was a one-night stand – well, a one-afternoon stand, to be more accurate. It's just that one of us didn't know it.'

'She's not for you, mate, no matter what comes next. You deserve more, better.'

Theo looked at his friend. 'Well, I have no choice, do I? She's clearly cutting me out of the picture. If it's a toss-up between Angus Thompson or me as the best possible father for her child, why would she choose me? Even if it is my child.' Theo closed his eyes and heard his mother's anguished words. '*This is the last straw, Peregrine. This is worse even than you cheating on me just after we got married, worse than you fathering that bastard boy, Alexander, worse than all of it!*' That revelation had cut him to the quick – and now here he was in a similar position. He was no better than his dad! This thought was one of the hardest to swallow.

Theo stood up from the table and reached for the letter. He folded it and tore it and tore it again and again, then dropped the fragments into the pedal bin alongside last night's pizza crusts and a couple of old tins.

'Do you want to talk? Or go and get pissed?' Spud offered help in the only way he knew how.

Theo shook his head. He wanted neither. What he wanted was to go to bed and stay there.

He climbed beneath his duvet and ran his fingers over the pillow where her red curls had lain.

'I won't tell a soul. And I don't blame you, Kitty. You know I don't know the first thing about being a dad – I'd probably be even worse than my own father. Angus will do a fine job, I'm sure. I will never forget our afternoon together. It was lovely.'

Eight

Theo was aware of a hammering sound. He lifted his head from the pillow and laid it back down quickly. The room spun and he thought he might throw up. The hangover clearly hadn't finished with him yet. He pulled the duvet up over his naked shoulder and wished whoever was knocking would go away. All he wanted to do was stay there, in his room, hidden from the world. He had nothing to get up for and nothing to look forward to, and it felt easier not to bother. Today, just like every day since he'd received the devastating letter, he woke feeling utterly worthless, unable to shake thoughts of Kitty from his head, wondering how she looked, how she was feeling, whether she knew yet whether she was going to have a little boy or a little girl. His little boy or his little girl. Was she happy?

The same lines went round and round his brain: *I'm going to be a father, someone's father, the father of Kitty's child, but they'll never know me and I'll never know them.*

He pictured Kitty and Angus Thompson exchanging duplicitous vows and cooing over the baby. He pictured Angus being the best father, doing all the things he'd wished his own father had done with him; he pictured him teaching the child to ride a bike. It was torturous. But a promise was a promise: he would keep out of Kitty's life and there would be zero contact. It was best for everyone. It was fruitless to be so preoccupied with it all; he was nothing to Kitty and had absolutely no role to play. After all, what was he to her? Merely the boy she'd sat next to in class. The weirdo.

Depression had locked Theo in an endless cycle of self-doubt with nothing but a bleak dawn to look forward to each day. He hadn't been to a lecture or even on to the university campus since he'd received the letter. For weeks now he'd ventured no further than the corner shop or the pub. He no longer cared about his degree, or about anything much. Spud had tried to cajole him into going to his tutorials. He'd tried to persuade Theo that letting his studies slip wasn't going to help anyone and was a terrible waste not only of all the hard graft he'd put in so far, but of the exciting future they'd discussed. But Theo just couldn't see it.

He rolled over and stuffed his head under the pillow, but the banging on the door didn't let up. Eventually he sat up, rubbed his face and scoured the floor for some clothes to put on. He could hardly open the door in the nude, even if it was probably only Spud. Spying his dressing gown, he shoved his arms into the armholes and fastened the rope belt around his waist. The banging continued. He cursed the fact that Spud repeatedly forgot his keys.

'All right! All right! For God's sake, I'm coming!'

He yanked open the door, but it wasn't Spud on the step. There, in his trademark navy suit, his expression a mixture of disgust and disappointment, stood his father.

'It's three in the afternoon,' his father said coldly as he studied Theo, all but tapping his watch face with his index finger.

'Hi, Dad. I know. I...' He couldn't think of an excuse quickly enough. 'Come in.' He stood back and watched his father's eyes roam the place. 'Would you like to sit down?'

'Where *exactly* do you suggest I sit?' His father stared at the sofa, hidden beneath a pile of clothing, sauce-splattered plates, chip wrappers and a stack of study notes.

Theo looked at the mess and felt embarrassed.

'You look dreadful.' His father spoke without sympathy.

'I was just about to shower.' Theo gave a short laugh, trying to convey that it was no big deal: his greasy hair and unwashed body were easily fixed. He walked over to the kitchen area, lifted a plate from the sink and looked along the crowded countertop, trying to work out where to put it. At a loss, he shoved it back in the sink.

'You smell like a brewery.'

'That'll be the beer.' He knew this would have made Spud laugh; his father, however, just stared at him.

'Do you find this funny, Theo? This the sum total of your life on the planet so far? All that money spent on your education and this is it? Living in a shithole and sleeping the day away?' He turned his gaze slowly and pointedly around the messy room.

'I...'

'No, let me finish. An education such as you have had is an investment, a huge outlay by me to make sure you have a future. And if you think this is how I saw my investment performing then you are very much mistaken.' His father shot his cuffs and jutted his chin. 'A letter arrived at the house yesterday from UCL.'

Theo looked up.

'Yes, I already know you have missed assignments and yes,

I know that it is likely you will not graduate.' He shook his head. 'What a bloody waste! Did you think you could lie to us? Pretend everything was just fine?'

'N... no, I...'

'And before you go any further, I was also fascinated to learn that you are no longer studying engineering.'

Theo's bowels turned to ice. He'd almost forgotten his parents were unaware he'd changed courses.

His dad snorted his disdain. Theo decided not to ask who the letter had been addressed to; it seemed pointless and he felt gutless. He couldn't cope with the interaction, not today.

'I... I didn't want to lie to you, Dad, and I've worked really hard up until this year. My grades were good. And then...' He paused. 'Things have... kind of fallen apart for me a bit.' He rubbed his face.

'What do you expect – sympathy? You're hardly digging roads – you're writing bloody essays, sitting in lectures and getting pissed, how hard can it be?'

Too hard for me. Too much for me right now. She's having my baby, but she didn't want me, so she went away. 'It's hard for me to explain,' he began, feeling tears pool.

'Jesus Christ.' His father ground his teeth and placed his hands on his hips. 'Get a grip.'

Theo gathered himself. 'I... I've been thinking that maybe I should apply to do the year again, Dad. I can—'

His father held up his palm and cut him short. 'Oh no, Theo. That is not what happens next. Your student days are over.'

'But I'm good at it, Dad. I know that if I—'

'There are no buts! And there's no more money, no more turning a blind eye to your drinking, your slovenly ways and your bloody deceit. Social fucking policy!' He was shouting now and Theo was glad Spud was out. 'I could have predicted this,' he yelled. 'You are to pack up your things and come back to Barnes. You're going to work. You're going to work hard and you're going to work for me.'

'But, Dad, I—'

'There's no discussion. That's it!' His father lifted his arms and let them fall back by his sides. 'I expect to see you home by Saturday and if you don't show up by then, you're on your own. Is that clear?'

'Clear,' Theo managed, feeling powerless, afraid, and humiliated at his dad's ability to reduce him to this childlike state.

He watched his father navigate the empty lager bottles and full ashtrays on his way to the front door. As he gripped the handle, he turned round to deliver his parting shot. 'And for God's sake, shave before your mother sees you.'

Theo sat motionless on the sofa and waited for Spud to come home.

'Oh, well, at least you're up!' Spud said chirpily. 'This is progress indeed. What happened, did you wet the bed?'

In no mood for humour, Theo rushed out the words that had played in his head all afternoon. 'I... I've got to leave, Spud.'

'Got to leave what?'

'The flat. Uni. Everything.'

'What are you talking about, mate?'

'My dad was here.' Theo looked down, feeling swamped by the shame of having failed to stand up to his father or be honest with him. 'He says I have to go and work for him. He knows I'm not going to graduate. They sent a letter to my home address and he opened it.'

Spud sank down on the other end of the sofa. 'How do you feel about that?'

'Like a fish in a barrel. I can't see a way out.'

'It'll be okay, mate.' Spud gave him a sympathetic pat on the shoulder. 'You're in a bad place right now and maybe this is what you need.'

'How?' Theo raised his voice, angry not at his friend but at the feeling of utter hopelessness that engulfed him. 'How is this what I need?'

'As much as I don't want you to go, right now you're so close to the edge, you're only just surviving. Some structure might be good for you, give you something else to think about. There has to be more for you than this, Theo,' Spud said softly.

Theo nodded, unable to voice exactly how he felt or what he needed.

* * *

Stella Montgomery poured the thick black coffee into the china mug and set it on the breakfast bar. 'This is such an exciting day, darling!' she trilled.

Her cheerful tone grated on Theo's nerves. 'It is?' He bit into his toast and loosened the tie at his neck. It was three years since he'd worn a collar and tie and he'd forgotten how much it felt like he was being strangled.

'Daddy is very excited about taking you to work.'

'He has a funny way of showing it.' Theo sipped his coffee. 'And you make it sound like a day out, an adventure, but it's my whole life we're talking about here.'

'It is your life, of course, but it's right that you take an interest in the business that will be yours one day. And there's no better time to start than the present.' She lit her cigarette and took a deep drag, leaning back against the countertop. 'There are a million boys who would give their eyeteeth to be in your shoes! Goodness me, a lovely job with your father, and a lovely home here. There's no reason for you to feel fed up. And let's not forget that you failed university. It's not as if you have a stellar academic career beckoning – you didn't even finish!' She turned and flicked her ash into the sink and ran the tap to dispose of the evidence.

Her words were like a punch to the gut for Theo. 'I know I went off the rails a bit, Mum. I... I've been really low – not just fed up but... There was this...' Theo stopped himself right there as the memory of his mother's cruel laughter that night at La Grande Belle filled his head. She wouldn't understand about Kitty; he couldn't bear it if she trivialised how he felt and once again laughed away his upset. Better to stick to more neutral ground. 'I loved my course. I had a plan, kind of. I wanted to work in housing policy – you know, do something relevant – and I wanted to carry on living with Spud, my friend.'

He fought back his emotion at the mention of Spud, who'd looked so downcast as he'd taken down his posters and packed up his case ready for a new bloke to move in. A bloke like Wilson, or Angus Thompson or his half-brother Alexander, a decent bloke who'd be fun to be around and wouldn't lie in bed feeling sad the whole time. A bloke who would graduate and flourish. A bloke who would one day make a brilliant dad. Not a weirdo.

'What kind of a name is Spud?'

Theo finished his coffee and left the room, hating how Spud's name was the one thing his mum had taken from that conversation. Was this to be his life? This half life, doing what his parents told him instead of following his heart? Once he set foot in Villiers House, in this suit, he'd be as good as clocking on for life, and that would be that.

'What the fuck are you doing?' he asked the grey face that stared back at him in the bathroom mirror. Not for the first time, he wished he was someone else. He turned over the lapel of his suit jacket and pinned his fishing fly to the underside, just as Mr Porter had done all those years ago. He ran his finger over the delicate green and blue feathers and the square red bead. 'I'm sorry, Mr Porter. Sorry I didn't fight harder for you, sorry I didn't stand up for you. If I had that time again—'

A knock on the door made him jump.

'Leaving in five!' his father called, on his way down the stairs.

Theo bent forward and rested his forehead on the cold glass. 'I keep waiting for my life to begin. And just when I think it might, I'm hauled back to the start line. What would you say, Mr Porter? What would you say to make it all better?'

He closed his eyes and stood like that for a while, letting the cool glass chill his head, until his mother called from downstairs.

'Darling! Daddy's getting in the car!'

* * *

'So what's your role exactly?' Spud shouted as he speared the scampi, dipped it in tartare sauce and forked it into his mouth. The music was too loud to allow for easy conversation, just as the lighting was too low to allow you to fully see the grimy residue on the tabletop or the matted stickiness on the carpet tiles.

Theo rubbed his palms together. 'I don't really know.'

'You don't know?' Spud laughed uproariously. 'Only you, Theo, son, could have a job and not know what it is.'

'Well, I mean, obviously I know the title. I am currently in the valuation department in an assistant, junior, valuation role.' He sipped his warm pint.

'Sounds interesting.'

Theo ran his hand through his hair. He couldn't joke about it. He was still too raw at having messed up and been forced down a route not of his choosing. It felt like he'd been knocked out of a race at the last hurdle and it hurt.

'You should be happy you have a job and that you're not in an industry Thatcher's bent on dismantling. Plus it seems like the routine suits you – at least you're not sleeping the day away any more.'

'I guess. And I am feeling a bit better. There are days, though—'

'Oh, mate, there will always be days.' Spud, as ever, spoke wisely. 'Graduation was a bit of an event. My mum, dad, nan, sister and her bloke all came down, but we were only allowed two tickets so Mum and Nan sat with me and the others stood at the back of the hall. Mine was the only family to cheer when I went up to get my scroll.' He shook his head, clearly chuffed.

'Quite right too.' Theo liked that Spud hadn't shied away from discussing graduation like most people would have. Instead he'd brought it up early on, so that once aired they didn't need to feel embarrassed about it any more.

'I'm looking at doing telesales in some grubby office block on Tottenham Court Road. Commission only and proper shitty, but it'll pay the rent, I hope.' Spud grinned. 'And fingers crossed it won't be for too long, just till I figure out how I'm going to fund my master's.'

It had taken Theo years to fully comprehend that for most people there was a direct correlation between money and opportunities and that if you lacked the former you would likely have far fewer of the latter. But Spud had never held that against him. 'God, you're going to be one of these eternal bloody students while the rest of us work for a living!' Theo slapped the table and used his dad's voice.

The two of them laughed.

Theo sipped his pint. 'I sometimes feel like everything I want and everything I think will bring me fulfilment is dangling just out of reach.' He recalled the feel of Kitty's skin against his fingertips. 'Can I ask you something, Spud?'

'If it was anyone else, I'd probably say "no" to that question, as I'd expect it to be followed by a demand for cash, but as you're loaded, I'm going to go ahead and say yes, fire away.' He grinned and chased a chip around his plate to catch the last few breadcrumbs.

'Are you happy?'

'Right now?'

Theo shrugged. 'Not only right now but in general. Do you wake up happy? It always seemed like you did.'

'No, I usually wake up hungover in my pants and with a mouth like a badger's arse.'

'God, please can we just have one serious conversation!' He took a breath. 'I feel like... I feel like everyone else has got life sussed while I'm still trying to figure it all out. And it's not new – I've always felt like this. Even when I was young, it was like I couldn't work out how to be around other people or be like other people. I'd watch boys in my year planning for the weekend, the next break, the following term – always looking ahead and comfortable, as if life was a travellator and all they had to do was stand on it and grab whatever they passed, whatever took their fancy. But for me…' He looked up as someone in the corner laughed. 'I struggled just trying to figure out the day ahead and I couldn't look any further and if I did I could only see more of the same, nothing good.'

The edge to his voice made Spud sit up straight and place the fork flat on the plate. 'Am I happy?' He considered this, wiping his mouth with the back of his hand. 'I think so. I mean, I'm not unhappy, so I suppose I must be happy.'

The two men looked at each other.

'But is that enough?' Theo asked. 'To say your life is satisfactory because you're not unhappy – is that enough?'

'I think you might be overthinking things. And…' He paused and stared into his pint. 'And I think you might still be a bit depressed.'

Theo glanced up at him, noting the way Spud avoided his gaze. He guessed it had taken a lot for his friend to say this. 'Possibly, but I've always felt this way. Like I'm waiting for my good times to start, as if I might go round the next bend and see a big neon sign with "Get your happiness here!" – a destination that I will arrive at. But instead, no matter how far I travel, it feels like there are only more bends.'

The music quieted, as if giving Spud the floor. He leant in with his elbows on the table. 'So maybe you've *always* been a bit depressed. Is that possible too?'

Theo shrugged. 'I guess. But are people actually born like that, is that what you think? Or did it start when I got to school and the shit began to hit the fan?'

Spud took a big slurp of his pint and wiped the froth off his lips. 'I honestly don't know. But I do think a lot of it is about expectations. As you know, I come from Wigan and my dad's been a miner at the Golborne pit all his life – though it looks like that'll be coming to an end very soon, thanks to Maggie. As kids we were just happy that he had a job, happy that we got proper hot dinners. When I was eleven, ten miners were killed in an explosion down the mine and we were happy that Dad wasn't one of them. Right now my family is happy that I've been to university and that they got a day out in London to watch me graduate. I don't try to look too far ahead.' He downed the rest of his beer and placed the empty glass on the table. 'You, Theo, son, have had one hell of a lucky life. I'm not knocking you for it.' He held up his palm. 'You were no more able to control where and to whom you were born than I was. I also know that the shit with Kitty has knocked you for six, but I think sometimes—'

'You think sometimes what?'

Spud wiggled his tongue up around his gum, freeing bits of scampi that had got caught. 'Sometimes I think you're looking for perfect where perfect doesn't exist. It's important you look at what you've got and not at what you haven't.'

Theo raised his eyebrows and looked at his friend. 'I hear what you're saying, but I had such a crap childhood that I think it might have damaged my ability to feel happy. It's like my calibration is out.'

'Then you need to find a way to recalibrate yourself, mate, or you're going to have an unhappy adulthood as well. And in my opinion that would be a bloody shame.' Spud picked up his empty pint glass and stood. 'Same again?'

Nine

1996

After eight years of working for Montgomery Holdings, Theo was well versed in every aspect of the family firm. The company bought land, built on it and acquired and renovated property in prime London locations, managing its portfolio to great effect. Because of its prudent, risk-averse strategy, the company's assets grew year on year. Theo found the 'profit before anything' mentality of his father and the rest of the board dispiriting, but in his quiet, unassuming way he had made it clear to staff and contacts in the industry that his values were more socially and environmentally oriented than those of his dad. He read articles on social policy and was drawn to the work of reforming organisations like the Joseph Rowntree Foundation, but he kept his head down, doing as he was asked and trying his best to fend off the depression that lurked inside him like a sleeping thing, curled and quiet but very much present. There was no denying he was still in his father's shadow and that rankled.

At least they were no longer sharing a house. Shortly before his twenty-fifth birthday, his mum had announced out of the blue that she and his father had bought him a lovely red-brick Edwardian house in Barnes and that Theo was free to do with it as he wished. The implication was that it should encourage him to find a wife and settle down to family life, but even if that wasn't on the cards, Theo was genuinely thrilled at finally gaining his independence. He could at last pursue his various flings without having to face a morning-after grilling when he didn't come home to his own bed. Not that there was ever anything much to tell. Few relationships made it past the second night together and none had lasted more than two weeks. Despite himself, the spectre of Kitty still haunted him, and the flash of red curls in a bar or on a dance floor was enough to make him do a double-take and step forward for a closer look.

Theo liked working in the City, close to the beating financial heart of the country, and he felt genuine affection for Villiers House, the handsome art deco building on Cheapside, a stone's throw from St Paul's Cathedral, which his great-grandfather had acquired in the 1920s. Theo appreciated the history of the building: each time he leant on the brass-topped handrails, curled his fingers around an ornate window latch or put his foot in one of the slight wells worn in the tread of the stone steps, he did so with a sense of connection to the relatives who had done so before him. Montgomery Holdings occupied the top floor, as it had since his great-grandfather's time, but the other six floors were rented out to financial trading companies.

Villiers House was mere yards away from several wine bars, and it was in these that he and Spud whiled away many an evening. But Spud was no longer free to stay out into the small hours, for fear of incurring the wrath of Kumi, his Japanese–American wife of three years. She wanted him home in suburbia at a reasonable hour, especially now that she was six months pregnant and not coping too well with the changes to her life. But, as ever, Spud appeared happy.

Theo noted that for the first time in their friendship, Spud seemed to be holding something back. He always shied away from giving specific details about Kumi's pregnancy and he quickly changed the subject when talk turned to his impending fatherhood. Theo presumed this was because Spud didn't want him to dwell on what he'd missed out on with Kitty. He loved that his friend was sensitive to this, but it had put the tiniest crack in their closeness. Spud was the only person on earth who knew he had a child; whether that child was male or female Theo still didn't know, let alone what their name was, but he did know that they would be turning eight very soon. He tried to picture them, tried to imagine the birthday party Kitty might organise for them, but he couldn't get beyond the dissatisfying image of a dark shadow of indeterminate features and size.

'Have you got the quarterly figures for Marcus?' Perry Montgomery stood in the doorway of Theo's office, impatiently tapping his signet ring on the wooden frame in double-quick time. His dark hair was now streaked with grey, but he still looked dapper.

Theo had been standing at his office window staring absent-mindedly down at the people scurrying back and forth on the pavement below. He turned now to answer his father. 'Nearly.'

'Oh good. I'll tell the board they can wait until nearly,' his dad shot back sarcastically.

The words flew across the room and almost choked Theo. As was usual, he averted his gaze.

'Could you be a little more specific or do you want me to ask Marcus to step in and give you a hand?' Perry's lips were set in a thin line and his eyes were fixed on the empty chair behind the desk, as if Theo had been caught shirking.

Theo's instinct was to dart back to his desk, take up the high-backed chair and start going through the spreadsheets, but he had a feeling that this false show of activity would only irritate his father more. He couldn't win. 'I don't need Marcus's help. I'm on it,' he levelled.

'Clearly.'

'I was just on my way out to grab some lunch – I'll do the figures the moment I get back. Can I get you anything?' He picked up his wallet from the corner of the desk and put his jacket on. The spacious office suddenly felt claustrophobic.

'Lunch?' His father's tone was so disdainful and was followed by such a lengthy sigh that as Theo walked past him he wondered if he'd accidently said he was going out dancing.

He decided to curtail his lunchbreak. Often he walked for a couple of blocks to clear his head, looked in the odd shop window or spent an age deliberating over the exact contents of his sandwich made freshly to order, relishing the change of scenery, but not today. His father would be watching the clock until his return.

London was hosting Euro 96 and the streets were uncomfortably rammed with football-mad tourists, many of them sporting their national colours. In the sandwich shop, Theo chose quickly, ordering the same as the woman in front of him to save on thinking time. He raced back to Villiers House, stepping into the road to avoid the throng of idlers who were clogging up the pavement and waving football scarves in the air.

'Hold the lift!' he shouted with his arm outstretched, brandishing the brown paper bag that contained the favourite sandwich of the lady who'd been ahead of him in the queue. He watched the doors begin to close, cursing his timing, but then felt a ridiculous sense of relief as he glided through the gap in the nick of time. Any win on a day like this was to be celebrated.

He took up a spot at the back of the lift and looked over at its only other occupant, a young woman with a dark bob who was standing in front of him.

'Sorry! I was trying to figure out which button might hold the doors, but they're all a bit worn,' she said, wrinkling her nose.

'Please don't worry about it.'

She glanced at him briefly over her shoulder and as her eyes swept his face he took the chance to do the same. She was not standard pretty, but she had an open face and a ready smile. *Great skin, bright eyes*. He liked the look of her. He liked the look of her very much.

'So, this is unusual.' Theo gave a small laugh as they took their seats in the snug of the Three Tuns. 'I meet you in a lift only this afternoon and now here we are. Cheers!' He raised his pint and clinked it against her small glass of white wine.

'You're a fast worker.' She sipped her drink, slurping from the top. 'I was really glad you asked me for a drink. Thank you.' She beamed at him openly.

'You're welcome. I'm really glad you said yes.'

Theo liked her lack of pretence, her down-to-earth manner. She made him feel relaxed. This was the exact opposite of the nervous state he usually found himself in on a first date.

The circumstances of their meeting had also been unusual. The creaky, sixty-year-old Villiers House lift had got stuck between floors, as it sometimes did, and when he'd realised that she was getting anxious he'd done his level best to distract her and keep her chatting. The more they'd chatted, the more interested he'd become and soon he'd forgotten they were waiting to be rescued by Bernie the maintenance man. He'd simply enjoyed finding out about the young woman, whose name was Anna. He'd been quite disappointed when the doors had finally slid open.

'So you live in Fulham?' he said now, trying to recall the various facts from their lift chat.

'Uh-huh, in a cupboard. Literally! My flat isn't much bigger than this table.' She rapped her knuckles on the surface as she placed her glass down and wiped her hands on her skirt.

She was unlike other women he knew. Nothing about her was pushy or presumptuous and she didn't seem to have any vanity or sense or self-importance. She wasn't one of the pouty, coming-on-to-him types he usually ended up with and neither was she sort of pretty, bright girl who expected to be adored – like Kitty. Theo realised that for the first time in as long as he could remember he was interested in someone. He was interested in her, Anna Cole with her shy demeanour and her cockney accent. He wondered how long Ned, the ex she'd mentioned, had been out of the picture and whether he'd been replaced. He hoped not.

'So you commute from Fulham? I come in from Barnes. I think the traffic in London is getting worse, don't you? It took me an hour to get over here in a cab from Paddington the other day. From Paddington! It might actually have been quicker to bloody walk.'

'I get the Tube to Mansion House usually, but sometimes I get off a couple of stops early and walk to Villiers House – to keep fit, you know.' She giggled. 'My friend Melissa's always going on at me to take up swimming or cycling, but I don't know how, do I, so that wouldn't be much good, would it?' She laughed again.

'You can't ride a bike?'

'Nope. Or swim.' She reached for her drink and sipped again.

'Anything else you can't do?'

She chortled. 'I think the answer to that is: considerably more than I can!'

He smiled, thinking of Kitty the swimmer, who might have grown her gills by now. *This girl…*

'Didn't you ever want to learn?'

'Which thing?'

'Both, I guess!'

'I suppose I did at one point, but swimming just felt wrong!' She wrinkled her nose with displeasure. 'And there was never any chance of me getting a bike, so I guess it would have been a bit pointless.' She tucked her hair behind her ears and seemed to consider this. 'But there *are* lots of things I wanted to do and didn't get the chance to – riding a bike was just one of them.'

'What things?' He was genuinely interested. He was attracted to her soft cockney accent and wondered where her thoughts had landed – she looked a million miles away.

Anna sighed and folded her hands neatly in her lap. 'Well, I would have loved to have gone to university. My grades were good enough, but…' She paused. 'It just wasn't possible.'

'Why not?'

She exhaled and hesitated. He guessed she was weighing up

how much to share on this, their first date. 'I was in care for part of my life and that kind of reduces your horizons, your expectations. The things I wished for were pretty simple, really. To stay safe, to keep out of the way of people who didn't like me... That sort of thing. I tried not to look too far ahead.'

Theo tried hard to mask his shock at hearing this. She'd been in care! He couldn't imagine it. They were from such hugely different worlds, but there was something about her that struck a chord. A sort of loneliness in her voice when she talked about her past, and a resilience.

'I can understand that.' He coughed to clear his throat, nervous about what he was going to confess, the shame of it; it was something he never normally shared. 'I went to university, but I didn't graduate.'

'Why didn't you graduate?' She held his gaze, her eyes steady and her expression non-judgemental.

'A number of factors. For a start I wasted the first couple of terms on a course I didn't want to be doing, engineering, when the thing that really interested me was social policy. So I switched, which was good, erm...' He faltered, searching for a way to phrase his story that wouldn't give too much away.

'Please don't tell me you were one of those students who couldn't possibly study until he had alphabetised his books and cleaned his whole apartment and made an apple pie! Whereas what you actually needed to do was get down to the studying! Or did you just get drunk and sleep?' She banged the table playfully. 'Was that it, Theo? Were you a lazybones?'

'Well, you're probably right about the avoidance tactics, though cleaning my apartment and making an apple pie are a little wide of the mark.' He smiled, thinking of how he and Spud had collected empty bottles of beer and lined them up around the edge of the room. He couldn't remember why they'd considered this to be a good idea. 'And actually I worked really hard, got good grades.' He paused.

'I feel a "but" coming on,' Anna said.

'And you'd be right.' He ran his tongue over his lips. Memories of that time were still painful.

'I kind of fell apart a bit.'

'Well, that happens.' She spoke softly. 'My brother had issues and it wasn't his fault, not really.'

She seemed to be close to tears and this new vulnerability made Theo's heart flex with tenderness and longing.

'I think we all go through things that shape us. I've always felt like an outsider.' She lowered her voice. 'I don't have tons of friends and I'm quite private. You just have to hope that when your time is over, you've lived a largely happy life, no matter that you had to dodge puddles of shit along the way.'

Theo laughed. 'I like that! And I myself have had to dodge some very large puddles of shit.'

'Does it bother you that you didn't graduate?'

Again, he liked her lack of guile. 'Not really, not now. Or maybe a little bit, sometimes.' He looked up at her. 'I'm definitely in the wrong job, though. I still daydream about working for social change, doing something that's not just concerned with maximising profits. I don't know…' He laughed to mask his embarrassment.

'Well, you're still young, you can do whatever you want. There's still plenty of time.'

'Yes.' He smiled at her. If only time really was the only barrier. 'I guess there is. Not graduating feels a little irrelevant now, but back then it felt like the end of the world.' He never wanted to go through that again – the taking to his bed and not wanting to wake up, the deep, black depression. 'I liked being a student, liked that life, but...'

'But life had other plans?'

'Actually, no, my father had other plans, but that's a whole other story.' He drummed his fingers on his thighs and reached for his pint.

'Well, I'm rather glad that your dad had other plans, or you would never have been in that lift and we wouldn't be sitting here now and there is absolutely nothing on the telly tonight.' She grinned.

'I'm glad to be a diversion.'

Anna smiled at him again, her beautiful, open smile. 'I think it's wonderful that you want to do a job that's for the greater good and not just chasing cash like so many people. I felt your kindness today in that lift. It made all the difference to me, more than you could know, and I get the feeling you can do anything you put your mind to, Mr Montgomery. There's something special about you.'

Theo stared at her, wondering if she knew what those words meant to him. She thought he could do anything he put his mind to! Him, the weirdo! Only she didn't make him feel like a weirdo. She made him feel... special.

'To puddles of shit!' She raised her glass.

'To puddles of shit!' he echoed and they both drank.

She wiped her mouth and reached for her purse. 'Same again?'

'I'll get them.' He made to stand.

'God, no!' She stood. 'You got the last ones. You should know I'm a girl who likes to pay her own way.'

* * *

'Hello, is this the correct telephone number for Mr Theodore Montgomery? Lover of Guns N' Roses, sore loser at Uno and lightweight when it comes to necking pints at speed?'

Theo laughed into the receiver. 'It might be. Who's asking?'

'My name is Spud and I used to be his best friend, but he seems to have gone to ground and the carrier pigeon I sent out has returned empty-handed, so I'm trying this number as a last resort.'

'Very funny.' Theo sat back in the chair behind his desk.

'How you doing, mate?'

'I'm...' Theo's grin pre-empted his reply. 'I'm great!'

'And does this or does this not have something to do with the mysterious Anna Cole you mentioned in our last chat?'

Theo laughed, loudly. 'What can I say? She's...'

'She's...?'

'She's bloody brilliant!'

'Bloody brilliant? High praise indeed. How long have you been seeing her?'

'Three or four weeks.'

Spud roared his laughter. 'That is funny! I know you know exactly and you're just trying to sound cool! "Three or four weeks!"'

Theo joined in the laughter. 'All right, you bastard. Four weeks to the day. Happy now?'

'Over the bloody moon!' Spud guffawed. 'You sound different.'

'I feel different,' Theo admitted. He looked up and out of the window. It was a grey day, but thinking of Anna made it feel like sunshine.

'So it's pretty serious?'

'I'd say so.' He grinned at the understatement. 'I feel like...'

'Go on! You feel like...?'

'I feel like she could be the one.'

'The one! Jesus, Theo, this is epic news!'

They both chuckled down the line.

'I'd say Operation Erase Kitty has finally been achieved. Took a little longer than expected, maybe, but we got there in the end.'

'It's completely different – real and brilliant and mutual!'

'So, sex good?'

'None of your business!' Theo smiled.

'That'll be a "yes" then. Met her folks?'

'No folks to meet. Both dead and she's pretty much looked after herself – she's a tough cookie, got her head screwed on.'

Spud exhaled slowly. 'Mate, I have to tell you that while that is undoubtedly sad, I have had Kumi's mum here for the last month, so the thought of hooking up with an orphan is pure genius.'

Theo laughed. 'That bad?'

'Worse. I made the mistake of reminding them that Kumi is not ill, just pregnant, and that millions of women give birth every day all over the world.'

Theo chuckled. 'What did they say to that?'

'I have no idea, but it was loud and furious and went on for a long time in Japanese. Both of them. In stereo. It might still be going on for all I know. Right now, I'd give my left nut for my wife to be an orphan. I'd give my right nut too, but Kumi already has that one in her purse. My life is over.'

'And yet you sound decidedly happy, considering your dire circumstances.'

'I am. Bit scared about the whole becoming a dad thing, but I am happy.'

'You're going to be a great dad.'

'Hope so. My parents keep calling me and asking, "What should we get for't baby? What do babies eat in Japan?" As if this child is going to arrive a fully fledged Japanese–American baby! They seem to forget that she's going to be half-Wiganer!'

Theo laughed, picturing the conversations with Ma and Pa Spud. 'I'm happy too,' he said, wanting to share this with Spud.

'Anna must be some girl.'

'She is, Spud. She gets me and she's a lot like me, even though we're from very different worlds. She kind of makes me feel better about stuff.' He sat forward in the chair.

'What stuff?'

'Everything, actually.'

There was a beat or two of silence and Theo knew what was coming next.

'We joke, but have you told her about Kitty, about… things?'

Theo closed his eyes briefly and felt the weight of the knowledge that he knew had to be shared. It sat in his heel like a sliver of glass that no matter how joyous the day or glorious the view, made its presence known with every step he took. 'No, not yet. It's hard to find the right time. It's a bit of a grenade and I don't want to spoil things.'

'I get that, and it's your call, but I think it'll be easier if you do it sooner rather than later.'

'You're right.' Theo rubbed his face. 'Anyway, mate, better crack on. Beer soon?'

'Yep, beer soon, and don't do anything I wouldn't!'

'Doesn't sound like you do much at the moment.' Theo laughed.

'Oh sod off!'

That evening, Theo and Anna sat in uncharacteristic quiet as the cab left the City and headed towards Anna's studio flat in Fulham. It was there, in her tiny, cupboard-sized space, that they did their courting. Little time was wasted on sleep; instead they laid the foundations for all that might come next. Both were high on what the future might bring.

Theo held her small hand and placed their knot of conjoined fingers on his thigh, where it rested comfortably. Tonight was the night. Spud was right: he had to confide in Anna about his child. But what if she despised him for it? Rejected him because of it? The prospect terrified him. The thought that his time with Anna might be coming to an end sent a shiver of sadness along his spine. His leg jumped with nerves.

They walked quietly up the stairs and into Anna's flat. Anna reached up to flick the light switch. Theo caught her wrist, knowing it would be easier to have the difficult conversation in the darkness. 'No, leave the light off, we'll just have the glow from outside.'

'I... I don't like the dark,' she stammered and his throat tightened.

'Me neither.' He laughed. 'But you've got me and I've got you, so we don't have to worry. Not tonight.'

'I don't worry, not when I'm with you. I don't worry about a thing. It's like everything is great in my world and it's the first time I've ever felt that way and I really like it!'

Theo placed his trembling hands on her face and Anna tilted

her head to receive his kiss. 'I… I feel the same,' he began, peppering his speech with light kisses on her face. 'It's like I know everything is going to be okay, because I've got you.'

'You have got me!' She beamed, nuzzling her cheek into his palm.

'There have been times when I was so sad…' He paused. 'No, more than sad – depressed. I have lived with depression,' he said frankly. 'My last terms at uni, they were hell.'

Go on, Theo, tell her! Tell her about Kitty and the baby! Tell her now! Get it out of the way!

'Oh, Theo…' Anna's voice trembled with compassion and for that Theo loved her more than ever. 'I'm sad you went through that.'

'I think I'm still going through it, I don't think it's really left me.' He bit his cheek. 'It engulfed me, knocked me sideways. I've come out of that phase, certainly, but it's like something that's always there, lurking just around the corner. I get the feeling it's never very far away.'

She nodded her understanding.

'But for the first time, I can see light and I guess that's why I don't feel as afraid of the dark.'

She met his gaze. 'You don't have to be afraid, not any more.'

Theo nodded. 'This thing that's going on with us, Anna…' He hesitated, wary of being the first to confess to the swell of love in his gut. 'I don't know what it is, but it's…' He exhaled.

'I know.' He could hear her voice smiling into the darkness. 'It really is.'

They kissed again and stumbled towards the bed at the end of her rather tiny living zone.

He did not want to break what they had – this, the most

perfect thing he'd ever been part of. This was not the time to tell her about a child he did not know, would never know; not the time to admit that his weirdness had led to Kitty rejecting him as the father of their child. No, this was the time to carry on falling for each other, for not worrying about a thing. He too had never felt this way about anyone and he too really liked it.

* * *

Theo looked at his reflection in the mirror of the office bathroom and stood tall. He took a deep breath.

'Would you do me the honour…?' He stopped. 'I ask this is in all sincerity…' He shook his head and coughed to clear his throat. 'Anna, from this day forth…' He felt the weight of the occasion, overly aware of the pose, tone and words required for asking this most important of questions. He had of course rehearsed before today, but now he was wondering if he should opt for something less formal. *Just make it count, Theo. Do it properly.*

It was a mere ten weeks since he'd met Anna Cole in the lift, but he knew with certainty he wanted to propose. Truth was, he'd known after one date and had spent the next few weeks looking for flaws, anything to test his suspicion that she was practically perfect. He shook his arms loose and turned his head until his neck cricked, surprised at how nervous he was. His mouth felt dry and his limbs were trembling.

Supposing she says no? What then?

If she said no, they'd be finished, they'd have to split up – they wouldn't be able to recover from that. The potential for disaster was significant, and that did nothing to allay his anxiety. He took another deep breath. Tonight, when he popped the question, it could be a beautiful moment; the start of a lifelong love, or it could be the worst of moments, the end of everything.

He could only liken it to standing on a cliff edge.

He entered the coffee shop with the advantage of not being seen and looked across at Anna, the woman he wanted to make his wife. The woman who loved him as no one had ever loved him and surely no one else ever would. The woman who, by loving him as she did, diluted his weirdness, robbed him of the 'loser' crown and turned him into the kind of chap that someone might want to marry. Anna made him feel like a man who was capable of becoming a husband.

As if confirmation were needed, her eyes fell upon him and her face lit up. He knew with certainty that there was no one in the world she wanted to see walk into that coffee shop more than him, and it felt amazing to be so wanted. To belong.

'So where are we going?' she asked, as, fifteen minutes later they settled into the back seat of a cab.

'I told you, somewhere special.' He smiled at her.

'I don't know if I'm dressed right.' She looked down at her work skirt and blouse.

'Don't worry. You look perfect.' He stared out of the window and tried to stem his nerves.

It wasn't until the cab drove over Hammersmith Bridge that the penny dropped and Anna realised he was breaking the code of a lifetime and was taking a girl back to his home. She looked at him with a knowing expression. He reached for her hand and the two sat quietly, each lost in thought.

For the hundredth time, he ran through in his head the many ways he might propose, wondering if it was absolutely necessary to go down on one knee, wary of making a fool of himself. After all, this would be a night they'd always remember. He swallowed – that thought did nothing to calm his racing pulse.

Theo paid the cab and retook her hand, guiding her along the gravel path, which crunched underfoot.

'Are you okay?' he asked, squeezing her fingers tightly.

Anna stared wide-eyed and he saw the grand façade as if though her eyes. She nodded up at him and that was how they stood for a second or two, in acknowledgement of the moment.

'Here we are.'

'Yes.' She bit her lip. 'Here we are.'

Theo fished in his pocket for his keys and gently pushed open the front door, elated to have finally found the woman he wanted to step over the threshold with.

It did indeed turn out to be a night Theo would never forget. Over a bottle of red, Anna talked freely about her life and her losses. There was no denying that to hear her story of losing first her mother and then her brother, Joe, who'd committed suicide, made him feel even more protective of her. And to top it all, she'd only recently discovered that the father she'd never met had also passed away. She talked fearlessly and frankly. Her story might have been too much for some, but for Theo it served only to bind them closer together.

Anna made no attempt to hide her tears. 'I feel like it's time,' she told him, 'and there is so much I want to say to you. I need you to *see* me.'

He nodded. 'I need you to see me too. There is so much *I* want to say.' He thumbed the skin on the back of her hand.

'We are from very different worlds,' she began.

'And I thank God for that.' He leant forward and kissed her gently on the forehead.

'I'm... I'm weird,' she managed, pulling away to look him in the eye. 'I've always been weird and I've had a weird life. A life I want to tell you about so that I don't have to worry about revealing it to you bit by bit. I think that's the best thing, like ripping off a plaster. I need to do it quick.'

Theo pulled her into his chest and held her tightly. 'Weird? Oh God, Anna, you have no idea...' He felt a bubble of relief burst inside his head. All these years, the toxicity of his weirdness had formed a barrier that kept other people at arm's length, and yet with Anna it was the very thing that joined them.

'I don't want to be on my own any more!' She raised her voice. 'I don't want to feel like sticks on the river! Like I'm being carried along, clinging on for dear life and hoping I don't drown.'

'I've got you, Anna. I've got you!'

'I've had enough, Theo. I'm tired. I'm so tired of being sad and being scared and lonely! So lonely!'

He kissed the top of her scalp and rocked her until she fell into a sleep of sorts. As she dozed, his confidence soared. They were meant to be together. She had to say 'yes'!

Later that night, after she'd woken and after more tears, more revelations, and more sadness about her family, her loneliness, Theo blurted out exactly what he was feeling, unplanned and heartfelt.

'I love you, Anna. I love you.'

'I love you too. I do, I really love you!'

They fell against each other, laughing, giddy in the moment.

'I always think you get the people in your life that you're meant to. I think we're meant to get each other.' Anna smiled.

'I think you're right. Two weirdos together!'

'Yes! Two weirdos with the lights left on.'

'I think…' Theo paused and reached for her hands, taking them both into his own. 'I think we'll get married and live here, together, just like this.'

This was very far from the formal proposal he'd practised so nervously and so many times, but it was no less perfect for it.

Anna couldn't halt the flow of tears that ran down her cheeks. 'Yes, Theo. I think we will get married and live here, together, just like this.'

Slowly he stood, pulled her up and guided her by the hand towards the staircase, towards a different life.

The next morning, as he came downstairs, he could hear Anna singing in the kitchen. He smiled. She was a little off key and hadn't quite got the words right. 'The things you do for love. The things you do for love!'

She was dressed in nothing more than his shirt and socks, and he stood in the doorway watching her fill the kettle, seek out tea-bags, rummage in the bread bin for a loaf and open several drawers and cupboards until she located butter knives, teaspoons and jam.

It was only when she turned to walk to the fridge that she saw him. She started. 'Oh! Theo!' She placed her hand on her chest. 'I was just trying to make breakfast. Is that okay?' She blinked, walked over and kissed his mouth.

'Of course it's okay. It's great.' He took a seat at the kitchen table and watched her navigate her way around the room, thinking how brilliant that he would be waking every day for the rest of his life in her lovely company. 'I feel smug.'

'Me too.' She raised her shoulders and his eyes fell on her exposed thighs as the shirt rode up. She walked over and leant against him, kissing his forehead. It was as if she couldn't stop. He understood this constant desire for contact. It was new and exhilarating.

'Smug and peaceful.' He rested his hand on her bottom.

'And engaged!' She pulled a wide-mouthed grin and raised her eyebrows. 'Can you believe it?'

'Actually, yes, I can.' He chuckled. 'I'd planned what I wanted to say and everything – but then all my plans flew out the window and I got nervous and the words kind of tumbled out on a stream of red wine.'

'I wouldn't have had it any other way. It was perfect.' She carried on with her tea making, only returning to the table when she had two steaming mugs.

She took a seat opposite and held her tea in both hands. 'Do you know, I always wondered who I might marry. I think lots of little girls do and it feels strange that now I've found out. I mean, I hoped it would be you—'

'Did you?'

'Yes, from the first time I met you, I hoped it would be you, but now I *know* it is and it's wonderful!'

Theo couldn't stop grinning. He had never felt this special before – ever.

'I wish my mum had met you.' Anna sat very still.

'Would she have approved?' he asked cautiously.

Anna shook her head. 'Now that's a daft question. She would have loved whoever loved me of course.'

Theo wished he had the same level of certainty about his own folks. 'Well, my mum and dad are a bit challenging at times.'

He smirked at the understatement, wanting to manage her expectations.

'In what way?' She blew on her drink to cool it.

Theo swallowed. 'They're quite selfish, preoccupied with their social lives. And I guess the older I get, the more I question the way they parented me. I was desperately unhappy at school and they did nothing about it. It would have made my life easier if they'd taken more of an interest or given more of a shit.'

Anna reached out and laid her hand on his. 'I hate to think of you being unhappy. I absolutely hate it. I wish I'd been your friend. I would have loved you then too. Especially when you were depressed, Theo.'

'Thank you.' He kissed her fingers, swallowing his guilt; he *had* to tell her about Kitty...

'And if you get low again, I'll be by your side,' she offered softly. 'Sometimes it's enough just to know you're not going to have to face things alone, don't you find?'

Theo's smile was unstoppable as, yet again, realisation dawned that she'd said 'yes'!

'I sometimes think, though, that the rougher you have it, the more you appreciate the good stuff – almost like the nice bits are a reward.' She continued sipping her tea.

'That's a good way to look at things. I find it hard to rationalise. My parents used to act like every day was a party and the world was sharing a joke that I simply didn't get. But whenever I tried to explain how I felt, Mum and Dad would just laugh, as if I was making a fuss about nothing, as if I was the problem. The onus was always on me to fit in, not on them to help me fit in or give me guidance.' He smiled ruefully. 'I could have done with my mum teaching me the alphabet game like yours did, to distract me from my loneliness. It might have helped me get to sleep better those nights in the dorm at school. A... appalling parents! B... bloody awful school... Is that sort of thing allowed?' He shot her a cheeky grin.

Anna giggled and shook her head in mock despair. Then her expression turned serious. 'You're not the problem, Theo! You're wonderful! I think you're very brave to be so open about what you've been through. And it means a lot. I don't want there to be any secrets between us. It's important.'

He held her gaze, letting her words permeate and feeling his shoulders sag under the weight of the secret he carried. He took a deep breath.

'There is something I would like to tell you.' He gulped his tea and placed it down with a trembling hand.

'Go on.' She nodded encouragingly.

His heart was galloping. He exhaled. 'I'm not like my dad.' As soon as the words were out, he felt a punch of sickness in his gut, because he was like his dad! They had both fathered children and swept them under the carpet, unmentioned, a source of shame... He felt his face flash with heat and the room swam a little. 'He has often been unfaithful to my mum, including with a much younger girl, a kind of nanny to me during one summer holiday, when I was fourteen.'

'Shit!'

'Yes.' He sat tall in the seat. He felt a strange sense of relief that the truth still lay hidden, out of harm's way and unable to damage what they had, the love they shared. But there was also guilt that he was letting her down, already defaulting on her 'no secrets' request. He wiped the corners of his mouth and sat forward. 'I tried to tell my mum that I'd support her and look after her, but she just laughed! And then she more or less told me that I was irrelevant to her and that no matter what my dad did, she would always pick him.'

'Oh my God, Theo!' Anna raced around the table and laid his head on her chest, holding him tightly and rocking him slightly. It was the most sincere and wonderful hold he had ever known. 'You've carried a lot inside you and you've had a shit time, but you know what? You've got me now and I love you so very much and I always will and we're getting married! And everything is going to be wonderful!' She kissed him hard on the face.

He nodded and inhaled the scent of her. 'Yes, it is. It's going to be wonderful.'

'I look at this wonderful house, Theo, and I know it will be the most incredible place to bring up our children. Not because of how grand it is, but because we live in it and we will never let our children cry themselves to sleep and they will always know how much they are loved. I can see us eating family suppers around the table where we can all chat about our days without fear of ridicule or rejection. A safety net, a proper family! It's more than I ever thought I could hope for. Mrs Theodore Montgomery!' She laughed.

'Mrs Theodore Montgomery,' he echoed. Theo swallowed the uneasy feeling that despite how much he loved this girl, the proper family she yearned for was still something that felt beyond his capabilities.

Later that morning, while Anna was luxuriating in the bath, Theo sat down at the desk in his study. He couldn't stop thinking about Anna's alphabet game. He loved this quirk about her, the fact that anyone else would simply let their thoughts tumble, but not Anna: she took control and played the alphabet game, working her way through the letters until mental equilibrium was restored. He flipped open the lid of his vintage pen box, selected a pen and wrote 'A' to 'Z' in a column down the left-hand side of a fresh sheet of paper. He laughed, wondering what Spud would make of him doing this exercise. With his pen poised, he thought of all the things he loved about Anna, his Anna, Anna who was going to be his wife!

A…

He looked at the window and pictured the girl he loved, before writing in a bold script:

Here we go, Anna, my first ever attempt at the alphabet game…

A… Anna

B… beautiful.

C… courageous. So much more courageous than me.

D… determined.

E… eager.

F… funny.

G… gorgeous.

Ten

Theo crept out into the garden straight after breakfast, went round to the kitchen window and waved through the glass at Anna, who was peering at the rather unpromising-looking lemon tree she insisted on keeping on the windowsill.

Anna glanced up and shot him a puzzled look. She wiped her hands and came out onto the doorstep.

'What's that?' she asked, pulling her cardigan around her form and nodding in the direction of the shed.

'What does it look like? It's a bicycle!' he beamed, excited.

'Well, I can see that, but what's it doing in our garden?' She took a tentative step closer.

'I can't have a wife of mine unable to ride a bike!' He pulled the bike around and stood with the back wheel between his shins. 'And now that we have officially been Mr and Mrs Montgomery for, ooh, four months, one week and three days, the time has come to rectify this glaring defect. So come on! Hop on!'

'No-wer!' She shook her head, laughing.

'Come on, Anna! I am going to teach you how to ride this bike. It'll be fun.'

'No, you are not.' She bit the inside of her cheek. 'And it won't be fun. It'll be rubbish.'

'I thought it was sad that no one had ever taught you how, and it bothered me that you never thought you would have a bike. I intend to put both of those things right.' He reached forward and patted the leather saddle. 'And before you know it, we'll be biking all over the place with a flask of tea in your basket and a picnic.' He thought of Mr Porter and the delicious sandwiches packed into his knapsack.

'That is really, really sweet of you, and I love the idea of it, but I think you might be confusing me with someone out of an Enid Blyton novel. I can't do it. I will fall off. I'm useless at stuff like that.'

'How do you know if you have never tried?'

'Because, Theo, I twist my ankle if I wear heels, I trip up kerbs and I can't navigate a turnaround door!'

He looked at her quizzically. 'A revolving door?'

'Yes! See, I don't even know what they're called!'

'Come on, Anna, I won't let you go, I promise.' He beckoned to her gently and held her gaze as she walked from the step, down the path and towards the bike. He liked the way she ran her fingers over the green-painted frame and smiled, as if coming round to the idea.

'You got this for me?' She bit her lip.

'I did.'

'Thank you, Theo. You love me, don't you?'

'I do.' He felt the surge of love for her in his chest.

Anna moved a step closer and looked at the pedals.

'That's it! Now climb on.'

She did as she was told, gripping his shoulder tightly as she gingerly put one leg either side of the metal frame and placed her foot on one of the pedals.

'It's going to wobble, Theo!' There was no mistaking the slight edge of panic to her voice. 'I don't like it!'

'It will, yes, but I've already promised you I won't let you fall.'

He relished the way she looked at him so trustingly. It was lovely to hold her steady and see her almost literally steeling herself for the challenge.

'That's it,' he said encouragingly as she lifted herself up and sat back on the saddle, her feet on the pedals and her hands clenching the handlebars as if her life depended on it.

'Look at you, Anna Bee Cole! You're on a bike!'

'Don't let go!' she squealed. 'Please don't let go!'

'I'm going to hold you upright but we'll move forward, so the wheels will shift but I'll be holding you at the back, okay?'

'No!' Anna screamed. 'Not okay!'

But he did it anyway and he could tell she didn't know whether to laugh or cry as she sailed along with him gripping the back of her saddle.

'See, you're doing great!' He beamed. 'Now we're going to try the same thing but along the pavement.'

'Oh God! No, Theo, please, I might hit someone!' she implored, but without the conviction of someone who was truly afraid. This he took as a sign that she was more willing than she cared to admit.

He steered the bike along the path until it was lined up with the wall at the front of the garden. He started to walk, still guiding her from behind. Her feet kept up with the turning pedals and she began to laugh. 'I quite like it! Don't let go!'

'Don't worry! I've got you,' he called, running out of puff as the bike gathered pace.

Soon she was going too fast for him to keep up. He stood back and watched with pride as Anna trundled on down the pavement, too focused on pedalling to realise that he wasn't holding her saddle any longer.

'Woohoo! This is great!' she yelled. She turned to her left to smile at Theo, but he was a good few paces behind now, staring after her with a grin on his face.

He raised both hands and gave her a double thumbs-up – prematurely, as it turned out. The shock of realising that she was now riding solo proved too great for Anna. She wobbled and lost her confidence. The bike careered into a neighbour's garden wall and with a mighty clatter Anna toppled over, the bike landing on top of her.

'Anna!' Theo called, running to catch up. 'Are you okay?' He bent down, moving the bike with his hands and kneeling to examine her scuffed leg with the type of scrape and bruise usually seen on the knees of six year olds.

Anna looked up and kissed his chin, she was breathless, exhilarated. 'I am more than all right – I can ride a bike, Theo! I did it all by myself!'

'Yes, you did. You were brilliant. But I think we might leave it a while before we try skateboarding and swimming.'

'My poor bike, have I damaged it?' she looked up.

'Forget the bike. I'd be more worried about the damage to the wall!' he laughed.

The two kissed, as they sat on the pavement without a care in the world.

*

Springing surprises on Anna was one of the many little pleasures Theo had come to relish about his new life as a married man. The two had fallen into a happy routine, making even the most mundane of chores seem like fun. He felt optimistic about the future when he considered the genuine humour and friendship that bound them like glue. It was very different to the show of unity that his parents felt the need to portray. The loud laughter and almost rehearsed ribbing that was traded back and forth in front of their friends was more than a little staged. It was a nice feeling knowing that when he and Anna were in the car alone or about to fall asleep there was not going to be the roar of anger and resentment that might have simmered all evening and which he had heard his parents voice on more than one occasion. It was a new and wonderful feeling to be at peace.

He couldn't wait to tell her about the Maldives holiday he'd just booked to celebrate their first anniversary, but whether or not that would be the place to try and teach her to swim, he wasn't quite sure. He was certain she'd love the Maldives though – she'd never been to the tropics and he could practically hear her squeals of delight. That was part of the joy for him, seeing things through Anna's eyes. He would tell her that night, he decided, after their dinner date with Anna's friend Melissa and her husband Gerard.

'Yours was a cracking wedding,' Gerard commented, as he filled Theo's wine glass with a warm red. 'None of the usual shenanigans. It was simple and so much better for it.'

'Neither of us wanted anything flashy.'

'And pure genius in the choice of venue, a great lunch and then a short cab ride home in time for the football, job done. In fact I remember saying something similar to your mother who looked none too impressed!' Gerard laughed, loudly. 'I think I was wearing my champagne goggles, I then asked her who she supported.'

Theo laughed at the idea. 'What did she say?'

'Nothing, she stared at me as if she didn't have the faintest idea what I was talking about and reached for your father's arm.'

'That'll be about right. Cheers!' Theo took a sip, as Melissa arrived from upstairs.

'Hello my darlings! So good to see you both. Sorry I am behind as always. This little scrap is the biggest distraction; I don't know where the hours go. Do you want to hold him?'

Melissa waved baby Nicholas in his direction. Theo stared at the little boy in his pale blue sleepsuit and felt his face colour, as he wiped his hands nervously on his thighs. 'I'm not very good with babies.'

'Well, you'd better get good at it, pal, because trust me before you know it there will be the pitter patter of Montgomery feet in the house and you are going to wish you had paid better attention!' Gerard laughed. 'At least that's how it was in my case. One minute I am married to the biggest party girl on the planet, out all night dancing,' he lifted his wine glass in Melissa's direction, 'and the next I'm queuing in the all-night chemist for disposable nappies and nipple cream watching men who used to be me, trot along the pavement with the wobble of drink and a silly grin on their faces, and do you know what I envied the most about them?' Gerard waited for a response.

Melissa tutted, 'Oh not this again!'

'Yes! This again,' he winked at Theo, 'what I envied in them the most was not their drunken antics or the freedom they had to plan an evening on the town and actually leave the house, no, it was the fact that I knew these men were going home to sleep! Imagine that? Sleeping in a bed for longer than two and a half hours before a wailing monster squawks into the night and we all have to jump to attention.' He took a slug of his wine. 'I was plain jealous.'

'Poor Gerard.' Anna smiled at him.

'Poor Gerard?' Melissa shouted. 'It wasn't poor Gerard who was sliding off the mattress too tired to stand so a child could brutalise his once lovely chest! Don't you dare give him sympathy!'

'You love it right?' Anna asked.

Gerard scooped baby Nicholas into his arms and kissed his little face. 'I do, Anna, I love it more than I can possibly describe. And don't tell him this,' he lowered his voice to a whisper, 'but I'd get up to him any time of day and night, just to get the chance to spend five minutes with him. I'm obsessed.'

Theo felt Anna's stare across the room and hated her look of hope. It was proving to be the biggest bone of contention between them, her desire to start a family and his attempts at deflecting the issue.

It was as they drove home to Barnes that Anna again broached the topic, as he had guessed she would.

'Nicholas brings so much joy to their lives, doesn't he?' Her words sounded off the cuff, but he suspected she had been mentally rehearsing them since they had left.

'He does. But I also get the impression that they have given up a lot. I mean, Gerard was saying they hardly ever get the chance to go dancing or go out.' He let this trail.

'Oh God yes, I would hate for us to have to give up our dancing!' she laughed and he joined in, knowing they had never done this. 'I just feel so excited when I think about it, Theo. I can't help it.'

'I know you do, but there are lots of advantages to not having kids.' He squeezed her leg.

'Like what?'

'Well, the sleep Gerard mentioned, can you imagine not being able to sleep? That must be like torture!'

'I promise I will do every single night feed and you will not be disturbed. The advantage of having a big house is you can sleep in the spare room.' She smiled.

'I can think of other advantages.' He coughed, preparing to announce his big surprise.

'I get the feeling you are going to suggest sex?'

'Actually, I was going to tell you that I have booked for us to go to the Maldives for our wedding anniversary, but if sex is on the cards...'

He watched her turn in the seat and place her hand over her mouth. 'Oh my god! Theo! Really?'

'Uh-huh. Our own villa, luxury all the way.'

He heard her sharp intake of breath. 'Oh Theo, that will be wonderful, thank you. Thank you, darling.' She reached over and kissed his face. 'The Maldives.'

He listened, as she practised the sound of the place and couldn't help but notice the slight edge of disappointment to her tone, as if no amount of fancy travel could make up for what she wanted most. A baby. He swallowed the guilt that swirled on his tongue and put the radio on.

Eleven

'Well...' Spud popped the last of his scampi into his mouth and wiped his hands on the paper napkin before flinging it into the puddle of tartare sauce and breadcrumbs that sat in the middle of his plate. 'I have to say that for someone who's just returned from the Maldives, you look mightily down in the dumps! Did none of that sunshine and relaxed living rub off on you?'

'Not exactly.'

'Half your luck...! I think Kumi and I celebrated our one-year anniversary by sharing a tub of raspberry ripple and having sex. In fact...' He sipped his drink. '... that might actually have been the last time we had sex.'

Theo abandoned his grey burger and chips and pushed the plate away with a sigh. 'I just don't know—'

'Well, we both know that you *do* know, but you're just deciding whether to confide in me or not.'

Theo gave a wry smile. It was impossible to fool his best mate. 'Okay...' He took a slug of his drink. 'The villa was incredible, right on the water, with a deck and all the bells and whistles. Anna was so excited to be there and it was brilliant seeing her happiness – it was the first time she'd been somewhere like that.

And there was the usual champagne on arrival, blue sky, bluer sea…' He rolled his hand in the air. 'You get the gist.'

'I do and I can see why you'd be so miserable – it sounds bloody awful.' Spud sipped his pint.

Theo rubbed his hand over his face. 'I love her.'

'I know.'

'But it's the having-kids issue that keeps on cropping up.'

'It's going to, mate. You've been married a year, it's what she wants, and rightly or not, it's what others expect too. And it's a big thing, a pressure, the biggest inside a marriage, I would think – certainly it is in ours. Kumi is already pushing for number two and I'm still trying to get my head around the fact that number one is here to stay!'

Theo wasn't in the mood for humour. 'Anna thinks having a family will be the thing that cements us.'

'It might be,' Spud offered supportively.

'But I don't think so, not for me. I haven't learnt the things you did. The way you talk about your dad, like he's your mate, and all the experiences you've had together…' He paused. 'And now you're a dad too and you just take it all in your stride. I've had none of that – I wouldn't know where to start.' He fingered the fishing fly on his lapel, trying to calm his agitation.

'Everyone feels like that and, trust me, no matter how or where or by whom you were raised, nothing prepares you for having one of your own. You just have to try and figure it out as you go along. Kumi and I have had such different experiences, but I think that's what makes it work. Miyu will have balance.'

Theo shook his head and shifted uncomfortably in his seat.

'You're shaking your head like you don't believe me,' Spud said.

'It's not that I don't believe you, it's just…'

'Is it partly to do with Kitty and stuff?'

Theo gave a small sigh and looked towards the window, tapping his fingertips on the tabletop. He was someone who discussed land prices, wine, the weather, cars, politics, food and sport – not 'stuff'. He swallowed and spoke slowly. 'I know very few people who grow older with the express desire not to become a parent; some do, I'm sure, but I feel like an oddity, like I'm going against the grain.'

'But you are a parent!' Spud said quietly.

'Yes. But not in any way that anyone would notice, not in any way that counts! Fucking hell, I don't even know if my child is a boy or a girl. And I do know that the mother took one look at me and ran for the bloody hills!' He said this a little louder and more sternly than he intended and certainly than he was comfortable with. He wiped the corners of his mouth with his thumb and forefinger. 'I'm sorry, Spud, it's a subject I find difficult enough to fence with at home, let alone having to do it here in the pub too.'

'No need to apologise, mate. It's raw, I get it, but the fact that it makes you so mad means it is unresolved.'

'I guess.' Theo stretched out his legs and crossed his ankles.

'Have you told Anna about—'

'No.' Theo shook his head. 'How can I? I tried when we first got together, I've tried many other times and I did actually try again when we were in the Maldives, but… well, we were having a row, and she looked so broken already, so I chickened out and ended up telling her about my so-called brother Alexander. And she thought that was shocking enough.' He shook his head. 'Christ, she is so intent on becoming a mother, she even writes to her future kids! She's given them names, Fifi and Fox, and she scribbles notes to them, telling them all sorts. Who the fuck does that? It's the most enormous pressure.'

'I think part of the pressure is that you're keeping a secret that's directly related to what she wants most. Your kid with Kitty, not telling Anna and her drive to become a mum, it's all different parts of the same problem.'

Theo looked at his mate. 'You think I don't know that?' He nodded. 'But how can I have another child when there is already one in the world that I have nothing to do with?' The nerve in his jaw twitched angrily. 'I can't do it.'

'I think it's a shame. You have so much to offer a child.'

'You mean the money, the house.'

'No, mate.' Spud laughed. 'Not the money! It's not about that, although that helps. What you have to offer are all the good things that make you you. You're funny and smart, and you're kind, Theo, one of the good guys, and those are not bad qualities to pass on, to share.'

'Thank you.' He meant it. 'And you're right, no amount of money in the bank matters when the world feels like a hostile place.' He pictured himself as a child crying into his pillow. 'But what I don't have, I suppose, is the... the confidence.'

'You think I don't know *that*?' Spud countered.

Theo gave him a dry smile; his friend's humour was stronger than his own dark mood. 'Truth is, I've always been worried about turning out like my father, and then the Kitty thing happened and it made me exactly like him!'

'No, it didn't. He had his circumstances, of which you know very little, and you had yours. All your choices were taken out of your hands – you are *not* a bad person, Theo, quite the opposite.'

'I'm not sure Anna would see it as different.' Theo downed the rest of his pint and ran his fingers through his hair.

'You'll never know unless you tell her.'

'God, Spud, to hear her crying herself to sleep, and to have to answer her questions over and over as to why we can't have a baby, it kills me to know how much anguish I'm causing her. If she knew there was a child out there, my child, it would destroy her.'

Spud took a deep breath. 'I can't imagine keeping something so big from Kumi. And I really think Anna would understand. I think her joy at becoming a mum would outweigh everything else.'

Again there was a moment of silence as Theo considered his words. 'I spent days and nights trying to hide from the world, trying to make myself invisible. I can't put a child through that. I won't. And it's made me this… this…' He struggled to find the right words. '… this glass-half-empty kind of guy, no matter what. And yet Anna…' He shook his head admiringly. 'She had the very worst of starts but doesn't let it define her, in fact the opposite, she's nearly always sunny. Whereas me…'

'I think that with you, Theo, it's more about your ability to shake off past unhappiness, to recognise you're a different person now.'

'Or rather my inability.'

'Yes. Exactly.' Spud lifted his pint pot and wiped his beer tash with the back of his hand. 'Well, I certainly thought tonight was going to be more of a celebration.' He folded his arms over his chest.

'I'm sorry. You're right.' Theo clapped his hands. 'So, the big old U S of A! Mr Mega Job. Working in a thinktank, whatever that is!' He grinned. 'I can only picture humans in a giant fish tank with thought bubbles and all wearing goggles.'

'And that would mostly be correct. Kumi's getting my flippers and trunks ready as we speak.'

Theo noted the slightest twitch to Spud's eye. 'Are you nervous?'

'A bit, but as I often say to myself, the decision you make is always the right one – that way you remove the self-doubt and just bloody get on with it!'

'Amen to that.' Theo raised his hand for a high five, which Spud made a show of ignoring.

They both laughed, then exchanged a look, before Theo, embarrassed, jumped up. 'Same again?'

'Yup.' Spud drained his glass.

* * *

It was raining as Theo and Spud left the pub and emerged onto the Strand. Theo lifted his suit lapels and held them closed over his cotton shirt, letting his finger run over the little fishing fly that sat discreetly beneath. 'I can't believe you're going to the bloody States. I'm actually going to miss you.' He punched his friend lightly on the arm.

'You must promise to come and see us. Kumi and Anna can enjoy the delights of Washington and you and I can drink beer.'

'You always say that, but we'd get stuck with Miyu while they go off, meaning beer will become coffee. The last time we babysat, I ended up getting a makeover!'

Both men laughed at the memory of how Spud's daughter with her dad's help had gone to town with her face paints.

'You should be honoured that you're her favourite godfather.'

'I'm her only godfather!'

'Good point.'

Thunder rolled overhead and the rain got heavier.

'It's only a plane-ride away.' Spud nodded, a little choked.

'Yep.' Theo looked at the pavement, where fat raindrops bounced on the grey slabs. 'Who'd have thought we'd be standing here like this all these years after I first met you. I remember when you knocked on the door of my room in halls. I hadn't even unpacked. And there you were, skinny and geeky and you called me Cleo, said it was because you were from Wigan!' He laughed.

'I was panicking! You were the poshest person I'd ever spoken to and it threw me. My mum told me to knock on the door of my neighbours and ask if they fancied a beer. I was bricking it, but she said it was a failsafe.'

'Turns out Ma Spud was right.'

'She usually is. Christ, I thought it would be one quick drink, I never expected I'd still be lumbered with you thirteen years later!' Theo smiled at him. This move was a big deal. 'This is just the beginning, mate – we have a lot of years to cover yet and a lot more beer to consume.'

'Do you think they have scampi in Washington?' Spud scuffed his shoe on the wet ground.

'Probably. But I think it's called "scayumpee".' Theo tried out his appalling American accent.

The two stood awkwardly, using the banter to mask their sadness.

'Come here!' Spud reached out and embraced Theo warmly, hugging him a little more tightly than was comfortable. He released him and shook his hand firmly.

'I'll see you soon.' Theo coughed and slapped his friend on the shoulder.

'Yes, mate. I'll see you soon. And you know where I am if you need me.'

Theo raised his hand in acknowledgement, then turned and walked away.

He was glad of the rain. Somehow it helped dilute the emotion of their parting. He disliked the hollow feeling in his chest, which felt a lot like loss. Unwilling to go home just yet, he wandered past Charing Cross train station and stood on the corner, staring at Trafalgar Square. The bronze lions gleamed majestically in the downpour and the lamplight was hazy overhead as raindrops punctured the surface of the fountain pools. This was the London he loved, when the shiny façade and the crisp flags laid on for the tourists were removed and the beating heart of the capital was laid bare. Running his hand through his hair, he dusted the rain from his short crop and rubbed his face.

Get a grip, Theo!

It was as he ambled towards Whitehall, dithering over whether to go back to the pub and sink another pint alone or whether to trot down to the Embankment and walk along the river, that the number 53 bus drew up alongside him. Something about the shape of the figure in the window of the top deck made him turn and look up. It was a silhouette he'd carried in his mind since he was fourteen. There in the front seat, gazing into the distance, sat Kitty Montrose.

Theo quickly glanced down the street, searching for Spud, wanting to point her out, needing if not his mate's support then at least someone to share the moment with. His heart skipped a beat. Just the sight of her made his pulse race faster, taking him back to his unrequited teens and then that glorious afternoon together back when he was at UCL. But then came the stab to his chest and the memory of her letter.

If our paths should ever cross, please respect my wish for us to never mention this. I beg you, Theo. This is the only way I can build a life. Please.

I say goodbye now...

'What if, actually, it wasn't only your call to make, Kitty? Why did I not have a say?' he muttered under his breath.

As if on autopilot, Theo freed his hands from his pockets and broke into a run, looking ahead at the traffic lights and thankful that they were still on red. With his eyes trained on the bus, he collided with a group of men, all in suits and all, like him, looking as if they'd enjoyed one or two drinks after work.

'Watch where you're going, prick!' one yelled.

Theo lifted his hand over his shoulder. That would have to be apology enough; he didn't want to lose sight of the number 53.

Running and slipping in his smooth-soled brogues on the wet pavement, he raced up the street, overtook the bus and came to a halt at the next bus stop. His chest ached and he had a stitch in his side. He smiled at the driver as he boarded, flashing his travel card and holding the rail as the double-decker pulled away from the kerb. Slowly, slowly he trod the narrow stairs.

The bus was warm; gloved hands had wiped viewing portholes in its steamed-up windows and the air was pungent with the smell of damp wool. With only a couple of other passengers upstairs, Theo had a clear view of the back of Kitty's head. Her hair, still red, had dulled a little and she had lopped it off to shoulder length. Suddenly shy, he wondered how he might justify his presence there – what should he say? He also thought of Anna, waiting for him at home, and he swallowed his guilt at having chased the bus for a chance to say 'hi' to Kitty. How would he explain that?

Why was he so keen to see her again? He stopped in his tracks halfway up the stairs, taken aback at the spontaneity of his actions. He was hardly still holding a candle for her. No, it wasn't that – there was more anger in him now. He wanted... He wanted to show her that she'd misjudged him. Wanted to show her he wasn't the weedy weirdo she thought he was. Wanted her to see that he'd found happiness too.

He gripped the rail at the top of the stairs and hovered in the aisle.

Kitty turned towards the window and looked out at the dark street ahead. It was as he studied her profile and prepared what he might say that a child's head bobbed up into view on the seat next to her. At this, Theo's legs turned to jelly. A child! His child!

He quickly sloped down the aisle and sat down as inconspicuously as possible. His heart beat loudly in his ears and his knees shook. The child was wearing a woolly hat. It was red with a blue band, the kind that a boy or girl might wear. The child's shoulders were slight beneath its navy duffle coat. Theo recalled owning a similar coat at a similar age and felt a flare of joy at this tiny connection of sorts.

He was transfixed by the pair, noting their gentle interaction as Kitty bent her head to better hear the soft voice by her side. He was touched by the way she laughed gently, placing a hand against a cheek he couldn't see.

It was a surreal situation. The child had to be about ten. His child, his flesh and blood, now sat no more than twenty feet away, but oblivious. Theo glanced towards the staircase and was wondering if he should leave when all of a sudden the child knelt up on the seat and turned to face the back of the bus. Kitty, still looking forward, placed her arm across the navy duffle coat to ensure that her child wouldn't fall if the bus braked suddenly.

Theo's breath caught in his throat as he stared into the child's face – the face of a pretty, bright little girl. *A girl! A little girl!* His daughter. She had her mother's freckles and the same upturn to the tip of her nose, but her dark curly hair, her brown eyes and the shape of her mouth were his.

She looked like him!

He remembered Anna telling him how as a teenager she used to flag down taxi drivers on the off-chance, hoping that one of them would be her dad and thinking that she'd instantly know when she found him because looks and shared genes would make it obvious they were father and daughter. *You were right, Anna. I am looking at her and she is looking at me and I know, I just know…*

'Sit round now, please, Sophie.' Kitty spoke sternly, loudly.

Sophie! Sophie! The word rang in his head like a note. His daughter was called Sophie.

'I'm waiting to go round a corner.' Sophie gripped the back of the seat and leant out towards the aisle, her tongue poking from the side of her mouth.

Adventurous and fearless – a warrior like your mum.

'You are not going to do that, you'll fall, so please sit round now!'

Yes, keep her safe, Kitty, keep her safe.

Maybe she was drawn by his stare, or perhaps she too sensed

the shape of a face she'd known since she was fourteen. Either way, Kitty turned round and looked directly at Theo.

There was a moment of stunned silence before she placed a shaking hand over her mouth and blinked furiously. Floored by her reaction, having anticipated something different, Theo again looked towards the stairs, wondering now how to leave without making a fuss.

They were both frozen in shock, anchored to the spot. Theo looked from Kitty to Sophie and she did the same, their frantic stares joining the dots.

'Don't cry,' he whispered under his breath. 'Please don't cry. I won't cause any trouble. I didn't know she would be here.' She! Sophie...

Kitty pulled a tissue from her sleeve, dotted her pretty green eyes and wiped her freckled nose. She popped the tissue into the pocket of her voluminous mac and reached into the small space on the floor, from where she retrieved her handbag. Theo noted a wide gold band glistening on the third finger of her left hand.

The two continued to stare at each other. Then she stretched up and rang the bell. The bus slowed.

'Come on, darling.' With false brightness and a sense of urgency, she ushered Sophie from the seat, following close behind.

'Why did you press the bell, Mummy?' Sophie asked, her voice well-spoken.

The two stopped at the top of the stairs, only inches from him now, both swaying a little, waiting for the bus to come to a halt. They were within touching distance, these two who in another life, if things had been different, might have been his family.

It was eleven years since he'd last seen Kitty. He noted the creep of fine creases at the edges of her eyes and the fact that her lips had lost some of their fullness. He lowered his gaze and was drawn by the unmistakeable baby bump protruding over the waistband of her jeans. She cradled her stomach protectively. He gave a small smile, thankful that things had worked out with Angus and hoping they shared the happiness he and Anna enjoyed.

'Where are we going, Mummy?' Sophie laughed. 'We aren't at Blackheath yet.'

Blackheath – is that where you live? Are you heading home?

Kitty pulled her head back on her shoulders and narrowed her eyes at Theo, warning him to stay quiet. 'I want to get off now, darling.' He felt a spike of guilt at the tremor to her voice, the fear in her eyes. 'We can… We can get the next bus.'

'Why are we going to do that?' Sophie asked.

'Just because!' Flustered, she snapped at her daughter in the Scottish accent that had always sounded to his ears like the sweetest music.

He made as if to rise, indicating he would get off with them, but she gave a single vigorous shake of her head, her mouth set.

Theo hardly dared breathe. Kitty's tears gathered again, and she cuffed them with the back of her hand. He smiled at Sophie as she passed and she returned his smile with a curve to her lips that mirrored his own. Her dark, shining eyes fixed on his; eyes that were just like his.

He listened to the sound of their footsteps and Sophie's stream of questions, which continued until they were out of earshot. He placed his daughter's sweet voice in the middle of his memory, knowing he'd probably never get to hear it again. Craning his neck towards the window, he looked down onto the rain-soaked street and saw nothing but darkness.

The bus trundled on. Theo sat for some time before jumping off in an open spot on the outskirts of Blackheath. Unsure of where he was heading or even in what direction, he moved briskly with his hands in his pockets, thankful that the rain had eased and too preoccupied to notice the chill in the air. He looked up at the purple bruise of sky as thunder rumbled over the river in the distance. It felt like an omen. The storm he thought he'd outrun was in fact catching up with him. *I must tell Anna. I need to tell her about Sophie.*

Crossing a main road, he found himself heading in the direction of Greenwich Park. And just like that he was crying, sobbing so loudly and with such force it became hard to take a breath. He cried for the fact that his best mate was leaving London for Washington, he cried for Sophie, who would live a life without him, but most of his tears were for his beloved Anna and what he was unable to give her.

As the strength left his legs, he sat on the kerb, hardly aware of the traffic that flew past. He thought of his Anna, who would be padding around the house waiting for the sound of his key in the door. Beautiful, sweet Anna who had been through so much and deserved so much more than this. Anna, who would give anything to feel the swell of her belly under a mackintosh, her skin stretched with his child, growing inside.

I'm sorry, Anna. I am so, so sorry. I'm not good enough. You shouldn't have picked me. Kitty was right; fatherhood is not the path for me. I am not that person. You should have picked anyone but me.

Twelve

Theo flattened his tie to his chest and wiped the corners of his mouth with his thumb and forefinger, a habit he'd developed to clear away any stray bits of food or spittle. He knocked and entered his father's office, which was across the corridor from his own.

'Dad, I—' He stopped.

A dark-haired young woman was perched on the edge of the oval table where the board usually met. She abruptly uncrossed her legs and stood up. Her smile faded, as did his father's. Theo felt self-conscious and unwelcome. It was the feeling he often had with his parents, the sense that he was an unwanted guest for whom no place had been set.

'Sorry, I didn't realise you had company.' He kept his eyes on his father, noting the slight flush to the bulge of fat that had recently appeared above his dad's starched shirt collar. His father wore the glazed expression he always had when in the company of a pretty woman. Theo felt the first stirrings of nausea. 'I'll come back later.' He pointed to the door.

'No, not at all. Theo, this is Marta, our new intern. She'll be here for the next few months, learning about the world of corporate property. She has a degree,' he added, as if this was something of a surprise. Theo's father and his cronies were always wary of women who had both beauty and brains.

'Good for you.' Theo smiled in her direction.

Clearly confident in her position, she responded by pulling a face at him that in any other circumstances might have been childish, with the hint of a snarl to her top lip.

'Tell you what, Marta,' Perry Montgomery said, 'why don't you take an early lunch and we'll see you back here in an hour or so?'

'Thank you. See you in a bit.' She bobbed her head and left the room, letting her challenging gaze linger on Theo.

The two men waited until the door had closed behind her before resuming their conversation.

'She's *very* smart.' His father coughed.

'So you said.' Theo really was heartily sick of his dad's roving eye and disregard for his mum's feelings. 'You know, Dad, any of the heads of department would be happy to show Marta round. You're the chairman of this company, you don't have to be so hands on, especially with something that's of no real benefit.'

His father stared at him and licked his lower lip. His eyes darted round the room and he seemed to be deciding how best to respond. Then he sat forward with his hands in a pyramid on the leather-topped desk, apparently having chosen to ignore Theo's comment.

'What was it that you wanted to see me about?' He pointed to the chair.

Theo sat. 'I've... I've had an idea.' He felt his confidence ebbing.

'Go on.' Perry lifted his chin, listening.

Theo gave a nervous laugh, wary of beginning. 'This is going to sound a bit leftfield, but it's something I've been thinking about for a while, a slightly different direction.' He waited for an interjection, a loaded question, but it didn't come and so he continued. 'I want to buy an old spice warehouse in the Bristol docklands that's come up for sale. It's semi-derelict and surrounded by wasteland, but it's very close to the redeveloped town centre and the waterfront and I'm sure the whole area is going to explode, which means it will only go up in value.' He paused, again waiting for his father to comment, but he didn't. 'And while we have this beautiful property, while we're waiting for it to go up in value, I've thought of a way that it can do some good too, for the community.'

A slight smile crossed his father's lips. 'Some good for the community, you say?'

Emboldened, Theo sat forward and, leaning on the desk, he spoke with passion. 'As you know, Anna is a rare graduate of the care system. She's strong and special, she's a success story, but there are so many kids who come out of the care system and fall through the cracks, as if the jump is too big from care home to regular life.' He recalled Anna telling him about her former roommate, Shania, who'd apparently become homeless and an addict. 'I want to convert the warehouse into pods, not overly grand or over-engineered but studios that kids leaving care could live in until they're on their feet and working or studying or whatever. It would be the missing link in the care system and it could make a massive difference.'

'Bristol? What do you know about Bristol?' his father scoffed, rather missing the point.

Theo held his nerve. 'Enough to know that its property prices are rising by a healthy percentage year on year. The rise in equity would be commensurate with some of our lower rental gains in other areas where property values are stagnant. The warehouse would be a valuable asset, but mainly, Dad, it's the idea of providing these places for kids who need them, kids who are vulnerable. It's the chance to help turn them into adults with self-esteem, into good citizens. We win, society wins.'

Perry looked down. 'And can I ask, did you recite that from one of your textbooks?'

Theo shook his head and chose not to take the bait. 'I'm serious, Dad.'

'Warehouses?'

'Yes, once used for tobacco and spice storage mainly, built in the 1800s. They're crying out for renovation, they'd be perfect for the sort of loft living that's done so well in London's docklands.'

His father sat back in his chair. 'It's one thing building flats in the suburbs or remodelling old cinemas within the M25, but sending a crew down to Bristol, out of sight and out of reach? And doing so to satisfy some liberal touchy-feely do-gooder need? It feels like too much of a risk.' His father took a breath and sized up his son. 'You need to remember, Theo, that we have close alliances with the planners in London. Very close alliances.'

'Close alliances,' Theo was all too well aware, was code for the brown envelopes stuffed with cash that were routinely handed over in exchange for permissions granted. These turned risky investments into dead certs and grew the bank balances of petty officials in the process. He had been told long ago that that was just the way things worked.

He ignored his father's jibe. 'I get that, but this feels like an opportunity and I was thinking it might be good to get away from London, breathe some different air and follow my dream of making a difference.' He let this hang.

'You want to get away?' His father narrowed his eyes and set his mouth.

'Not get away completely, no, but venture elsewhere... try something new.' His nerves bit.

'Yes, Theo, of course, why didn't I think of it? Why would anyone risk investing only in London, one of the world's property hotspots since... for ever, when I could convert a warehouse into homes for junkies!' Perry was on a roll now. 'It's bloody genius! And anyway, what would Anna make of you swanning off to Bristol, eh? Wouldn't she rather you stayed here and grew that family of yours?'

Theo flinched. His parents did this, used Anna as a bargaining chip whenever the need arose, and yet they made very little effort with her most of the time. But, again, he decided not to bite. 'I wouldn't be swanning off.' He looked into his lap, unwilling to admit that in his father's expressions he saw more than a hint of amusement at the fact that his marriage, like the rest of his life, was, in his view, far from perfect. 'I'd be based here but overseeing the project—'

'I won't be taking it to the board.' Perry stopped him short, lifting his chin. 'I just don't think you have it in you, my boy. After all, your track record, flunking university and all that, doesn't really inspire confidence, does it? As for Bristol warehouses, well, we'll leave those for the carrot crunchers to get stuck into!' He laughed.

Theo met his stare, frustration bubbling in his gut. He wasn't willing to roll over just yet. 'Maybe if I showed you the site plans and explained my ideas—'

'I have given you my answer, Theodore,' his father cut in, 'and as far as I know, it is still my name above the door, at least for a few years yet.' He gave a nasal chortle.

When he'd got home that evening, all Theo had wanted was supper and sleep. But he'd returned to Barnes to find Anna in a highly emotional state. Her half-sister had just given her a photo of Anna as a baby in the arms of both her father and her mother and, unsurprisingly, Anna had been over the moon about it. Unfortunately, though, this had led on to another discussion about Anna's desperate desire for a baby of her own. And, as was so often these days, this had developed into a big row, with tears and recriminations and a sense that they were never going to see eye to eye on this.

It had been a testing evening at the end of a testing day and Theo was relieved to finally get in the shower and let the cascade of hot water soothe away some of his fatigue. It irked him more than he was able to admit that his father had given so little attention to his proposition. He'd put so much thought into his pitch, had spent hours working out exactly how to present it, and all for nothing. What sort of father relished making his son feel so insignificant? What sort of father made his son feel like a failure however hard he tried?

Thinking about his own father inevitably led Theo on to thinking about Sophie. Ever since he'd seen Kitty and Sophie on the bus, the image of the two of them had rarely been far from his thoughts. He heard Sophie's girlish voice as he fell asleep, he pictured her big smile and innocent dark eyes, and he saw Kitty's horrified expression, her speedy exit from the bus. The message had been loud and clear, and it hurt. It hurt him more than he was able to express, and even if he had felt able, with Spud in the States he had absolutely no one to express it to. He found it hard to concentrate and he was conscious of the fact he'd been more irritable with Anna of late, on a shorter fuse. He felt bad about the row earlier on – it wasn't Anna's fault, he knew that, but even so... He just couldn't face discussing parenthood right now, not with Sophie in his thoughts so much, and the warehouse project, and his dad's intransigence. The black shadow of depression seemed to be coming scarily close again.

Reluctantly Theo stepped from the shower and put on his sweatpants and sweatshirt. He didn't know if Anna had let Griff, their new Alsatian-cross rescue puppy, out for his night-time wee and he thought he might run him quickly round the block. The fresh air might help clear his head and perhaps then he'd have a better chance of getting some sleep.

Theo descended the stairs and ran through what he wanted to say to Anna. He didn't want to go to bed on a row and he loathed seeing her upset. The least he could do was apologise and explain how he felt about his dad's behaviour.

Griff was making a low growl, which was curious because as long as their beloved pup was within sight of one or both of them, all was usually right with his world. As if urged by a sixth sense, Theo quickened his pace, just in time to see Anna stumble backwards and tumble to the kitchen floor. *What the hell...?*

'Anna!' he yelled, racing to her side. She'd hit her head and seemed to be out cold. 'Anna! Anna!' he yelled again, his voice loud and panicky now.

Griff growled and yelped. Theo kissed Anna's forehead, her hair, put his ear next to her heart. He couldn't tell whether he was hearing something or not, he was too scared, his own heart was racing like a train. He wasn't helping. Inhaling deeply, he made himself calm down. He gently lifted Anna's right arm and held his finger against her wrist, checking her pulse. He made himself pay attention. The pulse was there. He gulped and sobbed, then yanked the blue linen dishcloth from the Aga door and folded it into a cushion between her head and the cold floor.

'It's okay, Griff, it's okay, boy!' He tried to reassure the pup, who stood alarmed and whimpering now, next to his basket. Theo grabbed his phone from the tabletop and dialled 999. 'Ambulance! I need an ambulance, please, quickly. It's my wife, she's collapsed...'

As soon as he finished the call, he opened the front door wide, then raced back to sit on the floor with Anna. He took her limp hand inside his and cooed to her, kissing her fingers and wiping her hair from her pale face. 'It's okay, Anna. The ambulance is on its way. They'll be here in a second, don't you worry.' He kept talking, as much to allay his own fears as to reassure her.

With one hand still clamped to Anna's, he reached for the pen and paper that was lying on the table, thinking it might be helpful to note down Anna's pulse rate before the paramedics turned up. He never got round to doing that, because the top sheet of paper had already been used. Anna had written one of her letters to her imaginary children, Fifi and Fox, presumably while he'd been showering. His breath caught in his throat as he read it.

Fifi and Fox,
Here it is.

I have never been so close to giving up on my dream of you. Never.

I sit here at the kitchen table, writing with tears trickling down my face at these words. It's a hard thing for me to write, and an even harder thing to imagine. But, like always, I have to try and carry on, find the good, because there is one thing I know with absolute certainty and it's this – if I give in to the deep, cold sadness that lurks inside me, if I submit to the lonely longing for the people who have left me and the things I can't have, then the darkness will take hold. It will fill me right up and it will drown me.

I can't let that happen. Because while I am here there is always hope. Know, my darlings, that life is worth living. Life is worth living! It's up to us what shape that life takes. I had reason more than most to let my life crush me, but I didn't let it. I fought against it. And I will keep fighting – fighting to find the happy in this good, lucky life I have made, this life I share with Theo.

I will keep positive. I won't give up. I won't.

Anna
(I hardly dare write Mummy – it feels a lot like tempting fate.)

Theo howled as he reached the last line. 'Oh, my Anna, I am so sorry! I am. I can't lose you! I can't! You are all I've got. You are the only one who understands, who loves me. Please don't leave me, Anna, please, I'm begging you…' He bent low and kissed her again, feverishly and repeatedly. 'Where the fuck is the ambulance?' he yelled towards the door. Every minute felt like an eternity. 'Don't leave me, Anna, please! I'll do anything to keep you alive, to keep you loving me! I'll… I'll have a child with you! We can do it! We can make Fifi and Fox, we can.

I can't bear for you to not have what you want. I don't know how I'll cope, but I will, somehow, and I will do it for you! I will do anything. Just please don't leave me.'

Finally Griff started barking and there came the sound of footsteps on the gravel path. Two paramedics, a man and a woman, both wearing green overalls, ran into the kitchen and gently eased his wife from his grip.

'Is… Is she going to be okay?' Theo swallowed, placing his hands on his hips and trying to keep it together.

The female paramedic looked up at him. 'Let's get her to the hospital, then she'll be in the best place.'

The next few hours were a nightmarish blur. Anna was whisked off into the inner reaches of the hospital and Theo was left in the visitors' room with only his thoughts and a plate of custard creams for company. His mind couldn't settle and he kept going over the last few weeks, trying to recall if Anna had shown any signs of being unwell. Had she mentioned anything, any pains or headaches? He wracked his brain. He'd been so wrapped up in planning the Bristol project, and there'd been Kitty and Sophie, and Spud leaving… He definitely hadn't been giving her as much attention as she needed. And then there was the baby thing. He kept replaying the words of her letter. There was so much sadness there, so much grief. He paced around the visitors' room, desperate to avoid the obvious conclusion but coming back to it again and again: had she collapsed because of their row, because she'd been so upset? He stopped in his tracks, stood up straight and made a decision. He'd made a pact as she lay on the kitchen floor and he would stick to it.

The nurse came in and she was smiling! Relief flooded through him.

'Your wife is comfortable now, Mr Montgomery. She's asleep, so you probably won't get much out of her for a few hours, but you're welcome to come and sit with her if you'd like to.'

Theo needed no second invitation. He sat beside Anna through the dawn and on into the morning, clasping her, sobbing intermittently, willing her to be all right. As soon as she woke, he told her what he'd decided.

'So, I've been thinking, Anna, I want to give you what you want. I will need your help, but we should go for it, we should have our baby. Our baby! I decided, last night when you were lying there on the floor, I decided that I'd been selfish and unfair and cowardly and that I couldn't bear not to have you with me and so I made a promise to myself that—'

'Oh, Theo!' She hoisted herself up in the bed and stared at him. 'You mean it?'

'I do.' He smiled. 'We can do it together, right?'

'Yes! Yes, my darling, that's right, we can do it together!' She reached for him and snuggled into his arms.

Not five minutes after he'd told Anna about his change of heart, her room started filling up with visitors, rather robbing them of the moment. Much to his surprise, in came Anna's friend Melissa, then Sylvie, the mother of her ex, and then his own mother. He was touched at their concern, but he worried that the party-like atmosphere might all be too much for Anna. In truth, though, she had beamed at all the new arrivals and it seemed they were just the distraction she needed.

He decided to leave them to it for a brief while. He took a minute to sit outside the room, relishing the moment of solitude and glad to be away from the hubbub. He leant against the wall and tried to stem the shake to his limbs. The medics had discovered an irregular heartbeat, which Anna had tried to dismiss with shrugs and glibly offered statistics. But he was less convinced, all too aware of her mum's shockingly premature death and keen to find out what could be done to prevent her collapsing again in the future.

He was relieved when the visitors finally left, traipsing past him and offering to help in any way they could.

Melissa kissed him firmly. 'Call me, let me know what she needs, anything at all, and I can be there in minutes.'

Sylvie wagged a nicotine-stained finger at him. 'You take care of her, lovely boy, and you take care of yourself!'

'I will.'

His mother hovered, waiting until the other two were out of earshot. 'Keep us posted, darling.'

'I will, Mum, and thank you for coming.'

'Not at all. An interesting bunch.' She looked towards Melissa and Sylvie.

Theo chose not to react; a hospital corridor was neither the time nor place.

Stella cleared her throat. 'It wants keeping an eye on, that heart thing.' She nodded towards the door of Anna's room as she looped her pashmina around her neck.

'Yes, I know.' He watched his mum sashay along the corridor towards the exit. 'And I shall keep an eye on my own heart too,' he muttered, 'because if anything happens to Anna it will break.' He took a deep breath, assumed an air of confidence and opened the door to Anna's room.

He took up the seat next to her bed and held her hand.

It was only a few minutes later that the consultant reappeared. He flipped the pages of his notes, then held the clipboard behind his back. 'We have all your test results, Mrs Montgomery.'

Theo sat forward in the chair, trying to remain calm. He was a lot more concerned than Anna seemed to be.

'As we discussed earlier, your heart is nothing to worry about at this stage, but with your family history we will keep an eye on it.'

'Thank you.' Anna squeezed Theo's hand and raised her eyebrows as if to say, *ha, I told you, nothing to worry about.*

'There was something else, however.' The consultant paused and Theo felt as if those five words had sucked all the air from the room. He felt lightheaded and nauseous, desperately afraid of what might come next. With good reason, as it turned out.

'We ran some blood tests,' the consultant continued, 'and your hormones are drastically out of balance. It would seem that you are in the middle of an early menopause.'

Anna slowly let go of Theo's hand and sat up in the bed. 'What does that mean?' she whispered.

'It means, Anna, that your fertility is coming to an end.'

'No more periods,' she whispered. 'No baby. Oh, Theo! No... no... baby. Not now. Not ever. Not... with you. Not with anyone.' She sobbed into her sleeve.

The consultant left almost immediately and the two of them sat there with the ramifications of this 'something else' spinning around them. It was like they were caught in a tornado that was ripping apart everything they thought they knew. It did so at speed and with such force it left them breathless.

'No, Theo! Please, no! It's all I ever wanted!' Anna cried

noisily, messily, clinging onto him as if for dear life. 'I wanted my babies. That is all I have ever wanted! Please, Theo. Oh God! Please, no!'

Theo had no idea how to console her. What could he say? What could he do? Only hours ago it seemed like they'd finally agreed to do this thing together, and she'd been so elated, brimming with joy at the prospect. But now... God, what a mess. The worst day of his life by far.

As he sat there with Anna wrapped in his arms, rocking her gently, he realised with surprise that he wasn't only desperately sad for her, he was sad for both of them. The idea of becoming a father had started to take root, and now that the possibility had been so brutally taken away, he felt deflated, denied the challenge. There had to be another way, didn't there?

They continued sitting there until Anna had calmed sufficiently and felt ready to pack up and go home. Theo made his way to the bathroom, leaving her alone for a few minutes, and decided to call his mother as he'd promised.

'Yes, Theodore?' His mother did this, always made it seem as if now was the worst possible time to phone her. It took him back to Vaizey, to when he was a small boy standing in Twitcher's study, praying that she'd pick up the phone.

'The consultant has just left and, er, we've had some bad news, I'm afraid.'

'Oh, Theo, dear—'

He sighed, swallowed, and blurted it out. 'We've just found out that Anna is going through an early menopause. So that means—'

'Yes, dear, I am aware of what it means.' She tutted disapprovingly, as if reminding Theo that it was not the done thing to discuss bodily functions and especially not women's health issues. A wave of embarrassment washed over him.

He pictured the note sitting on the kitchen table:

I have never been so close to giving up on my dream of you. Never.

I sit here at the kitchen table, writing with tears trickling down my face at these words. It's a hard thing for me to write, and an even harder thing to imagine...

Oh, Anna! My Anna! Coughing away his emotion, he decided he was after all in no mood to talk to his mother. A bolt of frustration shot through him. What had he expected – support, kindness? He was about to phrase his goodbyes when his mother interjected.

'I did want grandchildren eventually – what a shame. And I think Daddy is similarly minded. Not that we've discussed it, but I know he would like someone to carry on the Montgomery name and all that. Still, life is a long and winding road, as they say. Who knows what's around the corner?'

Theo's anger boiled. What she was she implying? That he would leave Anna and find a second wife to provide them with a grandchild? His skin prickled with fury and he could barely find the words. 'You are fucking kidding me!' was what he came up with, and with that he ended the call.

He paced the corridor, his stomach in knots of anger and grief, steeling himself to go back into the ward.

'How are you doing?' he whispered to Anna, who looked small and fragile sitting on the hospital bed. It was as if the news of her infertility had made her shrink.

She shrugged and bit her lip. Her eyes were swollen from all the crying and she looked wretched. Theo's heart contracted. It tore at him to see her like that.

He took up the seat by her bedside and again reached for her hand. 'I meant what I said earlier about making a pact when you were on the kitchen floor, when I thought…' He gulped. 'When I thought I might lose you.'

She turned her head towards him.

'I meant every word – that we should have a baby, that I will be a dad for you, with you.'

Her tears fell quickly and her voice when it came was barely more than a whisper. 'Bit late now,' she managed.

Theo's stomach churned. She was blaming him and he deserved it. But he would make it right. He would try and put his past behind him and do right by Anna. 'No, my darling! There will be a way. We'll find a way. We could… We could adopt! We could become parents that way – we could do it, we could!' He gripped her tight, hoping this might be something they could focus on. 'You know more than most how every kid needs a home. We might not be able to… to have a child, but we can help one. Give one a happy home, just like you've always wanted. We can teach it like your mum taught you – how to be strong, how to survive!'

'Or two.' Anna managed a small smile. 'Two kids.'

His heart leapt with relief. 'Yes, my Anna. Or two.' He placed his head on the side of the bed and offered up a silent prayer.

Thirteen

'You have a lock of hair sticking up.' Anna spat on her palm and ran it over Theo's scalp. He found this both revolting and demeaning and he ruffled his hair as soon as she'd finished. She tutted at him, playfully. He pressed the front doorbell and stood in the porch, waiting, with her arm resting through his.

'I can't believe you don't have a key to your family home. That's so messed up.' Her words hung in the air like the afterburn of a sparkler writing in the dark.

'Anna, as you well know, there's lots about my family that is messed up. Denying me entry unless I come with a semi-formal invite to dinner is just one of them.' He gave her a false grin.

'Okay, well, I'm keeping a mental note, and your messed-up family is definitely not something we should mention at our adoption interview, okay?' She looked deadly serious.

'Okay.' He sighed, already wary of doing or saying the wrong thing at their introductory meeting, scheduled for the following week. 'I can't believe you're making us do this.'

Anna laughed. 'Honestly, you sound like you're twelve! I am not making you do anything! I just think that whatever beef you have with your mum is not going to be resolved by sitting at home and brooding. It's important you fix it – life is too bloody short.'

He smiled at her, his brilliant wife who was being so brave, with the news of her infertility still only a few weeks old. He had only told her vaguely about hanging up the phone on his mother at the hospital, but not the reasons why. 'I know you're right, but we're not staying long.'

'Wow! You have no idea how much I'm looking forward to tonight.' Her words dripped with sarcasm.

They were silent for a beat or two.

'What are we doing? They do this – they turn us into crazies!' He turned to her, his tone conciliatory. 'Shall we just go home and drink wine and have sex? Why don't we say you've got a headache?'

'Why do I have to be the one with the headache? You have the bloody headache! And besides, if I have a headache then sex is most definitely out of the question!'

'Actually, Anna, if you carry on shouting at me like that, I might just well have one.'

'Ah, there you are!' His mum opened the front door wide and greeted them warmly, kissing them both on each cheek as if there was nothing amiss. She had clearly dressed for dinner and was looking chic in her high-waisted navy palazzo pants and a cream silk shirt tucked in to show off her slender frame. There was a string of pearls at her neck and her hair was scraped back into a French knot.

'Come in! Come in!' She ushered them eagerly into the rarely used drawing room, her eyes bright.

He and Anna shared a look of mild concern. It had been years since Theo had seen his mother make such a fuss.

His father was standing by the fireplace; flames roared in the grate and logs crackled comfortingly. He was holding a glass of whisky and resting his elbow on the marble mantelpiece, looking very much like a portrait in oils.

There was a man sitting in the wing-backed chair behind the door. He stood up and Theo's eye was immediately drawn to the bootlace tie around his neck. The man's jacket was cut long, his jaw-length hair was slicked back with oil and he sported a large, drooping moustache. Theo guessed he was in his fifties.

Anna strolled across the room and kissed her father-in-law on the cheek.

'How are you doing now?' Perry boomed. 'The damnedest thing!'

'I am doing well, thank you.'

Theo's heart flexed as Anna painted on a smile, burying her sorrow. He knew she was well-practised at putting on a brave face; it was something she'd had to do a lot through her childhood. The weeks since the devastating news about her infertility had been terribly hard for her. Theo had taken some days off and they'd spent most of the time going for long walks with Griff, distracting themselves, focusing on their playful pup instead. Bit by bit Anna had thrown herself into researching the adoption process. Once he'd returned to work, she seemed to spend most of her days calling people, making appointments, getting books on the subject out of the library. Their conversations at night became dominated by her findings. He was pleased for her, and excited too. It was such a relief not to be arguing any more. Now at last they were united, and they were even able to laugh again together. He kept his doubts to himself and tried not to dwell on them, but every so often they surfaced. How much would he have to disclose, and did he really want to raise someone else's child when he already had one of his own?

His mother almost skipped back into the room, pulling him back to the present and to the strange guest standing among them.

'So, Theo...' She clapped and flicked her fringe flirtatiously. The blush to her cheek was one he hadn't seen in a while. 'This,' she announced with clarity and a determined emphasis, 'is Pastor Julian.' She gestured towards him as if she were a hostess on a TV gameshow highlighting the many attributes of a fridge-freezer.

The man stuck out his hand at an odd angle, making the handshake awkward. Theo knew that his father would be sharing the same thought: *not the Vaizey way...*

'*Pastor* Julian?' he queried.

'Please, call me Jules.'

The man had a deep voice that Theo could easily imagine preaching sermons of fire and brimstone. He was aware of his father's stare and the two exchanged a look that bordered on comical. To share anything with his father felt like a win and he enjoyed the interaction.

'This is my wife, Anna.' Theo held out his hand and pulled her over to receive her own odd handshake.

'Nice to meet you,' she offered and, as ever, Theo was touched by her sweet nature.

'Ah yes, Anna. I was so very sorry to hear about your recent bad news.' Pastor Julian nodded sagely, as if he had the measure of Anna.

It irritated and bemused Theo that this man had been given the lowdown on their lives. He looked at his mother, wondering what the hell was going on.

There was a pause while all five glanced from one to the other, unsure of what came next.

'Do you have a… Is your church local?' Theo faltered, wary of causing offence. His parents had never shown even the slightest interest in any religion. The only time he had seen them in a church was at weddings, christenings and funerals.

'It's not a church so much as a shed. In Putney!' his father interjected, loudly and with a wheezy rattle of laughter. This was followed by the clink of ice as he brought the tumbler of whisky to his mouth.

'Your dad's right. I minister in Putney, but the truth is my church is anywhere people need it to be.' Pastor Julian spoke with his palms upturned, as if halfway through a magic trick and keen to show he had nothing secreted up his sleeve.

His dad rolled his eyes behind the pastor's back and Theo had to admit that he found the man's theatricals more than a tad amusing.

'If you don't mind me asking, how do you all know each other?' Anna asked the obvious and most interesting question, pointing at them in turn with her index finger.

'Mrs Montgomery is a valued member of my congregation.' The pastor smiled at Theo's mother.

'My mother, a member of your congregation?' Theo laughed, waiting for the punchline. He didn't have to wait long.

'That's right, Theodore, isn't it marvellous! Your mother has found Jesus!' his father boomed. 'And not just regular Jesus, not your common-or-garden, couple-of-hymns, sign-of-the-cross type Jesus. Oh no. This church is something very special. It is a kind of magic church. I don't want to steal her thunder, but this week she has in fact been chatting to Great-Aunt Agatha

– the fact that the woman's been dead for nigh on thirty years is neither here nor there. Isn't it marvellous? Pastor Jules has a hotline to heaven! Who'd have thought it? Could you see your way to asking my Great-Uncle Maurice where he buried the family gold?' He chuckled and took another sip.

There was an uncomfortable silence while everyone waited for this new insight to settle. 'And as if that wasn't revelation enough, she found Jesus in the darndest place. Tell him, Stella. Tell the boy where you were when you had your epiphany.'

'Daddy is trying to be funny, but, yes, I have found Jesus. Or rather he found me.'

'And *where* did he find you?' His father wasn't going to let up.

His mother lost a little of her colour and Theo felt sorry that she was being put under the spotlight in this way. 'He found me in... in Marks and Spencer's.' She stuttered slightly but held his gaze.

The atmosphere at the dinner table was strained, to put it mildly. Theo's mother ferried the vintage tureens that had graced her own mother's dresser to the table and fussed over every detail, checking the saltcellar and wiping a smudge from Anna's wine glass. Eventually she perched herself on the edge of her seat, as if waiting for her next instruction.

Pastor Julian took in the sumptuous spread, coughed and announced, 'It would be my honour to say grace.'

This, despite the fact no one had asked him. Theo looked at his father, fully expecting a disdainful response, but Perry merely sucked in his cheeks, swirled an ice cube in his tumbler and stared at Pastor Julian, as though trying to figure him out. His mother clasped her hands earnestly and Theo did his best to avoid Anna's stare, desperate not to give in to the laughter that threatened.

The uncomfortable silences between mouthfuls meant that every dropped fork and each clang of a glass against a plate seemed to deepen the embarrassment of everyone present. Everyone except Pastor Julian, who seemed more than at home as he repeatedly dug the silver serving spoon deep into the dish of mashed potatoes and ladled chicken gravy over the top with relish. 'So, Anna, Stella tells me you were in care?' he said casually, almost as an aside.

Again, Theo was irritated by the pastor's tone. He watched Anna's face carefully as she responded, ready to swoop in and save her if need be.

'Yes. Yes, I was. From my early teens until I was eighteen.'

'You seem…'

Anna paused, holding her fork mid mouthful, waiting to hear what came next.

'You seem incredibly calm, astute, if you don't mind me saying.'

Anna's response was cool and well delivered. 'Well, that's very kind of you to say, but in my experience, people who have been in care are many and varied in their personalities and circumstances. I think it depends where you lived, who you lived with and why you were there in the first place.'

'And that is of course true, but still, the statistics would suggest that a life in care can lead to criminality, depression, drug abuse…'

Anna swallowed her mouthful and stayed calm. 'Sadly that is what the statistics say, but I'm not really one for statistics, 83.4 per cent of which are apparently made up on the spot.' She smiled at Theo and he laughed quietly, feeling a rush of love for her. 'Take my roommate, Shania. She and I were from not dissimilar backgrounds, and she nearly fell through the cracks after she left care. She was homeless not that long ago, in fact. But now she is clean, healthy and pregnant! I saw her just the other week, as it happens, for the first time in a long while, and it was a pleasure to see her doing so well.' She raised her glass and took a sip in honour of her friend. 'The secret is having somewhere safe to go when you leave care. Like Theo's idea for dedicated studio-homes for kids in Bristol, trying to give them a proper chance. Wouldn't that be wonderful?'

Theo held her gaze, quite overcome by her very public support for the project his father had been so derisive about.

Perry took the bait. 'Well, if Theo feels that strongly about those poor kids, he should fund the sodding project himself. How about that?' He banged the table. 'Or is that what this adoption malarkey is all about? Another do-gooders' attempt to make a difference? Can't see it myself, bringing up someone else's sprog – you surely never quite know what you're going to get! And the idea of him looking after a baby!' He pointed at Theo. 'He had a goldfish once, won it at a fair, don't think it lasted the night!'

The colour drained from Theo's face and he looked over at Anna, aghast. He'd told his parents in passing that they were exploring the idea of adoption, but of course they hadn't had a proper discussion about it – about that or anything in that vein. His dad's words cut him to the quick and he hated that it might be doing the same to Anna.

'It's okay,' she mouthed at him. 'I love you.'

He felt like weeping.

Stella sighed. 'Perry, please! That's quite enough! Do carry on, Anna.'

Anna was silent momentarily and then, to her absolute credit, she continued. 'I don't let my past define me, but also I don't forget it. I have learnt a lot through all of my experiences, I hope. Some good and some not so good.'

Theo eyed her across the table. *I am proud of you, my strong, lovely Anna.*

'And you were in care on account of losing all of your family?' Pastor Julian just couldn't seem to let the topic drop.

Theo clenched his teeth, holding back his anger.

'Yes, but I do have a half-sister and -brother here and a cousin, Jordan, but he lives in New York.' She smiled. 'But obviously that's far away and so I don't see him nearly as often as I'd like.'

Theo's dad had clearly had enough. 'Just going to let Rhubarb out for a shit,' he announced, standing abruptly and dropping his napkin into his chair.

'Nice.' Theo smiled at Anna.

'So, Theo...'

He braced himself for whatever crap the man was about to spout.

'Your mother tells me you're a troubled man? That you have an admirable social conscience?'

He looked first at the pastor and then at his mother and this time did nothing to stop the laughter from escaping. He made no apology, just swiped at his mouth with his napkin. 'No.' He shook his head. 'I wouldn't say I was troubled. A little pissed off, maybe, bemused, embarrassed certainly, but troubled? No. Could you pass the peas, please, Anna?'

Anna handed him the unwieldy tureen.

Pastor Julian failed to take the hint. 'I can tell you that there is no shame in not having everything figured out. Your mother tells me that school was very hard for you.'

'Actually, let me stop you there. Firstly, I don't know you and secondly, even if I did, I would not be willing to discuss anything as personal as my childhood.'

'Pastor Jules is only—'

'Only what, Mum? What exactly is Pastor Jules doing here?' Theo shook his head with annoyance.

'Theo!'

'It's okay.' The pastor patted Stella's arm and wiped his mouth, returning the napkin to his lap. 'I understand that when there is a lot unsaid, the messenger is often the one who is attacked. It's understandable.'

Theo glance at Anna and said, without attempting to whisper, 'Anna, did you say you thought you might have left the gas on? Do we need to leave *now*?'

They exchanged a look and he felt another flush of love for her. It felt good to have an ally in this shitty situation.

The pastor sat forward and stared at Anna. 'I am a messenger, Anna, and I have someone here that is trying to talk to you. His name is Jim. No...' He closed his eyes and held out his hand with his fingers splayed. 'James. Or John?'

Anna gasped. 'My brother?' she whispered, her face white. 'Joe?'

'That's enough!' Theo raised his voice and glared at the pastor.

Stella sat forward, looking cross, but Pastor Jules ignored Theo and continued. 'He says it wasn't your fault. He says he is sorry. And I can hear music... Let me see...' He cocked his head to one side, as if to hear it better.

Anna was almost whimpering now and Theo was incandescent with rage. What was this man trying to prove? How dare he upset Anna like that? 'I said, that's enough!' He slammed his cutlery down onto the table and stood, stopping Pastor Julian in his tracks. With eyes blazing he reached for Anna's hand.

Anna, as if in shock, stood too, her legs wobbly.

'Okay...' Theo reached out with a shaking hand and addressed his mother. 'I have no idea what the fuck is going on, but I want no part of it, not for me and certainly not for my wife, who has been through quite enough recently. Thank you for an interesting supper. It's been a blast.'

'What do you mean? We've only just started eating, you've hardly touched your food and I made tipsy pudding!' his mother whined.

'Trust me, Mum, I've more than had my fill. Come on, Anna. Say goodbye to Dad for us.' He placed a hand on Anna's back, guiding her along the hallway until they were outside, standing in the cool night air.

'What on earth...?' Anna gave a nervous laugh. Slipping her arm through his and bending over to laugh some more, this soon gave way to tears, which she swiped with her sleeve. 'I don't know why I'm crying.'

Watching her try to be brave tore at his heartstrings. 'I do, and I'm so sorry, Anna, that was truly awful.' He scuffed his sole on the pavement, trying to release some of the tension inside him. 'Are you okay? Did that scare you?'

'I honestly don't know what to think,' she levelled. 'It did scare me and I hated it, but at the same time, what if he really can do that?'

'Trust me, he really can't do anything, it's utter bollocks!' Theo shook his head.

'But it sounded like he knew things... About Joe... About... the music box he stole maybe? I've never told anybody about that except you,' she whispered. 'You didn't tell...?'

'Oh Anna, my lovely Anna.' He placed his hands either side

of her head and kissed her face. 'I've never told a soul, of course I haven't.' He hated what that vile man had dredged up. 'Do not give that so-called pastor a moment of consideration. It's a trick, and a cruel, dangerous trick at that. He was just fishing – it was all so bloody obvious, he just lobbed out some random names and hoped to get lucky.'

She nodded, and he could read the disappointment in her eyes. It was indeed the cruellest trick. Who wouldn't want to talk to someone they'd lost?

'Where did that guy spring from?' she asked.

'A shed in Putney apparently.'

'But how come your mother hooked up with him? It's nuts!' She twirled her fingers by her head, emphasising the craziness. 'I didn't even know she was religious!'

'Neither did I. And of course I have no problem with that if she has genuinely found faith, but *that guy*...'

'I know, right – *that guy*!'

Theo shook his head. 'I got the feeling she liked him.'

'I should say! Inviting him for dinner, sharing intimate details of her *troubled* child.' She pinched his cheek affectionately.

'No, seriously...' He pulled away a little. 'I mean, *liked* him. She seemed giggly and a bit besotted.'

'Two words I never would have associated with your mum.'

'Exactly.'

'Maybe it's a late mid-life crisis?'

'It's something all right.' He sighed.

'Okay...' She paused. 'Pastor Julian – another thing definitely not to be mentioned at the adoption interview.'

'On that we are agreed.' He nodded. 'God, I'm starving.'

'Me too. Chip shop?'

'Yes!' He grinned. 'Chip shop.'

They trod the pavement arm in arm, each pondering what they'd just been through.

'But just supposing—' Anna began.

'No, Anna,' he interrupted, 'there is no "just supposing". As I said, it is complete and utter bollocks.'

'I know,' she said quietly. 'I just wish it wasn't.'

An hour later, with the White Stripes CD playing, vinegar-stained chip paper littering the sitting-room floor, Griff asleep in the kitchen and a bottle of wine sunk, the two of them lay next to each other on the rug.

Anna ran her fingers over his chest and kissed his mouth. 'Troubled or not, I do love you, Theo, my little goldfish murderer.'

'Thank you for that. And for your information, the bloody thing died of natural causes, pretty much before I tipped it from the bag into the bowl. And also for your information, I love you too.'

She reached down and unfastened his belt.

'Wait a minute.' He grabbed her wrist. 'Do you think we should say grace first?'

Anna howled her laughter and climbed on top of him, kissing his mouth and running her hands over his chest.

He kissed her back, happy for the joy of contact and the happy abandonment of sex, which had been missing of late. In a paused moment they stared at each other.

'I love you, Theo. I really, really love you.'

He reached up and used the pad of his thumb to brush the sweet mouth that had uttered these words so sincerely. 'I love you too.'

'I can't stop thinking about it...' she began.

'Thinking about what?'

'That adoption might be the thing for us!'

And just like that, Theo's carefree mood was nudged out of the frame by the flicker of self-doubt he just couldn't shift. He was determined to try and make Anna happy, it was all he wanted, and he was going to give this adoption meeting his very best shot. But what if he really was destined to turn out like his parents? What if in twenty years' time their own child came round for the dinner party from hell? What if he simply wasn't father material, just as Kitty had surmised?

Fourteen

The ringing of the doorbell woke Theo, and then came the sound of Griff barking loudly in response. He opened first one eye and then the other. It was 9 a.m., late for them, and as always on weekends it was a joy not to have been roused by the alarm. Anna sat up and rubbed her face. 'Who's that?' She groaned, reaching for the glass of water on her bedside table.

Theo didn't reply, unable to think of an answer that wasn't obvious or a little sarcastic, considering he hadn't yet opened the front door. He threw his sweatshirt over his head and pulled on his pyjama bottoms.

'Mum! Hello.' He couldn't remember the last time she'd turned up at the house without calling first. It was usually when she needed a favour, like the dog walking or plants watering while they were away.

She was clearly agitated, fingering the pearls at her neck and blinking rapidly. Without any pleasantries or preamble, she began. 'I feel you let me down terribly last night, Theo!' She'd raised her voice and was speaking pointedly, as if the words had been cued up, waiting to be released. Judging by the dark circles under her eyes, she'd probably been mulling them over since the early hours.

'Come inside, Mum. Please.' He stood back with his arms wide, then glanced up the pavement as she marched in, to see if any neighbours were taking an interest. They weren't.

'I mean it. You let me down and you were rude!'

'Please calm down.'

'Calm down?' Stella continued at the same pitch. 'It was important to me! I wanted it to be a pleasant evening. You all knew that. I went to a lot of trouble.'

'I…' Theo struggled to know where to begin, torn between voicing his concerns about her and giving in to the anger that was brewing inside him.

'Morning, Stella. Would you like a cup of tea?' Anna had come downstairs in her dressing gown. Theo appreciated her soft, placatory tone, which felt like balm on their hot-tempered exchange.

'No, I do not want a cup of tea. I want an apology!'

'Right. Well, I'll pop the kettle on anyway.' Anna ran her hand over Theo's waist as she passed, a tactile show of support for which he was grateful. The happy glow of their union still clung to their skin and it would take more than his cranky mother to dampen it.

He followed her into the kitchen and his mother came on behind. Theo and Anna exchanged a knowing look.

'I mean it.' Stella's tone was accusatory. 'How often do I ask you for anything?'

'Quite often actually.' He kept his tone level.

She ignored him. 'My faith is now a big part of my life and all I asked was that you be civil to Pastor Jules, a guest in my home! My friend! A man of God! And you couldn't even find the decency—'

A man of God? He swallowed the many unfavourable comments that sprang to mind. 'Whoa there! I think, Mum, that we just need to slow things down a bit here. Firstly, it might have been an idea to call me, talk to me, and let me know about this big change in your beliefs so that I was a little bit prepared. And secondly, the man's a charlatan. He went way over the top last night, he was invasive and out of line.'

Behind his mother's back, Anna pulled a disapproving face at his frankness.

'That's what Pastor Jules says people with closed minds and people who don't have his vision will say.'

Theo pinched the bridge of his nose. 'Well, how bloody convenient. He's right, I don't share his vision and I don't share his moral code. How dare he say those things to Anna, how dare he? And I'm furious that you put her, put us, in that position.'

'Well, if you had stuck around and not marched out halfway through dinner, you might have learnt how his gift works.'

'Christ alive, his gift? Really?' He took a breath. 'You are free of course to do as you see fit, whatever is right for you – fill your boots!' He let his arms fall to his sides. 'But telling a complete stranger personal things about *my* life, about our life, aspects *I* would not want shared—'

'He's not a complete stranger to me!' she shouted.

'Well, that much was obvious.' Theo folded his arms across his chest.

'Have you been speaking to your father?' She shot him an anguished look.

Theo laughed. 'Since when did I speak about anything with

Dad? Ever? And while we are on the subject, he was horrid last night, just casually trashing our adoption plans – can he not see that it's important to us? I know it's too much to hope that it might be important to him. It's the same with my bloody plans for Bristol!'

'Oh, please, not that again!' Stella took a deep breath and pushed her thumbs into her brow, as if trying to relieve the pressure.

'Yes, that again. And for the record, Mum, you can't just come in here and wake us up with a row and then get mad when it doesn't go your way. You and Dad have always seemed to think that it's okay to put me on display when it's called for, but it's been on your terms and this is just another example of that. What you did last night with your crazy new friend and his parlour tricks was bloody disgraceful!'

'Don't swear,' she snapped. 'I haven't forgotten the way you cursed at me on the phone the other week – is it your new thing?'

'"Bloody" is not swearing. Shit, arse, bollocks and fuck, now *that's* swearing.' He regretted the outburst the moment it had left his mouth.

She looked at him with her mouth agape.

'Your tea, darling.' Anna handed him a mug and rested her hand briefly on his shoulder, a reminder to calm down.

He took it sheepishly and sipped, letting his pulse settle. 'I'm sorry,' he whispered.

The slight nod of Stella's head indicated an acceptance of sorts.

'But here's the thing, Mum. You have drunk, sworn, smoked and God knows what else for my whole life and then after one hour in the company of Pastor Putney, you expect me to just go along with the whole Julie Andrews charade? And worse still, he's fooling you – I don't think he's what you're looking for. I really don't. And I think he might be dangerous. Do you think you're being forgiven for all the bad stuff you've ever done and said? Is this a way of wiping the slate clean? Because I get that you might want to, but I'm not sure this is the right way.'

His mother shook her head. 'No, it's not that at all. I know that I'm not without faults, without sin, but it's more than that – I like the stillness, the quiet of the church, and the ceremony. It makes me feel better.'

Theo remembered how he used to lie in the dark at school with such longing in his gut, so desperate to return home that it physically hurt, and how it was made far worse because no one at home gave a shit.

'Watching you close your eyes in prayer as though it was the most natural thing in the world, even though you've never been a churchgoer, seemed a bit bonkers,' he said. 'And as for communicating with the dead...'

'It's not bonkers.' His mother stood her ground. 'And believe me when I say I wish I could go back and do a lot of things differently. In a sense, now I can – it's like being born again.' A smile flickered around her mouth.

'Oh, for God's sake, what next? A baptism?'

And then to his horror and acute embarrassment, his mother started to cry, properly cry, with a heave to her chest and a shake to her shoulders. Her mouth twisted and her eyes flamed.

'Stella, come and sit down.' Anna shepherded her to the kitchen table and helped her settle. 'I'm going to go and have my bath.' She winked at her husband, purposefully leaving them alone.

Theo sat opposite his mother and waited until her great gulping sobs had abated.

'I *like* feeling this way.' She sniffed. 'I *like* listening to Pastor Jules and what he thinks about life and I *like* the way he listens to me.' She pointed at her chest. 'I am a person too, and what I say and what I want has never been considered. Never.'

Welcome to my world... Theo buried the thought.

'I have never been heard!' Stella shook her head.

He felt the stirring of sympathy and tried to imagine living each day in the shadow of his father. He replayed some of the million ways his father deliberately made him feel worthless. He adopted a softer tone. 'I get it, Mum, I do, and if going to church is something you want to do and you get something out of it, then it can only be a good thing, but do you have to go to *that* church?'

'You know nothing about it!' she replied. 'You have made up your mind based on what – ten minutes in Pastor Jules's company? Why do you think that's okay?'

He swallowed the words that rattled in his mouth, took the path of least resistance and conceded. 'You're right, Mum, I probably could have been more civil. What I think about Pastor Jules and his shed in Putney stands, but for embarrassing you, I am sorry.'

His mother sat still, letting his apology percolate. She straightened her back. 'Daddy is being so horrible to me about the whole thing – he finds it all most amusing. He doesn't understand that I need the calming space to keep sane.' She curled her fingernails into her palm as she spoke. 'I need the quiet contemplation of prayer to get my head straight.'

'*Possibly the most important lesson of all is that when you're still and quiet, that's when your thoughts get ordered, when your mind sorts out all its problems and when you're able to see most clearly. Don't ever underestimate the value of stillness.*' Mr Porter's words came into Theo's head; he heard his distinctive accent and felt a smile forming at the vivid recollection of that conversation.

'I do understand, Mum.' He spoke softly. 'But I wouldn't be doing my job, would I, if I wasn't looking out for you, making sure you were safe and that there wasn't something I should be doing to make you happier.'

Stella reached across the table and placed her hand over the back of his. 'You have always been a good boy.' She gave a long, slow blink that looked a little like a prayer and smiled at him.

Theo suspected that she, like him, was picturing that night in the upstairs corridor of La Grande Belle when he had summoned all of his courage and had tried to act as her protector.

* * *

Anna fidgeted in the plastic seat, adjusting the cuffs of the blouse she had deliberated over for almost an hour. 'I want to look smart but motherly, trustworthy but fun – which do you think, Theo, the pale blue or the white?' She had held the hangers out alternately.

He had stared at her, trying desperately to get in the swing of it but knowing the biggest barrier to their adoption plans would probably not be which shade of blouse she chose but something far more fundamental. *Please let me get it right*, he urged himself, over and over. *We need this*.

They'd already had a massive row about where his priorities lay. The Monday morning after the Pastor Julian dinner, Theo had gone into work with his dad's snide aside running on a loop through his head: '*If Theo feels that strongly about those poor kids, he should fund the sodding project himself.*' He was damned if he was going to let his father reduce him to tears over something he cared so much about, just like he'd done to his mum and her new interest in all things religious. Before he had a chance to think better of it, Theo had called the Bristol agent and bought the warehouse – funded the sodding project himself, lock, stock and barrel. Anna had been furious when he told her: she worried that his attention was no longer one hundred per cent on their adoption plans (probably true) and that tying all their money up in this gamble of a project endangered their future security (also probably true). It hadn't exactly made for the most peaceful run-up to the adoption meeting. And to make things worse, Anna's pregnant friend Shania had just asked Anna to be her birthing partner in a few months' time. Theo was pretty sure that the experience of seeing her friend give birth would not be helpful and he was dreading the upset that would surely follow. Why did things have to be so damn complicated?

But here they were nonetheless, sitting on a couple of narrow seats along a plain wall in a waiting room that was probably no different from the waiting rooms of countless other municipal buildings. He could feel waves of excited energy coming off Anna. 'Don't be nervous,' he whispered. 'All it will take is five minutes in your company and it'll be blindingly obvious to anyone that any child's life would be infinitely better with you in it.'

He saw relief spread slowly across her face. 'Thank you for saying that, Theo. With you by my side, I think I can do anything!'

'Exactly.' He smiled at her.

'Mr and Mrs Montgomery?'

Anna shot up and grabbed his hand, marching him into the office. The woman used her foot to hold the door ajar as she beckoned them in. Theo took in her stocky build, the muted tones of her mustard and green skirt and the blunt cut of her grey hair. A neat, square woman in her mid sixties, she wore stout lace-up shoes and looked more like a dog walker than an adoption official, not that he'd tried to paint a picture of her beforehand, but if he had, this wouldn't have been it.

'Come in.' She gestured with her open hand towards the bland, sparsely furnished room. Bar a table in the centre, six leggy, school-type chairs and a set of royal blue vertical blinds, there was little else. No distractions.

'It's good to meet you, Mr Montgomery. I am Mrs Wentworth.'

'Theo, please.' He felt a small flicker of embarrassment that she didn't extend the same courtesy, then smiled as he caught her eye, desperate for her to like him, to approve.

'And Mrs Montgomery.' She shook Anna's hand.

'Anna, please.'

'Please, do sit down.'

He watched Anna deliberate over where to sit, as if this too might be part of a test. He wished she would relax. He was, as ever, immaculate. It was important to him, this first impression. He hitched up his suit trousers, twisted his signet ring, straightened the Windsor knot of his pale blue tie and adjusted the lapels of his jacket, running his thumb along the silk underside and taking courage from the feel of his fishing fly. Then he coughed to clear his throat.

'So, all we're going to do today is have a chat. I can tell you about the process that you're considering embarking upon and it's a chance for you to ask any questions you might have before you make that decision. How does that sound?'

'It sounds wonderful!' Anna fired back, sounding to him like the try-hard girl in school, keen to get the answer right, desperate to be picked. It tore at his heart, because he knew she was perfect. Perfect for him and perfect for any child that might need a home. But then again, maybe she was right to be this way; maybe it was the little things that would make the difference. He thought about getting stuck in the lift with her that day, three years ago, a little thing on a seemingly insignificant day. A day, no, a minute that had changed his entire life. And hers.

Conscious of Mrs Wentworth's scrutiny from the seat opposite his, he became hyper aware of his every facial tic. He found himself trying to suppress the flurry of thoughts that swirled in his mind, as if her incisive gaze could penetrate deep inside his brain. What if she could see his doubts, what if she could tell he had a big secret in there, had deceived Anna for all these years? What if she somehow intuited that he already had a child and therefore shouldn't be allowed to take on someone else's?

He inhaled and shook himself out of this stupidity – it seemed his mother wasn't the only gullible one in the family. Mrs Wentworth was some sort of social worker, not a psychic!

Mrs Wentworth smiled and rested an elbow on the arm of her chair. 'I can tell that you're a little nervous, and that's perfectly understandable, but there is really no need.'

'I guess that's because it's so important to me.' Anna jumped in again with the textbook answer.

'And that I understand, but this really is just a chat.'

'Okay.' Anna exhaled. 'I will try.'

'And what about you, Mr Montgomery? How are you feeling about this?'

He didn't like the slant to her head, as if she really had seen something in him that might be a tick in the wrong box. He held her gaze. 'Er… I'm a bit nervous too, I guess. It's more the fear of the unknown for me, I think.'

'Would you like to expand on that a little?'

'Er… I don't know.' He paused, feeling like an idiot. He decided to change tack. 'I just wish Anna would show you her true self, because she's—'

'I am being my true self!' Anna shot back, cutting him short.

'I didn't mean it in a negative way, I was only thinking that you are perfect and you don't need to perform.'

Mrs Wentworth raised her pen. 'What do you mean by "perform", exactly?' This had clearly caught her interest.

And, awkward though it was, that exchange turned out to be the least uncomfortable of the day…

They drove home in a fug of hostility distilled from all the words left unsaid and bubbling under the surface, waiting for release.

'How do you think—'

'Don't talk to me, Theo.' Anna raised her palm. 'Don't say anything!'

He took her advice and kept quiet.

It was she who broke the silence, a few minutes later. 'Did you deliberately try and sabotage the whole interview? Was that your game plan?' She shook her head, muttering something acidic but inaudible.

'Of course not! I got flustered, I—'

'What was all that about me performing? It made me sound like a fake!' she yelled.

'I was only trying to say that the real you, the everyday Anna, is more than good enough to adopt a child and that you didn't need to be so on edge!'

'The everyday Anna? And who is that exactly? I *was* being myself! Not that Mrs Wentworth would believe that, not now! Jesus, Theo!'

'I just—'

'No, don't say anything!' She turned and pointedly stared out of the window, staying like that for another good few minutes.

'Then she asked you a basic question, Theo! Basic! "Why do you think you would make a good parent?" And you... you just... Urrrrgh!' She shook her head and looked furious.

Theo's mouth went dry at the recollection.

'Why do you think you would make a good parent, Mr Montgomery?'

Twisting in his seat, he'd seen the image of Sophie smiling at him on the bus and then Kitty's face, horror-struck at the prospect of any interaction, and his confidence had evaporated. *Why do I think I would make a good parent? I don't, not really! I'm not sure I could be. I am weird, toxic, useless.* He then heard his father's voice, loud and clear: '*The idea of him looking after a baby!*'

And then he'd given his stupid answer, mumbled from cracked lips. 'I don't...'

'You don't think you *would* make a good parent?' Mrs Wentworth had prompted.

He'd sensed Anna sitting ramrod straight in the seat next to him, her words a decibel higher than her normal speech, her tone urgent. 'He'll... He'll be great. He's just nervous! He's kind and he listens and he has a good, good heart...'

Her rapid and heartfelt defence only made him feel worse. He shook his head. 'No, I was going to say, I don't know exactly, but I will try very hard.'

Glancing across the car now, he noted his wife's set expression, the tension in her jaw. Her hand was clamped over her mouth as if to prevent her from saying the wrong thing, the hurtful thing.

I want so badly to be the man you want me to be, Anna. I want us to adopt, but I don't know how to jump through hoops and be the smiley, untroubled father you have in mind. I don't know how! And that's the truth.

Fifteen

'Your dad's asking for the projection figures on the Deptford development.' Marta stood in the doorway to Theo's office, clinging to the frame with her red, talon-like fingernails, her lips painted to match. She tapped the toe of her black stiletto on the floor impatiently.

She bothered him.

'I'll give them to Marcus.' He spoke without looking at her again, keeping his eyes on the unopened envelope that had just been delivered to his desk.

He heard her sigh as she closed the door. Sitting back in his chair, he tried to imagine working as an intern and feeling confident enough to treat the chairman's son with such disdain. Was that how everyone saw him – a walkover?

A few seconds later she opened the door again. 'He says, can you—'

'Look, I'm sorry, Marta,' he said, cutting her short, 'but if my dad wants to speak to me, he is capable of coming in here himself and if he isn't, he can use this.' He picked up the telephone and held the mouthpiece towards her. 'And if for whatever reason neither of those things are possible, then you too can use the phone and call me. I'm trying to concentrate here and that's a little hard to do when you keep popping through the door like a bloody cuckoo clock.'

He wasn't sure why he was so irritable, or where his confidence had come from, but the way Marta pursed her glossy red lips and slowly walked backwards told him that he'd got the message across. And it felt good.

He picked up the brown envelope. His heart beat a little too quickly and he felt lightheaded. He breathed deeply, trying to quash the surge of excitement. This was it, the letter from the planning office in Bristol. He ran the pad of his thumb over the postmark and slid his finger under the gummy flap. The single sheet was officious, peppered with words, dates and departmental logos, all in red, but the only thing that drew his attention, was the single sentence informing him that planning permission for his twenty-four self-contained studio units had been APPROVED. He read and reread the word, feeling a fire of achievement in his belly – and this was before he'd shifted a single brick.

He contemplated calling Anna but instantly decided not to. He felt disinclined to argue with her today or hear the inevitable disappointment in her voice. The fallout from the adoption meeting was still tarnishing things between them and it took the edge off what should have been a day of celebration.

Sitting back in the leather chair, it felt as if his bowels had turned to ice. It wasn't just that all their money was tied up in this pile of vintage bricks; he'd also paid for security, started clearing rubbish from the site and engaged the best architect he could find. It felt like he had a mountain to climb and, much worse, it felt as if he was climbing it alone.

He sighed and leant back, feeling the tilt at the base of the chair as he stared up at the same ceiling his forefathers must have stared at many a time, plotting and scheming to build up the business. He closed his eyes.

'Are you asleep?' Marta woke him with her question.

'No!' He let the seat tilt forward again, aware of dampness on his chin. He had drifted off and he must have been drooling, but there was no way he was going to admit to either. He wiped his face with the back of his hand.

'It looked like you were sleeping to me.'

'Did you want something?' he asked, recalling their conversation about using the phone not an hour since.

'Yes. I've been to sent to ask if you're coming in for the quarterly review? It's just that everyone's waiting to start.' Her blouse gaped open to reveal a lacy camisole and she stood there with her right hip sticking out and her hand resting on it, as if striking a cover pose. It made him feel uncomfortable.

He'd forgotten that the quarterly review was today – he'd been too distracted. 'I'll be in in a minute.' He hurriedly opened the file on his computer that would provide him with the information he needed to share with the board.

'You might want to…' Marta touched her own fringe.

The moment she left, he checked his reflection in the window and cursed the wayward flicks of thick curl that stuck up vertically around his face. He used his fingers as a makeshift comb and tried to calm them. With his laptop under his arm, he gulped down the cold coffee sitting in the mug on his desk and winced at the bitterness, then crossed the hallway.

His father's terse glance at the wall clock did little to assuage his anxiety.

Theo felt only semi-present, nodding as reports and updates were given slowly and methodically, a stream of numbers and information in which he had only the vaguest interest. All he could see was the letter of approval from the planning department, as if it was tattooed on the inside of his eyelids. His mind whirred with all the possibilities.

'Theodore?' His father's voice drew him into the proceedings.

'Yep?' He straightened his tie and sat up in the chair.

'Sorry, are we keeping you from something more important?' Perry Montgomery asked. 'We are waiting for your input.' He nodded at the men assembled around the table.

'Yes. Of course.'

He tapped the keyboard, trying to find the damn spreadsheet, unsure of where they were up to and what had been said. 'Sorry, just give me a moment.' His face flared with embarrassment.

'If my son is a little distracted, it might be because he is fixated on buying a property in Bristol, would you believe! He wants to drag us down the M4 and get involved in *social housing* or some such.' A strained chortle rippled around the room.

Theo heard the laughter. It felt the same as it had that day in the library at Vaizey College. '*Right, Mr Homo, gather your books and leave! I will not have disruption in my library. There are people trying to work. Off you go!*' He felt a jolt in his gut and before he knew it he had closed the lid of his laptop and was standing.

'Actually, it was more than a fixation, it was a sound business proposal. But I can see there's no point in regurgitating the details here and now. As it happens, I believed in it and so I bought it, a little while ago now.'

He enjoyed the look of surprise on his father's face.

'Well, well. Interesting.' His father nodded and tapped his fingertips in a pyramid at chest height. 'Can we now get back to the task in hand?'

Theo looked at the gathered group and felt a shiver of dislike. These men were his father's cronies. In a sudden moment of clarity he decided he no longer wanted to be part of the gang. 'I'm sorry,' he mumbled, before buttoning up his jacket and leaving the room.

'Finished already? That was quick,' Marta called out as he walked past her desk and into his office.

He ignored her. Standing at the window, he looked down at the pavement, as he was wont to do, drawn by the hundreds of dark suits traipsing up and down, presumably every one of them trying in their own way to make their mark.

I'm thirty-one years old, not a boy. It's time, Theo. Time to do something different. He thought of Mr Porter, pottering in his front garden, sitting at the table, taking brightly coloured feathers between his leathery fingers and turning them into something wonderful. He felt beneath his lapel where his gift of a fly on a safety pin nestled.

I wonder if you're still alive? How old would you be now, dear friend? If you were nineteen in 1944, blimey, you must be in your seventies. I always thought of you as an old, old man back when I was at school, but you weren't all that old, were you? Just grey-haired and dealing with all life had thrown at you. I am sorry, I will always be sorry. I should have done more, said more... I didn't realise until it was too late and you were gone.

The door of his office flew open, pulling him into the present. He closed his eyes briefly and steeled himself. His father was the only one who came in like that, without introduction or forewarning, making the point this was his building, his company and that they had to play by his rules. It had the effect of making Theo feel like a guest, keeping him on his toes, and this too was familiar.

'Well, well, well, that was quite a display.' Theo noted the hint of amusement in his father's tone. 'When you have calmed down, do you think we might be able to continue with our meeting? There are six good people sitting around a table waiting for you to deliver your report. The report you are paid to deliver. They're not used to being kept waiting and I'm not used to having to explain away such unprofessional behaviour. So if you don't mind…' His father gestured towards the door.

Theo stayed by the window and shook his head briefly. His limbs were trembling. 'I received a letter today from the planning department in Bristol. They've approved my plan for the warehouse.'

He wasn't sure what he wanted from his father by way of response. Good advice? A little bit of support?

His father sank down into the chair on the other side of the office and crossed his legs. His eyes were bright, his stare challenging, and there was a nasty smirk on his lips. 'Well, what a surprise!'

Theo had imagined this moment often, but it didn't feel half as good or victorious as he'd anticipated. He paced behind his desk. 'How can you sit there as my father and not be happy that I've succeeded in something? Would it kill you to give me a bit of reassurance? Why do you always make it feel like I've lost!'

'Is that what you're after, boy? A pat on the back? A medal? Trust me, I know good men who've received medals for doing great things…'

Theo stared at him, dumbfounded.

'... and you haven't succeeded at anything yet. Buying a pile of bricks and turning them into something are two entirely different skills. And your business model is flawed!' He was yelling now, wiping spit from his damp lower lip with his handkerchief. 'That challenge, however, now sits firmly on your shoulders, but it's not important, not to me. My loyalty is here with the company my father and grandfather built.'

Theo got the picture. He had let them down, all of them. 'If you'd given me room to move within Montgomery Holdings, then maybe I wouldn't have felt the need to do something outside. But you've never valued me, you've always assumed the worst, treated me like a failure without giving me the chance to prove otherwise.' He faced his father and placed his hands on his waist.

'So this is my fault now?' His father chuckled. 'I am the reason you need to throw all this away?'

His dad's laughter was like a punch to Theo's already fragile confidence. His temperature flashed hot. He was furious. 'You could say that.' He breathed heavily, unable to list the many ways his father had hurt him and let him down.

'Is that right?' Perry sat back in the chair. 'Have you ever looked at it from my perspective, Theodore? I was overjoyed to get a son – *a son*!' He balled his fist, as if he'd won the jackpot.

Theo desperately wanted to ask if he was his father's first or second son – just how old was Alexander? But this was neither the time nor place.

Perry continued. 'I tried to coach you, influence you, tried to lay the foundations that would turn you into the man I wanted you to be. But, Jesus Christ, you never even picked up a fucking rugby ball! I used to place one in your hands and try, but you simply weren't interested.'

Theo could just about see the funny side of this. Was this what his old man's disappointment boiled down to – his lack of interest in the game of rugby?

Perry wasn't done. 'Why couldn't you have been like every other Vaizey boy, the sort I grew up with, men I loved and admired? Was it too much to ask for you to try and fit in a bit, find one thing in common with everyone else – just one thing? Even as a toddler you were always running off to hide behind you mother's skirts like a nancy boy. What was the matter with you?'

Theo stared at his father, wondering how much of his unhappy childhood to dredge up, not wanting to make things harder for his mother than they already were. The air between them was thick. The shadows of their words crept into the cracks in the ceiling and hid between the drawers of the desk. They weren't going to disappear any time soon. He took a deep breath and rounded off the sharp edges of his response.

'I don't think there's anything wrong with me. And I don't think not having an interest in a particular sport should be the thing that defines whether I'm a man or not.' His voice was calm. 'And actually, Dad, if I found you hard to approach as a toddler, if I preferred to run to Mum, was that my fault?' He let this sink in and saw the faint twitch to his father's left eye. 'Sometimes trying to force a square peg into a round hole results in it breaking. But I didn't break.' *Not quite.*

His father stared back at him with the beginnings of a smile on his face. He was hard to read sometimes. 'I like your frankness,' he said. 'And I have to say, knowing that you actually had the balls to follow through with something that caught your eye, this Bristol business, knowing you had the nerve to follow your instinct, is bloody marvellous! That, Theodore, is what makes a businessman.'

Theo felt the strength leave his legs. He had waited years to be thrown even a crumb of congratulation by his father and here, at this moment of exhaustion and in the face of his triumph, here it was. It was sickening to him just how overjoyed he was at his old man's self-styled compliment.

Perry had more to say. 'Following your heart, that's what it's all about. Not following orders or toeing the line. It's about challenging those orders and carving your own path. That's when things get really interesting.'

Theo opened his mouth to respond to this, but his thoughts were three steps ahead and he was as shocked as his dad when he gave them voice.

'I'm leaving the company, Dad. I'm setting out on my own. I can't do this any more and I think putting space between us can only be a good thing, a healthy thing.'

The smile fell from his father's face and something close to hurt flickered in his eyes. Far from feeling triumphant at having gained the upper ground for the first time in his life, Theo instead tasted the familiar guilt, this time tinged with fear.

'Be bold, Theodore.' His father stood, straightened his cuffs and held his son's gaze before he left the room. 'Always be bold.'

* * *

Anna laughed loudly into her fist before grabbing a piece of kitchen roll and wiping her nose and mouth. 'For real?' She gazed at him and refilled her wine glass. 'You've quit your job?'

'Yes. For real. I'm going to find a way to make that site work and when I've found the magic formula, I can repeat it. I can make an honest living while changing lives, Anna.' He took a slug of beer from the bottle in his hand.

Anna shook her head in disbelief as she paced round the kitchen. 'Did our conversation about openness not resonate with you at all? And what about the adoption process?'

'Yes, it resonated! It's not like I planned it. It was one of those spur-of-the-moment things. Dad was pushing and I—'

'Oh God, Theo!' She placed her hands in her hair, looking and sounding exasperated. 'Don't you see that you don't have the luxury of making spur-of-the-moment, unplanned decisions! You are married – to me! I'm not saying don't do it, don't follow your heart, and I'm not saying I don't admire what you're trying to achieve – I do! But we should have discussed something as fundamental as this!'

'I know, and in the cold light of day, away from the office—'

'How are we going to pay for the build and the house bills while it all gets going? How are we going to show we've got the stability and security to support a child?'

He hated the way she managed to turn his project into something fanciful, impossible, less a plan than a whimsy. 'I don't know yet.'

'Well, that's a good start.' She sighed. 'My wages won't cover our fuel bills, much less anything else.'

'I've already told you that I've never seen either of our contributions as anything other than all going into the same pot. We're a team.' He hoped the subtle reminder that he had pretty much funded their entire life together might be a prompt for kindness and understanding.

'A team?' She shook her head. 'It takes more than simply saying the word to make it the truth.'

'I need you to support me on this, Anna.'

'And I needed you to commit to the adoption!' She took a deep breath. 'It's not like I have any choice, is it? You've already jumped.'

The telephone in the kitchen rang. Anna rushed to the countertop and lifted the receiver in anger. She shot a look at him from across the room.

'Yes?' she answered sternly, before closing her eyes. 'Oh, sorry, Stella, I thought it might be a sales call. Yes, I'm fine. No, not at all, I'll just grab him for you.' She laid the phone on the surface and left the room.

Theo held the receiver and spoke slowly. 'Hi, Mum.'

He was greeted by the sound of his mother crying. Her words were off rhythm, burbled amid the breaks for her tears. 'I don't… I don't know what to say to you! Daddy told me… and I thought it was a wicked joke. I could never have imagined you walking away from everything that the Montgomerys have built up over the years! I just don't understand it, Theodore! Why? Why would you do this to us?'

He sighed and pinched the top of his nose. 'Because it's time. And I'm not emigrating or abandoning you and Dad, just trying a new career path, that's all.'

'That's *all*? You are our only son and heir! How can you say "that's all"! I have prayed for you all afternoon. I asked Pastor Jules to pray for you too.'

Well, that's all my problems solved! He bit his lip, angry that once again she was talking to the greasy pastor about his private life. 'Look, Mum, I'll be happy to discuss this when you're calmer, but there's no point going back and forth like this when you're so upset.'

His mother changed tack, her voice now clipped. 'Daddy says you need to collect your things from the office and you need to do it tomorrow!' And with that she ended the call.

Theo reached into the fridge for another beer. He knew that this edict came from her and not his father, a way to vent her hurt, and it took him right back to his school days, when he'd felt like a pawn in the middle of whatever drama had been unfolding between them. This only served to reassure him that he'd made the right decision.

'Well, this is going to make tomorrow's birthday celebrations interesting.'

He turned and looked at Anna, having quite forgotten that tomorrow was his birthday. His head felt like it might explode.

Sixteen

The next day, Theo slept late, uninterested in his day of supposed celebration. He took Griff for a run and did his best to stay out of Anna's way until she left to meet Shania for a hospital appointment, part of her duty as birth partner. He waited until early evening before making his way into town, knowing that by six o'clock his father would be at his club and the seventh floor would be mostly deserted.

He let himself into his office, flicked on the desk lamp and scanned the room. He would always view Villiers House and his time in it with nostalgia. It was after all where he'd met Anna. Opening his leather sports bag, he took a couple of social policy books from the windowsill. This made him think of Spud. What wouldn't he give for a pint with him right now, today of all days, when things with Anna were tense and he'd just taken his great leap into the unknown. Spud would have been full of good, practical advice.

He picked up a picture of himself and Anna on their wedding day with Big Ben and the Houses of Parliament as the backdrop. Pausing to run his fingertips over her beautiful face – *Oh, my Anna* – he then placed the lot into the bag and, rummaging through the drawers, retrieved his various bits and pieces: a mini desktop golf set, a Christmas gift from Anna, three spare ties, and several travel books purchased spontaneously from Stanfords during lunchtime jaunts up to Covent Garden.

He heard a sound coming from the corridor outside and looked up. With his heart thudding, he crept across his office floor, glancing around for something he might use as an impromptu weapon. He swiftly gave up on the idea – the thought of having to bash someone made him feel sick. He'd never been good at all that macho stuff; his plan had always been to run should the need arise.

Out in the corridor, he was surprised to see a thin shaft of light coming from under the boardroom door. He opened it an inch or so and narrowed his eyes.

The first thing he saw was a bottle of champagne on the table and two half-empty glasses. The second thing he saw was his father, sitting on the edge of the table. His shirt was undone, and he wasn't alone. Marta was, as ever, looking suitably alluring in red lipstick and some sort of very revealing black lacy garment. Unseen by either of them, he watched his father lunge forward and grab Marta's slender wrist, yanking her to him; his other hand held the back of her neck as she slid against him.

And just like that, Theo arrived at a place that he knew was a beginning and an end, a destination to which he'd been running ever since that holiday on the Riviera, if not before. He looked down at his palm and fingers and balled them into a fist. As a boy, he had once longed for the big hands of his father, hands he had seen drag his mother from the edge of a pool in a drunken rage, hands he had seen wrung together in frustration at his own many acts of perceived ineptitude. It wasn't until this moment, however, as Marta lifted her foot and rested her heel on the wall for leverage, that Theo finally acknowledged the grown-up hands of the man he had become. And they were honourable hands, hands that had to put things right.

He slammed the door against the wall and watched them both jump. Marta let out a small, theatrical scream and clasped her blouse over her near-naked form as she fled the room. His father, however, took his time, seemingly unflustered; he smoothed his hair and buttoned up his shirt before casually reaching for his glass of champagne, sipping it as Theo walked closer.

Is this bold enough for you, Dad?

'Well now, do you have permission to be here, as an ex-employee? Don't we have to change the locks or something?' his father asked with something akin to amusement in his voice.

'I thought I might hit you.' Theo wiped the sweat from his top lip with a trembling hand. 'But, unlike you, I have enough regard for Mum not to put her through that.' His voice was steady but his breath came in bursts.

'Well, there's a shock, you choosing the sissy-boy way out!'

Theo bit the inside of his cheek and tasted the iron seep of blood on his tongue. 'I feel sorry for you, Dad.'

'Don't.' Perry emptied his glass and put it down sharply.

'No, I do.' Theo held his stare. 'You are a sad old man. Do you think Marta would be the slightest bit interested in a pot-bellied old boozer like you if you didn't own the company?'

'And do you think I give a shit?' His dad laughed, his arms wide open. 'Have you seen her?'

'I remember the way you looked at Freddie at La Grande Belle – it was revolting, predatory.'

'Who the fuck is Freddie?'

She had clearly been expunged from his dad's memory, probably like countless others. That horrible holiday had proved so pivotal in Theo's life, but to his father it was nothing. It was Theo's turn to laugh. 'I guess it must be easy to forget all the women you've had, every one of them just another distraction, a game you play with no regard to the damage you're causing.'

'You think I'm unique? Get real, boy! You think your mother and I should sit around watching good documentaries in our slippers, drinking cocoa into our dotage?'

Theo ignored him. 'Let's talk about Alexander.' He spoke the name clearly, loudly, the name that usually hid at the back of his mouth, whispered only in the solitary darkness. 'Do you remember his mother? What damage did you do her, and him?'

A flicker of surprise crossed his father's face and it felt good to have the upper hand.

'Yes, Dad, Alexander. Is he younger than me? How did that feel, knowing that expensive Vaizey education was being wasted on me while he was living God knows where in God knows what situation?'

Perry was smirking now. 'You think you're so clever, Theodore. You think you have it all figured out.' There was a moment of hesitation while the two men stared at each other. 'But here's the thing.' His dad took a step towards him. 'Alexander did have the benefit of a Vaizey education. He was a couple of years older than you. How do you think I knew about your woeful performance on the rugby pitch? Your fucking weird antics with the gardener? Did you think I was psychic? No, Alex told me. Alex who works in the City, Alex who is a bloody success!'

Theo felt as if he'd been punched in the gut. His body folded and he gripped the table for support. 'He... He was in my school?'

'NO! He was in MY school!' his father roared. 'A Theobald's boy of course! Xander Beaufort.'

Theo's mouth dropped open. Xander Beaufort! He struggled to recall the boy's face, but he remembered that he'd been a prefect at Theobald's and he hadn't cut Theo any slack. 'Did... Did he know about me?'

'Of course he bloody knew about you!'

Theo felt as if the room was spinning. His father reached for his jacket. *You win, Dad, you win. I am done.*

'You see, Theo, life is about planning, it's about putting things in place so that all the bits of the jigsaw fit together. The fact that you are starting to see the whole picture is, I suppose, inevitable.'

'Did... Did Mum know Alexander was at Vaizey?'

'What do you think?'

Theo felt winded by the revelation. He'd felt helpless and inadequate that night at La Grande Belle all those years ago, but this took it to another level. He'd said only recently that despite his father trying to force him, a square peg, into a round hole, he hadn't broken. But that was then. Now he felt quite broken.

Perry walked around the table and made for the door. 'Oh and happy birthday, Theodore. Save some cake for me!'

Theo left the office and stood in the street, breathing in the cold evening air and trying to clear his head. The depth of his father's duplicity took his breath away and, try as he might, he couldn't stop thinking of Sophie, and Kitty, and Anna. *Like father, like son.* Was he really so different from his dad? There was only one person he wanted to talk to right now, but sadly he was in Washington DC. He saw he had a missed call from

Anna, probably wanting to know where he was, but instead he pressed the button to speak to Spud. Given the time difference, he wasn't surprised to get an automated answerphone; Spud would be working.

'Mate, it's me.' He took a deep breath. 'It's my birthday, but that's not why I'm calling. I feel like I'm falling apart. I told my dad I knew about Alexander and...' He paused. 'Well, it didn't go how I thought it might. It's made me think about my situation. I don't ever want Anna to feel how I felt tonight, to find out I have a little girl, a child in this world who doesn't know me... I'm gabbling. Call me when you get this. I need to talk to you, Spud.'

He hung up the phone and hailed a cab to take him home.

Trying to quash the turmoil that swirled inside him, Theo straightened his tie and paid the cabbie before running up the steps to the front door. Taking a deep breath, he tried to erase the previous hour. He didn't want the image in his mind of his father and Marta together, nor the memory of his father laughing at him. The revelation about his brother was still hard for him to accept. It felt like a bad dream. All he wanted was a drink, a shower and an early night. He hated his birthday, always had. He found the whole celebration a little forced and pointless, not to mention embarrassing. Anna, however, felt differently. It distressed her that his parents had been all but indifferent to his birthdays as a child and he knew she'd want to make a fuss today, as she always did, a sort of compensation for past lacks, with the obligatory opening of presents, a steak dinner and a fancy cake. To deny her the joy of organising these little celebrations felt mean. Although, right now, he'd never felt less like celebrating.

He let himself into the hallway and dropped his keys on the dresser. The house was darker than he'd expected – almost pitch black, in fact. He was grateful for the glow of the street light that filtered through the sitting-room window and cast an intricate flickering pattern over the hall floor.

'Oh God, please not a surprise party,' he whispered, ditching his jacket. He couldn't face having to make small talk with Anna's clutch of girl buddies and their other halves, with whom he had zero in common, or, worse, having to deal with his mother, knowing what he now knew and listening to the excuses for his father's absence: '*Daddy's been caught up at the club… Dad's at a planning meeting… Your father's gone to an auction…*' He'd heard them all.

He fixed an expectant expression and opened the door with gusto. The sight that greeted him took him aback.

There was no party. No steak dinner, no gifts and no cake. The room was eerily quiet and cold. Even Griff sat with his muzzle on his extended paws, as if in contemplation.

Instead of a crowd brandishing blowers, standing under a homemade banner and wearing elasticated conical hats, there was just Anna, sitting alone at the kitchen table in the semi-darkness. As his eyes adjusted to the low light, he could see that her hair had been pulled back into a messy ponytail and that she'd been crying. Her eyes were red and swollen and she was rolling tiny sausages of shredded kitchen roll between her fingers.

'What's going on?' he asked, looking around the room for clues as to her state of mind but finding none.

'Please sit down, Theo.' Her voice was small, cracked.

'What's the matter? Are you okay? Has something happened?'

She waited until he was seated before reaching for her phone. She laid it on the table between them and played her answer-phone messages. 'You have one message,' the robotic voice informed.

Theo braced himself and cocked his head, waiting to hear what devastating news had made her so upset. Something to do with Jordan maybe? He mentally began planning her trip to the States, wondering how quickly he could get her packed and on a plane to New York. He slid his fingertips towards her hand, hoping that physical contact might bring some comfort. Anna flinched, quickly pulling her hand beneath the table and resting it in her lap.

The moment the message began, he knew.

His head swam, his stomach dropped and his mouth went dry. His heart was racing fit to burst as the bile rose in his throat.

'Mate, it's me. It's my birthday, but that's not why I'm calling. I feel like I'm falling apart. I told my dad I knew about Alexander and, well, it didn't go how I thought it might. It's made me think about my situation. I don't ever want Anna to feel how I felt tonight, to find out I have a little girl, a child in this world who doesn't know me… I'm gabbling. Call me when you get this. I need to talk to you, Spud.'

This was how his beloved Anna had learnt of the secret he had tried so hard to keep from her! After all that time spent fretting, plotting, dissembling… The countless restless nights worrying about whether it was better to tell her or not to tell her, waiting for the right time, the time when the news would do the least damage to her, to them. And that time had now been forced upon them, dropped like a bomb on their future.

It had all boiled down to one slip of a finger on an answerphone message.

'You have a little girl?' she rasped.

'Yes.'

'You're a dad.' She swallowed, shaking her head. 'Is Kitty her mum?'

He closed his eyes and nodded. God, this was worse than he could ever have imagined. She was sure to be jumping to horrible conclusions. Christ, why hadn't he listened to Spud? Why hadn't he come clean with Anna in their first weeks together? They could have got it all out of the way early…

'I knew it. I always kind of had this feeling about her, the way you looked when you told me she was just some girl from school, the way you changed the subject when her name came up. You were always so evasive. I just knew.'

And there it was – the damage was done. Damage he might never be able to undo, however hard he tried to convince her.

'Do you… Do you love Kitty?' she asked quietly.

'No, not at all. I was infatuated with her at school, but no.' He shook his head.

The two of them sat quietly, on opposite sides of the kitchen table, in close physical proximity but miles and miles apart.

He tried again. 'I don't have any relationship with either of them, Anna. None at all. And I didn't plan it – it just happened,' he whispered. 'It was long before I met you, a one-time thing, and I was told in no uncertain terms that I was not to make contact because, unlike you, Kitty knew that I would be a shit father and a fucking useless addition to any child's life!'

Anna shook her head. 'Don't you fucking dare! Don't you dare compare me with some woman you had a one-night stand with who doesn't know you like I do! Don't you dare suggest that it is for reasons *she* came up with that *I* have been denied motherhood! You are my husband!' Her voice squeaked, sounding raw with sadness. 'You've been cheating on me since the day we met.'

'I have not!'

'Yes, you have, Theo.' She was cool now, her voice barely quivering. 'Lying through omission and lying by keeping a secret, a big secret!'

'I haven't lied to you, Anna. Not intentionally. I might have held back, but—'

'Held back? You have a *child*!' She laughed, wiping her nose with the back of her hand. 'Have you any idea what it's like living with you?' She looked up. 'You have never given yourself to me, not fully. I have tried to be content with the little bits of you that you cast at me like pieces of a puzzle. And I scamper to catch whatever you throw because I love you.' She broke off, crying again. 'I love you so much, but every time you give me a new piece of you, you take away an old piece and I now know that I can never, ever complete the picture of you. Never. And as if that wasn't punishment enough, I find out you have a little girl. A little girl you share with a woman who isn't me, a little girl you phoned Spud to discuss while I was running around trying to make a party for you, collecting a fucking cake!'

'Anna, I... I wish I had told you. I do! But every day, every month that passed made it seem harder and harder to come clean.'

'Well, bravo, Theo.' She clapped. 'But I doubt you would have "come clean", as you put it, if you hadn't misdialled that number today.'

He looked away and both knew this to be the truth.

⋆ ⋆ ⋆

Creeping up the stairs, he trod with caution into their bedroom, a room in which he now felt like an intruder. He snatched items off hangers and rummaged in the drawers like a thief, only half conscious of what he was doing, wishing he was somewhere else, someone else. Eventually, with his suitcase in his hand, he walked slowly back downstairs to say goodbye.

Anna glanced up at him and his heart tore to see how wretched she looked. How had it come to this?

'I don't know what's happening, Theo. I don't know if we're ending, and I don't know what to do.'

'I'm sorry, Anna. I love you.'

'Please don't keep telling me that you love me – it's like wiping away the blood after you've cut me. It doesn't help the hurt or excuse the act, not even a little bit.'

He hovered awkwardly by the fireplace and stuttered out his plan. 'I've decided to go to Bristol. I need to see to some things there anyway, and I need to sort my head out. I'm sure you do too.'

'I'm sad, Theo, but I'm not surprised.' Her voice was a harsh croak. 'I've been waiting for this conversation since we went to the Maldives. I think deep down I knew then that we were on a timer.'

'You did?'

Anna nodded. 'I think possibly since the day we married. I mean, I was never right for you as far as your parents were concerned – I don't speak right, I don't know the wrong and right way to do things and I never went to that bloody school they bang on about.' She gave a false laugh. 'And for someone who cares as much about what others think as you do, especially your shitty parents, whose approval you still crave...' She let this hang.

'Don't say that.' He choked back another wave of sobs. He hadn't even had the chance to tell her about his earlier confrontation with his dad, or Marta, or bloody Xander Beaufort.

She followed him into the hall as he unhooked his coat from the newel post and ferreted in the pocket for his car keys. He bent towards her with arms slightly open, unsure whether or not to hold her, both of them instantly and painfully aware of how in such a short space of time the boundaries had shifted between them, to the point where he no longer felt able to take his wife in his arms and offer comfort.

'Just go, Theo! Fuck off to Bristol or anywhere else!' She jumped up and ran to the front door, holding it ajar, standing with her jaw clenched, waiting for him to pass.

'Anna, I... I can't be the man you need me to be.'

'So you've said.' She wiped away a stray tear. 'And actually, tonight, for the first time ever, I am starting to believe you.'

Theo headed west in a daze, driving on autopilot, his head swimming with hurtful snippets – '*you've been cheating on me since the day we met*' – his heart aching so much he didn't know if he'd even make it to Bristol. He heard the long beep of an angry horn and was momentarily blinded by the flash of headlights on full beam. He swerved to retake the inside lane, unaware that he had drifted through lack of concentration. He swallowed, slowed his speed and took a swig of the coffee he'd picked up at the service station. He shook his head and put the radio on, desperate for something, anything, to distract him from the noise that filled his head.

Seventeen

Theo woke a fraction of a second before his alarm. He rubbed the grit from his eyes and lay back against the soft pillow, breathing deeply, knowing this was how best to shrug off the memory of the nightmare that lurked. He flexed his muscles against the cool sheet, a little damp with his sweat, and clicked on the lamp, careful not to wake Anna. He glanced across to where her sleeping form lay… but of course she wasn't there. This was not their bedroom at home in Barnes, this was the hastily secured bedroom of a budget hotel beside the river in Bristol. The place where he'd spent the last couple of weeks. By day he paced the docks, taking in the majesty of his red-brick warehouse and wondering how his life could have gone so spectacularly wrong in such a short space of time. By night he covered his ears with the spare pillow to block out the shouts of revellers coming and going at all hours, students mainly, pouring out of the famous Thekla nightclub, a former cargo ship which was moored opposite.

Contact with Anna had been minimal, each conversation curt and to the point. She wasted no time on pleasantries, and the lack of kindness in their exchanges deepened his sadness still further. *What did you expect, Theo?*

But despite his torturous dreams, today was going to be a good day, and that was enough to encourage him into the bathroom at such an ungodly time of the morning.

A couple of hours later he was pacing the arrivals hall at Cardiff airport with eager anticipation, checking his phone repeatedly. It was while he was distracted by the noisy reunion of a mother and daughter to his right that a familiar voice called out, 'Mate!'

Spud wrapped him in a big hug. They only ever embraced before or after significant time apart; to do so at routine hellos and goodbyes had never crossed their minds when they were younger, but now that they lived on different continents, it would probably become the norm. It was over six months now since they'd last seen each other.

'Liking the sideburns.' Theo pointed at Spud's hair. 'Even if I can spot a bit of a grey fleck. Very distinguished.'

'Got to do something to keep down with the kids,' Spud said, laughing.

Theo grabbed the folded suit carrier from his hand.

'You can mock my smattering of grey, but I see you're going a bit thin on top there.' Spud stood on tiptoes, an unnecessary charade as he was taller than Theo, and peered at his friend's crown.

Theo ran his palm self-consciously over his pate. 'Probably! The month I've had, nothing would surprise me.'

Spud patted his back, brotherly and affectionate. 'Glad you've not opted for the comb-over. Better to just get rid, as you have. Nice and short.'

'Thank you for that advice, Mr Sassoon. And it's not that bad! Any other comments on my appearance?'

'Not that I can think of – you're looking good, Theo, been working out?' Spud patted his own flat stomach.

The two laughed and Theo was grateful for how easily they always picked up where they'd left off, no matter how long they'd been apart. 'So, a whole five days in Blighty, eh?'

'Yep. Been in London the last two days – where you clearly were not – and now it's here for three days, for a conference and back-to-back meetings, but at least they're in beautiful Wales, which makes it slightly more bearable. If nothing else, I can look out of the window and enjoy the view. Thanks for coming to get me, by the way.'

'No worries. It's a good chance for a catch-up, otherwise wasted if you were sitting in a cab. And it's no distance from Bristol.'

Spud flashed him a thin-lipped smile when he mentioned Bristol. They had much to discuss, but that could wait.

'And of course you can take time out of your day as you're now your own boss! Must be great to do what the hell you like.' Spud grinned and punched Theo lightly on the shoulder.

'Oh yes, mate, I am living the dream.' Theo grinned. 'Only a couple of weeks in and I am indeed my own boss. Not a penny of income, rising costs, dwindling savings, loneliness, self-doubt, one single employee, and the only thing stopping me from jacking the whole thing in and going for a long swim off a short pier is the fact that I still, in some tiny crevice of my mind, believe that what I am doing might just be the right thing.'

'Well, as a wise man once said, the decision you make is always the right one.'

'It was you that said that!' Theo tutted.

'And I was right.'

'So, a good flight from town?' Theo asked as they made their way across the car park.

'Is there such a thing? I hate it. Sitting high above the clouds in a tin can. Planes are nothing more than a necessary evil for me, a way to hop across the pond and get around.'

'How are Kumi and the kids?'

'All good. Really good, in fact. Miyu is talking as well as walking now and she bosses me around when Kumi is otherwise engaged – they're like a tag team! And I swear to God they agree with each other on anything I am opposed to on point of principle, ganging up on me – my life is not my own and when her granny is around, I have to deal with the three of them!' The big grin on his face belied his words. 'I am secretly learning bits of Japanese so I can listen to what they say about me without them knowing. It's been illuminating.' He nodded.

'What do they say?'

'Essentially that I am not only stupid but I might actually be the most stupid man ever to grace the earth, like perennially stupid.'

'I don't think the stupid have Master's degrees and I don't think they use the word "perennially".'

'You might be right.' Spud chuckled. 'Tom is a sweet baby, the opposite of his sister in every way. If she is a tornado, Tom is a gentle breeze.'

Theo flipped the boot of his new black Mercedes SL. 'So you prefer Tom?'

Spud stared at him as he unloaded his bags from the trolley to the boot. 'You don't prefer one of your kids over the other!' He laughed.

'You don't?' Theo was only half joking.

'No! God, they're just different!' Spud shook his head and ran his eyes over the sparkling metallic paintwork of the car. 'Flipping heck – this is a beast! And if this is the car you get with no income, then sign me up!' He rubbed his hands together at the prospect of a ride.

'A legacy from Montgomery Holdings, mine for the next eighteen months, and then the way things are going, it'll probably be Shanks's pony. Want to drive?' Theo held up the keys.

'Mate, I am jetlagged, out of practice at driving on the left and more used to an automatic minivan – think I'd better pass. But I won't pretend I'm not insanely jealous and insanely excited at the thought of doing so!'

Theo slid onto the cool leather and watched his friend do the same in the passenger seat.

'Oh, she's a beauty! What's the most you've got out of her?' Spud clapped. 'Kumi would never let me have a car like this, even if we could afford it.'

'Well, Anna doesn't drive it.' He had mentioned Anna, done the thing they had seemingly been keen to avoid until the time was right.

'How's she doing?' Spud asked soberly, as if only now remembering that there were more important questions to ask than what top speed Theo had managed in his awesome car.

Theo concentrated on fastening his seatbelt and starting the engine, which purred. 'I don't know, is the truthful answer…' He raised his hands and let them fall. 'Our conversations are very formal and I don't know what she's thinking. Christ, I don't know what I'm thinking!'

'It must feel like you're in limbo.' Spud gave him the words.

'It does.' He gave a glum nod and looked straight ahead, unwilling and unable to discuss this further right now.

Spud lowered his voice, his words sincere. 'It will get easier. Everything will become clearer. You know that, don't you? It just needs time.'

Theo gulped down the embarrassing lump that sat in his throat. He looked across at his friend, who now ran his palm over the hand-stitched leather of the console. The temptation to open up to him properly before they'd even left the car park was strong. 'So where first?' He coughed. 'Celtic Manor – that's where you're staying, right?'

'Yes, and as long as they have good coffee, take me there. Right now I can think of nothing better.'

Theo shook his head in mock disgust. 'And to think we used to drink beer with our cornflakes every morning!'

'We used to do a lot of things.' Spud laughed. 'And at least one of us had a lot more hair!'

Theo pressed the stereo into action and the familiar strains of Guns N' Roses' 'Sweet Child O' Mine' filled the car.

'Oh, mate! Yes!' Spud began his impromptu air-guitar routine, while Theo banged the steering wheel as though it were a drum. They might have been two grown men with responsibilities, travelling in a high-end executive car from the airport, but for the five minutes of the song, they were nineteen again, scruffy and living in their grotty flat in Belsize Park, where the plumbing was leaky and they mostly slept or hung out in their underpants.

It was late by the time Theo arrived back at his Bristol hotel. He settled back on the bed and opened his laptop, dialling up for an internet connection. His email pinged repeatedly. He glanced up at the ceiling, imagining he was in the kitchen in Barnes, and smiled fondly at how Anna used to get irritated if any noise filtered up the stairs. He thought about Griff the puppy and felt a wave of longing for that house and those in it. He looked at the phone and considered calling, but another stilted exchange with Anna was the last thing either of them needed.

He liked working there in the quiet at that late hour. Catching up on emails from planners, architects, the team at the council and Jody, the young woman he employed remotely as his right hand. It was a world away from his plush office in Villiers House. He shook the image of his father and Marta from his head. Jody had emailed him the CVs of candidates who'd made the first and second cut for the role of project manager, to oversee the renovation – someone with more building experience than him. Theo smiled. If only he'd studied engineering!

He yawned, scratched his stubbly chin and gave the CVs only scant consideration, wondering if he really wanted the egg and cress sandwich that had been warming in his briefcase since he'd picked it up on the way back from dropping off Spud. As he debated how hungry he was and prepared to call it a night, his attention was drawn to one CV in particular.

'It can't be.'

He swallowed, sat forward and squinted at the screen. His pulse quickened as he clicked on the attached document. There it was: confirmation that Mr Magnus Wilson, of Bath, former pupil of Vaizey College and with a whole list of qualifications and achievements to his name, was asking Theo for a job. Not that Wilson would have known; there was nothing at a glance to link Theo to the company. Theo's reaction to seeing Magnus Wilson's name was surprising. Even now, more than a decade later, he felt a stab of discomfort at the memory of the boy who had made his school life hell. His leg jumped as if he was back in Theobald's House.

Sitting back on the bed, he thought long and hard about what to do. Would it be a good thing to see Wilson again or was it better to let sleeping dogs lie? He pictured the way Wilson had stood triumphantly after beating him up, his eyes showing no remorse.

Theo was unnerved. Instead of going to sleep, he reached for his briefcase and grabbed the slightly squashed sandwich. He was hungrier than he thought. He tried to stem thoughts of Wilson, already looking forward to meeting up with Spud again the next day.

The two men sat at a table in the sticky-floored pub in Wood Street, Cardiff.

'So are you going to interview him?' Spud asked through his mouthful of scampi.

'I honestly don't know,' Theo said. 'What would you do?'

'I'd be tempted to, just to get a look at him, and the vile, vengeful part of me would want to take him so far in the process and then let him down in a withering way.' He pretended to twirl an invisible moustache in a villainous manner.

'You don't have a vile and vengeful part, that much I do know.' Theo held his mate's gaze.

'True, I'm an old softie, but I like to think that if there was a call for it, I could do mean and macho.' Spud laughed and sipped his pint. 'Ah! I tell you what... crap food and a warm pint, I have missed home!'

'I'll bet. So do they have scayumpee in Washington?' Theo chuckled.

'Yes, but they call it "shrimp" – go figure! Not that I'm allowed to eat it. Kumi watches what I eat.' He pulled a face.

'So you are going for a pud?'

'Absolutely!' Spud grinned. 'I've got my eye on a hefty rum baba with extra cream.'

Theo shook his head in disgust.

'It's bothered you, hasn't it, this guy popping up after all this time.'

Theo sniffed. 'It has. You know how you have those people in your past who just...' He balled his right hand into a fist and punched it into his left palm. 'They have that ability to get under your skin because the memory of them is so powerful. It doesn't matter that years, decades have passed – he was a thorn in my side for so long.'

Spud paused, placing his pint on the tabletop. 'It does you no good to harbour those thoughts. They cause stress and stress is not something you want building up inside. You've got enough going on right now.'

'Haven't I just.'

'So, this move to Bristol, is it permanent?' Spud asked, his tone neutral.

'I don't know.' Theo looked towards the window. 'I know we both need a bit of space to get our heads straight, but I don't know if she wants me back, and I don't know if I can go back.'

'That's a lot of "don't knows".'

Theo nodded. 'Anna wanting a baby has always been the

biggest thing for her, and so to find out about Sophie…' He paused. 'It's knocked her for six and it's all my fault. If only I'd told her on our first date… But the longer I left it, the harder it became and there was always a reason not to bring it up.'

'Because you were scared to.'

'Yes, I was scared to and now I'm scared of what comes next.' He sighed. 'I want Anna to be happy, she deserves happiness more than anyone, and I wanted to be the one to make her happy. But now…? I'm not sure if I can.'

'And the Kitty situation?'

Theo coughed. 'No change. I have no part in her life. She doesn't want me to muddy the water for either of them, and I get it.'

'My advice would be to let it go, let a lot of those memories go, the ones that trouble you.'

'I know that, but what if I can't let them go, what if they're ingrained in here…' He tapped his forehead. '… springing up when I least expect them to?'

'I'd say you need to find a way to let them go, try harder.'

'The problem is…' He sniffed and exhaled, trying to compose himself. '… that right now I am very, very unhappy. And I shouldn't be. In truth, I am sick of it, mate, weary with being this sad.' He sighed for the umpteenth time. 'I had everything and I was loved.' He pictured Anna, again. 'But it's like I have nothing and it's… it's been this way for my whole life. I've been good at hiding it at times, but I'm aware of these fault lines running through my mind, and what leaks out of the cracks is sadness.' He clenched his jaw. 'And I've always felt that one jolt of fear, one huge knock and those lines might open up and I might fall into the abyss.' He looked up at his friend.

'Like when you got that letter from Kitty about Sophie,' Spud said, 'and you seemed to give up. I was worried about you then. Mind you, I'm worried about you now.'

Theo gave a dry smile. 'I know that if I fall, I might never resurface. I've faced depression many times, felt it breathing down my neck, and it's a hostile place to live and a place I never want to go to again. And I've always refused to talk to anyone about it. I took some pills and battled through. And it got better, a little.' He clenched his fists. 'But the state I'm in now feels different, it doesn't feel like depression, it feels like failure.'

'It's not failure – it's life.'

Theo shrugged. 'I guess. I'm just thinking of the times when I have been happy. The moments, often quite brief, when I was with someone I wanted to be with in a quiet place.' He thought of falling asleep next to Anna under a canopy of fairy lights in her tiny flat, and of the night spent on a camp bed in the front parlour of Mr Porter's crooked cottage with the smell of wood smoke and kerosene permeating the walls. 'This means I am capable of happiness, right?'

'Yes, absolutely, and that's really important.' Spud spoke plainly. 'Knowing when you're happy and what it was that made you happy is like learning the code.'

Theo nodded, feeling an overwhelming sense of longing for his wife.

'You're a good man, Theo, you always have been, and you're one of the very few people I trust. You're brilliant – I just wished you believed it.'

Theo blinked at his friend. 'I tell you what I wish: I wish we had another pint.'

He raised his empty glass, doing what he did best, skirting over the sentiment, making light of the moment and swallowing the howls of distress and regret that rumbled in this throat.

⋆ ⋆ ⋆

Theo revved the engine and slipped the gearbox through its paces. He was edgy. Not even Guns N' Roses on the stereo could lift his sense of apprehension. Having deliberated long and hard over what suit to wear and which shirt, he looked at his reflection in the mirror, satisfied with his appearance at least.

The traffic was heavy coming out of Cardiff, where he'd just dropped Spud at the airport for the first leg of his journey back to the US. As he crawled along the M4 towards Bristol, he began to lose his nerve. He put in a call to Jody.

'How's it going?' she said when she picked up, knowing he had to be at the hotel in Bristol by 11 a.m. to interview the two final candidates.

'Yep, good. Anything to report this morning?' A small part of him hoped for a cancellation, a change in plans that would mean he could peel off at the next junction and go and find some breakfast. *What were you thinking, Theo? What part of you thinks this is a good idea?*

'No, nothing to report. We're all good,' Jody chirped.

'Righto. Well, have a good one and I'll call you later.'

He ended the call and watched as the traffic miraculously vanished, leaving him plenty of time to make his appointments. He turned up the volume for 'Sweet Child O' Mine' and hit the gas.

⋆

Theo stood and shook the hand of Phil Marshall. 'Thank you for coming in. We'll be in touch.' He smiled as the man got to his feet and buttoned his suit jacket.

'Thank you for seeing me and if you need any more information or have any other questions, then just shout.'

'We will. Once again, thanks for coming in today, Phil.'

'My home phone is best – I'll be on it all day. So…'

'Yes.' Theo sensed Phil's desperation. 'Thank you.'

He watched him reluctantly leave the room; it was obvious he wanted to stay there and work on Theo until he said yes. He thought of Spud and the way Miyu wore him down. He smiled at the image of his browbeaten buddy, trying to picture him holding court on Capitol Hill, advising senior politicians on fiscal policy with confidence and then going home to try and negotiate bedtimes with a headstrong little girl.

He felt a new and unwanted pang of regret over Sophie, tried to imagine going home to her. Spud's words filled his head. '*My advice would be to let it go, let a lot of those memories go. It does you no good to harbour those thoughts.*' Theo wished it were that simple. He was going to miss his mate.

He stood and walked across the spacious top-floor meeting room of the city-centre hotel, taking in the waxed wooden floor, comfortable leather furniture and painted brick walls. He liked the nautical overtones, the porthole mirrors and the oversized rope-wrapped lanterns, approving of the nod to Bristol's maritime heritage. They were a welcome distraction as he waited. He swallowed the bile that rose in his throat and wiped his sweaty palms on his trousers.

He was nervous. Very nervous.

He stared out of the window onto the cobbled courtyard

beneath and tried to slow his breathing, thinking of how best to approach the meeting and wishing he was somewhere else. His eyes scanned the far wall to see if there might be another way to leave, a different exit, but there was none. He glanced at the door and tried to imagine Wilson walking through it. His stomach jumped when he realised that at any moment that was exactly what would happen.

There was no way he was going to give Wilson a job. No way on God's earth, but the temptation to see his tormentor again, now that he had the upper hand, was one Theo could not resist. He had already decided to be gracious and kind, to be the better man. What he wanted more than anything was not revenge, nor even to gloat; he wanted answers, answers that might help keep his nightmares at bay. Not that he would ever have admitted this to another living soul. He now wondered if Wilson would even recognise him. It occurred to him that it was most unlikely that he haunted Wilson's dreams in the way Wilson did his.

Theo made his way back to the desk, fingering the CV that sat in front of him, taking in the few facts: married, three children, aged thirty-four. It seemed almost impossible that that amount of time had gone by. It was as he read further that the door creaked and in walked a man Theo would have passed in the street without recognising. It was only his eyes that marked him out as the Magnus Wilson of old.

Shorter than Theo had remembered, and slighter, Wilson sported a dark, close-cropped beard and had been liberal with his eau de toilette. He smiled and walked forward with his hand outstretched, mimicking the many masters who had taught them that this was the Vaizey way. '*Make an impression, boy!*

Hold eye contact! Command the room!' 'Magnus Wilson,' he announced as he neared the desk.

Theo drew himself up to his full height and liked the advantage it gave him. He too held out his hand and met Wilson's gaze. As they shook hands, he saw the faint hint of recollection cross Wilson's brow; he was clearly trying to place the face, no doubt running through the database in his head, attempting to find a match.

'Theodore Montgomery.' Theo nodded and released the man's hand.

'Christ alive!' Wilson smiled broadly and opened his mouth, seemingly uncertain of what to say. 'Theo?'

'Yes.' He sat.

'Good God! We were at Vaizey College together!'

'Yes, we were. Please sit down.' He spoke with an air of indifference, indicating the chair and watching as Wilson took up the seat.

'How long is it since we've seen each other?' Wilson shook his head in surprise.

'A long time.'

'I can't believe it! Did you know it was me?' Wilson glanced at the CV sitting on the desk.

'I did, but only just before you arrived,' he lied.

Wilson shook his head. 'This is nuts, Theo! I can't believe it. It feels crazy to ask how you've been, with so much water under the bridge. How would we start?'

'How indeed.' Theo wasn't sure if Wilson was playing nice, had forgotten their violent relationship or simply didn't give a shit. Either way, he kept his guard up.

Wilson carried on. 'I went to a couple of the OVB reunions,

but they weren't really my thing. I know a couple of the lads that still go, but I've not kept in touch with many people.'

'I would have thought the reunions would have been right up your street.' Theo sat back in the chair.

'Are you kidding? An army brat like me? I only had a place because the military were paying the fees and there were plenty who never let me forget it.' Wilson shook his head. 'I always felt like an unwelcome guest.'

Theo stared at him, shocked to hear Wilson describe his feelings for Vaizey in the same terms he himself used. 'I didn't know that. You certainly didn't let it show.'

'Yep, it's true. My mum left my dad when I was a toddler, which now I have kids myself I cannot begin to fathom, not at all. I don't remember her.' He shook his head. 'Even though my dad wasn't an officer – officers' kids routinely went to Vaizey – the MOD helped him out and so it was boarding school for me while he was in the army. He was often on tour and it was deemed better for me than going into care, and better for my dad, of course.'

In care, like my Anna, like the kids who will benefit from this project.

Wilson continued. 'I used to spend the holidays with my old nana in Dorchester. For me it was like two worlds colliding: one minute I was roaming the privileged halls of Vaizey College and the next I was sharing a bunk bed with my cousin and doing paper rounds to get cash. I even had two voices – my school voice and my home voice.' He shook his head. 'I always felt split, like I didn't belong in either world, not really. In fact I don't think I properly became me until I met my wife, Julie.' He licked his lips. 'God, I am over sharing. Please put it down to nerves and the fact that we have history.'

Theo noticed that his voice now was a mixture of the two worlds, not overly posh and overbearing as it had been, but softer, more pleasant.

'Are you nervous?'

'Yes, of course! I want this job and I can't decide whether our school days makes it more or less likely that I will get it, if I'm being honest.' His eyes settled on Theo's face and Theo watched his Adam's apple rise and fall.

'You treated me quite badly at school.' Theo spoke the words slowly, a watered-down version of the long diatribe he had practised countless times over countless years. But today, with Wilson sitting in front of him, this measured approach seemed more appropriate.

'I did, and I remember it.' Wilson nodded. 'I remember us fighting.'

Not fighting – you beat me up.

'You came back from the summer break looking tanned and happy and I'd been stuck indoors for the best part of two months, staring at a rainy window, and my dad had only just gone back on tour and I was pig sick with jealousy.' He smiled at Theo like they were old friends reminiscing, which only served to confuse Theo more.

A jolt of nerves fired through his gut, the reminder of not only the fight but that summer at La Grande Belle. 'I can assure you I might have been tanned, but I was far from happy and even if I had been, that was surely not sufficient grounds for beating me up.'

'No question you are absolutely right. I was a little shit to you. A proper little shit.' Wilson chuckled, as if they had shared a joke. 'Theo…! Well, I never.' He spoke his name fondly. 'I was made house prefect just before you arrived…'

A Theobald's house prefect. Like Xander Beaufort – my brother.

Wilson coughed. 'Anyway, I was cleaning Twitcher's study one day when he took a call from admissions to say that you were arriving. I was earwigging and heard him say you were a close family friend. Oh my God! We were all panicking, convinced you were going to be a right snitch, running to your dad's mate, spilling our secrets.'

Theo shook his head. 'I don't think I'd even met Twitcher until I started school.'

'I hated you so much!' Again, Wilson's tone was warm, almost affectionate.

'Why? Why did you hate me?' Theo sat forward and rested his arms on the desk, keen to understand why he'd been the target, what exactly he'd done to incur Wilson's wrath.

'Are you kidding? There you were, jetting off on a plane in the holidays. You had everything I wanted. The best I could hope for was making cakes with my nana in her little kitchen and eating cheese on toast, squashed next to her and my cousins on the sofa. I'd never been on a proper holiday, much less on a plane!'

Theo pictured this and knew that he would have loved to have spent time in a cosy house, eating cheese on toast on a crowded sofa.

Wilson was still talking. 'You were rich, like mega rich, and I had to put up with a second-hand uniform out of the lost-and-found box. And your dad used to turn up in that sweet navy blue Aston Martin.' Wilson whistled. 'She was a beauty – I remember it now, it was the talk of the school. And your mum…!' He smiled. 'I don't want to sound disrespectful, but your mum was smoking hot! And how she fussed over you – I think we were all a bit jealous of you.'

Theo laughed. 'Yes, that car was a beauty.'

'Fucking smell... vomit!... bloody expensive... idiot!... what the fuck is wrong with him?'

'But remember, that's my mother you're talking about!'

'I know! I know!' Wilson placed his hand over his mouth. 'But she was something else. We knew you had a flash house in London – the rumours swirled. God, you even had old Porter to keep an eye on you at school, and he gave it to me with both barrels every time I saw him. He cuffed me one right on the head.' He rubbed his temple, as if the pain still lingered. 'I was shit scared. Scared of him and scared of getting another one if my dad found out. You had it all, Theo, and I had nothing, and I found it hard to stomach. It wasn't personal. I was just a messed-up kid. A very messed-up kid who was missing his mum.'

'I guess that's easy for you to say, but it was *very* personal to me,' Theo levelled.

Wilson nodded. 'I can imagine, and the thought of anyone treating my boys how we treated you...' He shook his head. 'I am sorry.'

The two men sat, letting the apology hang between them like a bridge. Theo visualised Mr Porter and heard his words as he reprimanded Wilson. *'Here's the thing, Mr Wilson. You need to be very careful that you respect everyone in your path, as you never know where they'll pop up again. And, trust me, the path we walk is long and winding.'*

Theo smiled at the irony. *Isn't it just...*

Wilson sat forward. 'Would you like to see a picture of my family?' Without waiting for a response, he pulled out his wallet, holding up a slightly faded image of a homely blonde woman flanked by three young boys. 'My oldest, Joe, only nine but plays good rugby!' He nodded with pride at the photo. 'And the other two are Max and Ben. Ben is our surprise. We'd agreed to stop at two, but you know what these women are like – persistent! – and after a bottle or two of Lambrusco, she took advantage and got lucky.' He laughed.

Theo pictured Anna and felt sadness on her behalf. She too had been persistent but hadn't got so lucky.

'What about you, Theo, any kids?'

'No. No kids.' *Apart from you, Sophie... Apart from you, and to deny you cuts me to the quick.*

'Oh, I'm sorry.' Wilson folded away his wallet and it occurred to Theo that those who did have children, Spud included, could only see his supposed childless state as regretful.

'So, about the job...' Theo coughed and brought the meeting back on track.

'Oh God, I'd almost forgotten why I'm here. Excuse me while I switch into professional mode.' Wilson sat up straight and adjusted his jacket lapels. 'I have a lot of experience on projects like this. Last year I worked on a similar build in Hereford – vast industrial barn conversions that were made into holiday studios, but a similar principle. I control budgets, oversee materials, the whole shebang.'

Theo cast his eyes over Wilson's CV and tried to think of an appropriate question.

He drove down the M4 with a peculiar feeling of peace. Seeing Magnus Wilson had helped draw a line under the years of persecution and given him greater insight as to why things had happened as they did. It wasn't that he forgave Wilson, not at all, but he came away from their encounter with a better understanding, and he hoped to build on that foundation. He smiled at the metaphor, then put in a call to Jody.

'Evening, boss, you heading back to London?'

'Yes, I've got the bank meeting tomorrow and I need to do a few personal things. I'll let you know how it goes.'

'Does this mean we can guarantee my pay for the next few months?'

'Yes, if the loan gets approved. Otherwise I shall give you a glowing reference for whoever is lucky enough to employ you next!'

'You are too kind,' she said. 'How did it go today?'

'It was good, actually.'

'Have you made a decision?'

'Yes. Yes, I have.' He smiled. 'And assuming we get the funding, we are good to go. Can you get me Phil Marshall's number.'

Night fell as he reached Barnes. Heading there had been a spur-of-the-moment decision as he'd hit London. A quick drive past his house had revealed nothing. The hall lamp was on, but the curtains were drawn. He'd hoped to see Anna in the street, on her way home or walking Griff, and in his mind he'd played out how he might make their meeting look casual, but she was nowhere to be seen. He decided to pop in and see his parents. He hadn't spoken to his mother since his resignation and he wanted to smooth things with her at least.

He parked up, rapped on the door and waited while his parents flicked on the various lights and slid the many bolts to allow him entry.

'Theo! Is everything okay?' His mother gripped the thick shawl at her neck. Her immediate concern indicated that their angry call was now at the back of her mind and he was thankful.

'Yes, just thought I'd pop in and see you.' He walked forward and grazed her cheek with a kiss.

'Well, this is most unexpected!' She smiled nonetheless and ushered him into the sitting room, shuffling a little in her slippers.

'Theo, is everything okay?' His father roused himself from his chair; he had clearly been dozing. There was no particular animosity in his tone, nothing to indicate that this was their first meeting since the damaging encounter in the boardroom at Villiers House.

'Yes, I was just passing. Well, kind of.' He sat on the sofa.

His father stared at him quizzically. 'How's the Bristol thing doing?' He reached for his glasses and rested them on his bulbous nose.

'Good. So much red tape.' He nodded, wanting to give only the minimum of detail, which was as much as his father deserved. He noted the change to his father's once athletic frame, the slight bowing under the extra weight. His mother, in contrast, had lost the curves that had apparently so enraptured his peers and was now reed thin. Theo recalled the way Wilson had admired her. He yawned and rubbed his face; it had been quite a day.

'Daddy and I were just having cocoa, darling. Here's yours.' His mum handed him a mug.

'Thanks.' He took it gratefully between his palms. 'I was in Bristol today, interviewing. I met up with an Old Vaizey Boy – he was on the shortlist for the position of site manager. Magnus Wilson?'

'Magnus Wilson,' his mum repeated, tapping her mouth with her finger. 'That name rings a bell for some reason.'

'Was he a Theobald's boy?' his father asked, loudly.

'Naturally, Dad. Theobald's through and through.'

His father's face split into a grin of pure joy and he clapped his hands. 'Well, good for you, Theo! Good for you! How was he?'

'Good. Yes, good, I think.'

His father sat forward in the chair. 'It's wonderful to share those memories, isn't it? A unique experience, I've always found, and it binds you for life.'

'Yes, I would have to agree.' Theo smiled ironically and sipped his cocoa, knowing he would always be mystified by the esteem in which his dad held the place. It had felt so important to share the news with his father, but at the same time he hated that at some level he still sought his approval and, worse, that it was all wrapped up in that bloody school. 'I have a meeting with the bank tomorrow, to sort a business loan, funding for the renovation and so forth. Fingers crossed.' He remembered his conversation with Jody and sincerely hoped he wasn't going to have to let her go.

'You don't need a loan, darling – you're still a shareholder of Montgomery's and you can use company money.' His mother spoke matter-of-factly.

'I…' He looked at his father – this hadn't occurred to him. He wasn't sure but thought there might have been a flash of something like regret in his dad's eyes.

'Your mother is right. Loans cost money. That's just basic, boy. Don't borrow if you don't have to. Speak to Marcus, he can go through the funding. And you should take offices at Villiers House too, and claim your start-up costs, that makes it tax-efficient. Have you considered registering as a charity? There are tax breaks to be had there too, means you'll have more to plough back in where it's needed.'

'Thank you.' He meant it, sincerely.

'Don't thank me! It's not a case of thanks, it's a matter of birthright!' his father boomed.

And right there and then, the moment seemed appropriate. 'There's something I'd like to tell you.'

His mother peered over the rim of her glasses. 'Are you referring to the fact that you have been lodging elsewhere?'

'I wasn't, actually, but you've heard that Anna and I are taking a break?' He didn't know how else to phrase it.

'Oh yes, dear. I mean, it's none of our business, of course, but gossip spreads like wildfire in Barnes.'

Theo bit his tongue, knowing it spread like wildfire because she liked to set the kindling and apply a match. 'Yes, well, we're apart right now, regretfully, but we'll see.' He sipped his cocoa, a taste that took him back to childhood, to school. 'As I say, that wasn't what I was referring to.'

'Oh?' He had her interest.

He took a deep breath. 'The reason I fell apart in my last year at university was not because I was being lazy or partying too hard – it was because I was depressed.'

'I think we rather gathered that.' She sniffed.

'Yes, but maybe not the reason why.' He paused. 'I fathered a child. I have a child, a little girl.'

His mother gave a gasp and slopped her cocoa onto the arm of the chair. His father remained unnaturally still, alert, waiting to hear more.

'She's not so little now,' Theo continued, keeping his gaze on his mug. 'I'm not in her life, but Anna knows, and I don't really know why but I wanted to tell you. It felt important. No more secrets.' He caught his father's eye.

'A granddaughter?' his mother asked with a wistful air. She placed her cocoa on the table by her chair and reached for her handkerchief. 'And does the child have a name?'

Theo nodded. 'Her name is Sophie.'

'Sophie,' his mum repeated, taking the corner of her handkerchief to blot whatever was in her eye.

His father picked up the remote control and turned up the news.

After saying goodbye to his parents, Theo grabbed his briefcase and checked into the local pub, where the rooms were overheated and the floors creaky. His phone buzzed.

'Hey, mate.'

'Hey! You home?' He tried to picture Spud's whereabouts.

'Nearly, thank God. How did it go?'

Theo smiled, knowing that Spud had probably spent most of his day envisaging Theo's great showdown with the school bully. 'Better than I thought it would, actually.'

'Did you punch him over the desk? Kick his shins? Nick his lunch money?'

'No!' Theo laughed. 'You've been watching too many of Miyu's cartoons.'

'You might be right.' Spud sighed.

'It was weird. I got really worked up before he arrived, I was nervous, but I don't think I would have recognised him, to be truthful. I realised that the boy I pictured doesn't exist, not any more – and he hasn't for years. If anything, he looked—'

'Looked what?'

'I don't know.' Theo huffed. 'Ordinary. Not like someone that would pose a great threat or be the total bastard that he was as a kid.'

'Well, people can and do change.'

'Some, yes. If anything, I felt quite sorry for him.'

'Bloody hell! You did?'

'Yup.'

'And did he recognise you?'

Theo recalled the way Wilson had eyed him over their handshake. 'Yes, almost instantly, and he wasn't embarrassed or overly contrite. I think his memories have a different filter. He made the whole school thing and his behaviour sound like they were par for the course, and I realised that for him they might well have been. I don't think he had the easiest time as a child, but for very different reasons to me.'

'So what did you do, send him packing? Spit in his eye?'

'Actually, no.' Theo loosened his collar and spun his keys on his finger. 'I chatted to him civilly. Not a punch was thrown.'

'You were civil?'

'Better than that – I was almost chummy.' He closed his eyes and held the phone away from his ear while Spud laughed loudly, as if this was the punchline he'd been waiting for.

'I'm proud of you, Theo.'

'Thanks. You don't think I'm a mug for not challenging him more?'

Spud's laughter again filled the gap between the oceans.

'What are you laughing at?' Theo asked.

'Oh, mate, I am sitting in a cab, it's late afternoon, traffic is horrendous and I have a mountain of work to do. I've got emails pinging in left, right and centre. And all I want is to be at home with a cup of coffee, but instead I'm heading to a toy shop because I promised Miyu a Sylvanian Families tree house and there wasn't one at the airport, surprise, surprise. I'm on a mission to keep a promise when there are a million things I should and would rather be doing, and you ask if I think *you* are a mug? Still, the joys of parenthood, huh?'

'I guess so.'

'Ah, shit, bad choice of words. How are things? Have you seen Anna?' Spud adopted a softer tone.

Theo opened the rickety sash window and looked up at the night sky, listening as a duck squawked and landed on the water. 'No. I haven't seen her. Did you ever wonder if you were accidentally living someone else's life? You know, like when there's a mix-up at the hospital and people get the wrong kid?'

'No, I never felt like that.'

There was a beat of silence while both waited for more. Neither took the lead.

'I need to go, Spud, I need a leak. I'll call you back later in the week.'

'Okay, but what happened with the Wilson bloke? How did it end?'

Theo took a deep breath and gave a small laugh. 'I gave him a job.'

Eighteen

Theo had been living in the little flat in Bristol for six weeks. He kept it bare, wary of making it feel like home as that would have given it a permanence that he feared. There were no pictures on the walls, no crockery or cutlery in the cupboards and no landline. He preferred to treat it as he had the hotel not too far from the flat, nothing more than a base. Just until...

It had been strange to wake up in his childhood home in Barnes that morning, and not for the first time in recent weeks he'd come to with a start, wondering where he was. He fastened the towel around his waist and stared at his reflection in the bathroom mirror.

The call from his mother the previous day had shocked him and the sense of disbelief hadn't lessened. It was a strange time, a day he'd always known would come, but one he'd assumed would be far into the future, giving him a chance to mentally prepare. He could only imagine how Anna had coped, having had to deal with something similar when she'd been nothing more than a little girl. His heart flexed for her.

He was yet to feel the sadness that he'd anticipated; right

now he was simply exhausted by the weight of the news. He guessed this was shock. He felt floored, angry even, as his brain struggled to accept the finality. His nerves twitched and his limbs jumped, as though surprised. He felt cheated; he'd figured he'd have more time. At the back of his mind a fantasy had hovered for longer than he cared to admit. It was one where he and his father sat in front of a roaring fire, pints in hand, as they gave each other the floor and spoke openly about their clashes and their differences before hopefully arriving at a place that resembled calmer waters, if not understanding. He knew it was ridiculous – he was a grown man, and how many people reached his age without considering the inevitable loss of those they loved? But Theo had, as ever, felt in some way immune.

There was so much he had yet to say to his dad, so many conversations started but not finished. Worst of all were the apologies that had danced around them over the years. Both men had failed to reach up and grasp the words, unable, for reasons deeper than he could fathom, to make peace. The wounds of their recent battle, where harsh and hurtful truths had been exchanged in the boardroom, had healed a little, but the skin that wrapped them was thin, new and still tender.

And now it was too late. It was all too late.

He stared at his reflection, wiping the steam from the mirror with his hand, and wondered what else was slipping beyond his reach faster than he realised.

Two memories were proving especially hard to shift: his dad leering at Freddie from the bedroom window of La Grande Belle, and his dad trying to hide his anger when Theo had thrown up in his Aston Martin. Both events so long ago now and yet still stuck on replay in his head. Spud's good words of advice came to him once more: '*Let it go, let a lot of those memories go, the ones that trouble you.*'

If only it were that simple. He wished he could replace them with something more agreeable, like the Christmas morning from his childhood when he'd watched as his Dad tore open yet another pair of socks before throwing the packaging at his mum, who ducked and giggled, trying not to spill her breakfast Bellini. Or the time he'd spied the two of them through the crack of the kitchen door, dancing with each other, both in their pyjamas and neither with any clue that he was looking. But it was the negative memories that persisted. His father's face livid: '*The idiot!... What the fuck is wrong with him?*'

'It's a good question. What is wrong with you?' he asked the face that stared back. He jutted his chin and ran the back of his fingers over his neck and face, taking in the deepening furrows on his brow.

He shaved, dressed slowly and made his way downstairs. The sound of Stella's sniffing filled the air. He was ashamed at how much the noise grated his bones. It was more than he wanted to deal with. He resisted the urge to put the radio on and dilute the atmosphere with something, anything, unsure of the correct etiquette in this situation. He watched her make cups of tea as a distraction and wipe the sink and countertops with a bleached dishcloth, going over and over the same pristine surfaces, until, spent, she sat slumped. Her usual upright posture was bowed under the weight of her grief. She drew random shapes with her finger on the tabletop. She looked... She looked old.

'Are you going to say something at the service?' she eventually managed, looking up. She blew her nose into a paper tissue and balled it into her handbag.

'I hadn't really thought about it. Would you like me to?'

'Of course I'd like you to! It's very important. And you have six days to think about exactly what.' Her voice cracked, the sandpaper vowels rasping in a throat raw with distress. She resumed her invisible doodling.

'Sure.' He nodded. 'If you think that's a good idea.'

She rolled her eyes, as if the answer should be evident. 'And I think we should go and see him. Together.' She stared at him, her eyes brimming.

He felt the rise of nausea. 'Do you… Do you think that's wise, Mum?'

Her reply was instant, her voice shrill. 'It's not about what's wise, it's about what's right! I *have* to say goodbye to him. My husband, my darling husband…'

'But you said goodbye to him at the hospital,' he reminded her, keeping his tone neutral, 'and he won't know if you go and see his… his body or not.' Saying the word 'body' felt both disrespectful and uncomfortable, reducing his father to a thing. A thing that was now gone. This thought hit him with force in the centre of his breastbone. 'I just don't want you to be upset by seeing him after he's passed, that's not how he would want you to remember him, and I don't think it's healthy that your last image of him might not be a pleasant one.'

'I don't get to choose, Theodore! I can't help what I find, but I *will* do the right thing by him.'

'But that's just it, Mum, who says it's the right thing? There is no right thing. There is only what's right for you. You don't have to do anything you don't want to. I just think—'

'I don't need to know what you think!' Stella raised her voice. 'Don't be like him! Don't tell me what to think or what I can or can't do!'

Theo took a deep breath. 'I'm only trying to look out for you, Mum. Even though this is the worst possible thing that could have happened, try not to forget that we are both going through it and I am trying to make it the best it can be for you. Because I love you.'

'Well, good.' She reached into her handbag for her packet of cigarettes. 'Because the right thing for me is going to see your father before he is laid to rest, and the right thing for you, as his only son, is to come with me. Okay?'

She jammed the cigarette into her mouth, once pretty and full, now pulled thin and puckered with creases which fanned out from her top lip. She held the lighter to the end of the cigarette. It had the usual effect of making him want to smoke, which annoyed him as much as it tested his reserves.

He threw open the kitchen window.

'It's already quite cold in here,' his mother snapped, gathering her fur stole around her narrow shoulders with her cigarette-free hand.

'Yep, but I don't particularly want to breathe your cigarette smoke, so what are we going to do?'

He folded his arms across his chest, holding his position. He watched her draw on her cigarette and wondered how many mothers, when told by their child at a time like this that they loved them, would have answered that they loved them too... He left the room, rubbing his temples to try and alleviate the first signs of a headache.

* * *

The funeral felt flat, predictable, and after Theo had given his rather rushed eulogy, his mind wandered. In the lead-up to the day, he had suspected, in fact hoped, that the service at St Mary's might be the point at which he'd experience the full force of his grief. He wanted to succumb to the tsunami of emotions that he figured must be bubbling inside him somewhere – but no. Instead, he remained almost dazed by the proceedings, unable to relate to the outpouring of grief from his mother, which made him feel more than a little uncomfortable. He had assumed she'd be more contained, a quality she had always admired in her peers, but, as so often, it seemed that such rules only applied to other people.

The speeches were numerous and heartfelt, given by glum-looking old men who stared out over the congregation from the lectern. He suspected they were considering their own fates as much as they were mourning their friend. Several Old Vaizey Boys spoke of a man who was smart, successful and benevolent. But as for the principled family man whose door was always open, Theo hardly recognised that description.

He remembered something Spud had said long ago, when as students they'd strolled round Highgate Cemetery, drunkenly searching for the grave of Karl Marx. '*I wonder where they bury all the shitty people? I've only ever seen gravestones for the good, the beloved and the wise. Do you think there are any that say "My husband was an absolute arsehole"?*' They'd giggled at the thought. He wished the memory hadn't popped into his head right now. Spud had sent a simple card of condolence with a simple message: *Ever onwards and upwards, my friend.* Theo coughed and returned his attention to the service.

Back at his parents' house for the wake, Theo grabbed a drink and, turning, saw Anna walking in. *My Anna.* A smile crept over his face; his default setting whenever he saw her was happiness. She looked beautiful: make-up-free and neat in her black dress with a white crocheted collar. He saw her bite her lip and knew she was feeling nervous. He walked towards her.

'Hey, you.'

'Hi, Theo.' She reached out and squeezed his arm, and he fought the temptation to sweep her into a hug and hold her tight.

'How's Shania doing?' He searched for common ground and was rewarded with the beginnings of a smile.

'Good. Getting close to due date – she's going to be such a great mum. Did you get my card?' She spoke quietly.

'I did, and thank you. And thank you for bringing Mum food and checking on her, she did mention it.' He had studied her words of condolence, scouring them for any hidden note of forgiveness, any hint of a possible reconciliation, but finding none.

'Not a problem. Of course.' She looked down. 'I was genuinely sorry to hear about your dad. I don't think any of us were expecting it. I mean, of course you never are, but you know what I mean.'

'I do, and thank you.' He hated the formality with which he had offered thanks three times in as many minutes.

'How are you doing?' She placed her hand on his chest, a gesture that brought a lump to his throat.

'I'm…' He lifted the tumbler in her direction, as if that might be explanation enough.

'I thought it was a nice service.'

'Yes, it was.'

'And let's face it, Theo, it could have been so much worse.' She pulled a face.

'In what way?'

She leant towards him and he inhaled her particular, intoxicating scent, somewhere between clean laundry and summer. 'Your mum might still have been going through her Jesus phase, which would have meant that Pastor Jules, he of the legendary bootlace tie and magnificent tash, might have been conducting affairs from a shed in Putney.'

Theo laughed, feeling instantly self-conscious that he should find anything funny today but at the same time so glad they could chat like this. 'God, I'd almost forgotten about him! But at least she'd have been able to chat to Dad and find out where he left the key for the shed.' He laughed, recalling some of the pastor's excesses. 'That was some night.'

'Yep.' She gave a faltering smile, as if the mention of a good night inevitably led to thoughts about the bad one, when he had walked out and she had let him. 'Anyway, I'm sure you have to mingle.' She stepped backwards and it took all of his strength not to reach for her and pull her close.

Saskia, his mother's friend, closed in. 'Come on, Theodore, eat up.' She held up a foil platter of bite-sized morsels, all pink and sitting on something crunchy, the sight of which made his stomach lurch.

'I'm okay, thank you.'

Saskia winked, then continued on her mission. 'We have no space in the freezer – I need to make sure everyone in the house consumes at least one of these. Or it will be doggy bags – really, not the done thing!'

The kitchen felt like the safest place to hide, among the

lavender- and mothball-scented crowd of well-wishers. From somewhere in the middle of the throng, his mother let out a loud cry. He looked over to see Nancy, another friend of old, supplying her with tissues and a steady forearm on which to lean. He pushed his way through to where Nancy seemed to have hemmed her in. His mother glanced up at him with an expression of relief.

'Theodore, you remember Nancy?'

'Yes, of course. Hello, Nancy.' He smiled at the woman, whose orange lipstick and green eye shadow reminded him of the crude makeover Miyu had given him with her face paints. 'Thank you so much for coming.'

'I wouldn't have missed it. Peregrine was a dear. Besides, we go way back, your parents and I. I think the last time I saw you, Theo, was on the Riviera – you were no more than a tiddler.' She wagged her finger at him, as if he still merited no more than tiddler status. 'I remember Leopold thought you were a fine young man, not at all giddy-headed like some of a similar age, my own included.' She sighed.

He was embarrassed that this woman and her husband had been present at La Grande Belle. The whole gang must have been aware of his father's drunken infidelity. He felt his face colour. They probably knew a lot more besides. He pictured Xander Beaufort, whom he had half expected to attend today. Poor Alexander, just another aspect of his father's past to be smudged into the background until no one could see it clearly.

His mother seemed indifferent to what her peers did and didn't know. He wondered if it was the fog of old age that coated anything unpleasant with a veneer of acceptability or whether it was simply a deterioration of the memory that meant events were not so sharp, so damaging. Or, of course, it might have been that she now didn't give a shit. His smile faded to a watery imitation.

Nancy raised her voice, as if this might make her point more valid, or perhaps it was that she was used to addressing her friends whose hearing was on the wane. 'I was just saying to your mother that I think it would be a good idea if she went to speak to someone.'

'And I have told Nancy that I have no intention of doing anything of the sort.' Stella spoke determinedly.

'Well...' Nancy gripped her elaborate, bead-encrusted handbag to her chest. 'That's what you say now, but when Leopold died I went to speak to a therapist. It helped me enormously. I needed to make sense of it all, and talking things through made a difference.'

'Darling, I really don't think that kind of thing is for me.' His mother gave a sharp nod, signalling an end to the topic.

Nancy, however, had other ideas. 'And I didn't think it was for me either, and I have to admit, I *was* okay for a while, but when the fuss of the funeral had died down and Douglas and the grandchildren had gone back to Zurich, I was at a loss. I needed to talk to someone who wasn't family and who was going to listen and help me stay on track. And she did. She was wonderful. I really owe her so much – it's hard to explain. Her name is Miss Garcia and she is based in Bloomsbury.'

'Oh, I can just see me popping off to Bloomsbury each week! It's hardly convenient!' his mother scoffed. 'Thank you, Nancy, but no.'

'Well, I shall leave her card on the side here. She is very expensive but worth every penny. She's clever, and all I know is that when I was at my lowest point, she helped me find happiness.'

Nancy's words had a profound effect on Theo. He wondered if it was possible, that there really could be someone, a clever someone, who could help him sort his muddled thoughts, help him find the equilibrium he so craved. He pictured it in that second, his happiness as a rainbow-striped thing hiding under a bed or lurking in the back of a cupboard behind long-forgotten boxes...

'Theo?'

He turned at the sound of Anna's voice and raised his eyebrows in reply.

'I'm off.'

'Right.' He wished they were alone; there was so much more he wanted to say. But as he was ordering his thoughts and summoning the courage to voice them, she called to his mother.

'I shall speak to you soon, Stella.' And just like that, she was gone.

* * *

It felt strange walking into Villiers House again, knowing he was now the last Montgomery in the place. And for possibly the first time, he considered what his parents meant by birthright – would all this be Sophie's? How would that work – a letter like the one Anna had received from her unknown father, Michael Harper, sent after his death? The thought was as depressing as it was cowardly.

He walked past the desk once occupied by Marta, suppressing the unease he felt at the memory of his last sighting of her, and smiled at the young man sitting there.

'We were all very sorry to hear about your father.'

'Thank you.' He stared at the man, trying to recall his name from when they'd been introduced, a while ago now.

'Stephen.'

'Yes, sorry. Thank you, Stephen. My memory…' He tapped his head, as if that was all the explanation required. 'My mind's all over the place at the moment.'

'I can only imagine. Marcus said you'll be taking over your dad's office when you're ready and so I just wanted to say that if there's anything you need or anything we can do…'

'Thank you.'

Theo opened the door to the big room. It smelt of his dad, of woody cologne and nicotine, with a hint of peppermint and whisky, the former used ineffectively to mask the latter. He opened the window and welcomed the cold breeze that whipped around the furniture. The uncomfortable coolness seemed to help clear his thoughts. Settling back into his father's chair felt illicit. He ran his palms over the cracked leather of the arms where the old man's hands had rested over the years, and still his reaction was subdued.

Pulling open the top drawer, he touched his fingers to the black and white picture of his father in his cricket whites. He was kneeling on one knee, one of a team of eleven: two rows of smiling, bright young things, wearing striped cricket caps that proudly displayed their house colours and with the Gothic architecture of Vaizey College providing the impressive backdrop. Anyone could see that those fortunate young men would go places. Theo felt a stirring of sadness, but it was Mr Porter he pictured, bending low and painting the cricket crease with a stubby paintbrush.

'Can I get you a hot drink or anything?'

Theo hadn't heard Stephen come into the room. He popped the photograph back into the drawer and stood, adjusting his jacket. His finger lingered on the feathered talisman that always brought him comfort.

'No, thanks, Stephen. I'm only popping in. I'll come back soon. I need to...' He ran his hand through the air in an arc, hoping this might hint at all the things he needed to do but was currently unable to voice.

'Where shall I put this?' Stephen bent low with a bundle of mail in his hand.

'Oh, just here on the desk is fine.'

'I've given all the corporate stuff to Marcus. These are more personal.'

'That's fine.' Theo smiled and watched Stephen walk slowly out of the room.

He blew out through bloated cheeks and flicked through flyers for executive car services and an offer from the golf club his father and the rest of the board played at. Lastly, he picked up the magazines from the bottom of the pile. A building magazine, several devoted to classic cars or classic boats, past editions of which cluttered up the windowsill in his parents' downstairs bathroom, and there at the very bottom a copy of the *Old Vaizian* with the outline of the most beautiful school buildings plastered all over the front. Theo had never subscribed, being far from interested in anything anyone old or new at the school had to say. For some reason, call it nostalgia, call it sixth sense, he pulled it from the plastic covering and flicked through the glossy pages.

His heart fluttered as his fingers splayed to hold two pages open.

There was a picture of the crooked cottage, pretty much as he remembered it bar a new roof and a fresh lick of paint on the front door and windows. It surprised him, the wave of emotion that broke over him. He lifted the page to his face and read: *Mr Cyrus Porter, former groundsman of Vaizey College, passed away…*

He rolled the magazine, placed it in his pocket and grabbed his car keys.

Nineteen

It felt strangely emotional to wake to the feel of a hard bolster beneath his head. Theo had arrived at the old-fashioned B&B on the outskirts of Dorchester the night before, exhausted, and had slept with the deep-set window slightly open. The chill air, cold bedding and quiet Dorset countryside placed his memories back at Vaizey College. He lay back on the mattress with his arms locked behind his head and wondered, as he did every morning, how Anna was doing. He reached for his phone, hesitated, then placed it back on the nightstand, nervous of calling to say he was thinking of her, mulling over whether or not it was a good idea, aware of how such a small thing had now become so much more complicated.

He showered, then declined the kind offer of breakfast that was, said Mr Whittaker, the portly owner of the establishment, now being kept warm on a hot plate on the Aga, given the late hour. Theo had no appetite and decided he would grab a coffee later. Hitching his bag onto his shoulder, he gave his thanks and offered praise for a night well spent.

'Actually...' He hesitated, twisting his brogue on the patterned hall carpet. 'I don't suppose you could point me in the direction of a good sports and tackle shop?'

A couple of hours later, with the boot of his Mercedes full to bursting, he pulled the tag from his new, waxed-cotton hat, which sat askew on his head, a size too small, and punched in a call to Jody, who was fast becoming his most valuable asset.

'Just to let you know, I won't be in today or tomorrow and maybe not for the rest of the week.'

'You okay, boss?' She cut to the chase.

'Yep, I'm fine. I'm handing you the reins. Keep me posted if you need anything and I'll phone in when I can. Stephen is taking all calls at Villiers House, but do check in with him.'

With Wilson running the build and Jody's remit now extending into all operational areas – she excelled at just about everything she did – the team was coming together nicely. Theo's dreams were becoming a reality. His worries were now giving way to a sense of pride and excitement, as if he could see the finished building and all that it would achieve. And it felt good.

He pumped the gas on his sleek Mercedes and headed off into the countryside. With his window down, he breathed in lungfuls of the clear Dorset air.

It was two full days later that Theo stomped the mud from his boots and climbed into the comfortable front seat of his car before making his way back along the lanes to the homely B&B with the white bolster pillows that he'd been dreaming about.

Bathed now and with a cold beer in his hand, he went down to the library, fancying a read to distract his thoughts.

'Well, good afternoon to you, Mr Montgomery.'

Mr Whittaker the owner was kneeling by the grate, restacking the log pile and filling the coal bucket from the scuttle. 'Nice to have you back, sir. Been off exploring? I saw the wellies outside!'

'I have actually spent the last couple of days thigh-deep in cold water in the middle of bloody nowhere with a fishing rod and a box of warm sandwiches for company.'

Mr Whittaker chuckled loudly. 'Fishing, eh? Did you enjoy it?'

'No.' He shook his head. 'I absolutely hated it. I was cold, miserable and bored witless.'

'Well, I guess it isn't for everyone.'

'I'll give that a true.' He laughed. 'Anyway, thought I'd grab a novel.'

'Be my guest.' Mr Whittaker indicated the shelves and shelves of dusty books, which again made Theo think of school.

Maybe it was a subconscious decision. Theo hadn't planned on going near his old school, but like a scar that screamed to be itched, and given that it was almost en route to St Barnabas' Church, Wrendletown, he couldn't stay away. Slowing the car, he approached with caution, not intending to stop but figuring he would simply have a quick look and drive on. He was surprised to feel none of the angst he associated with the place. It was just a building after all, and a pretty building at that. He thought of Wilson, busily at work on the Bristol project and doing a fine job. It was a revelation that the more time he spent with him, the more he liked him. It was an odd thing to admit that they were slowly building a bridge between colleague and friend.

He pulled the Mercedes across the entrance to the car park, whose gates his father had driven through in his beautiful Aston

Martin on many an occasion. The sense of nostalgia left a lump in his throat. He knew that Peregrine James Montgomery the Third, of Theobald's House, Vaizey College, would have been delighted to see his son returning to the place he'd held so dear.

A car beeped behind him. He looked into his rearview mirror at a man trying to pull in from the lane. Theo raised his hand in acknowledgement and drove forward into the car park. The silver Range Rover rolled past and parked up next to him, disgorging two boys in full games kit. It made him smile, how only a blink ago that had been him, albeit without the enthusiasm these two now showed for getting to their match.

He watched a woman, bent over, struggling with a cardboard box as she lifted it from the boot of an old Golf. And as she straightened he felt his stomach shrink around his bowels.

It was Kitty.

'Jesus Christ!' He swallowed and looked behind him, keen to make a hasty retreat, unable to cope with another painful encounter, unwilling to deal with a rerun of the 'stay away' glare she'd fired at him on the bus. But with the Range Rover tight behind, he was hemmed in. Trapped.

Becoming aware of his stare, Kitty looked up, blinked and squinted, before placing the cardboard box on the ground and walking over. His heart raced and he was unsure of what to do or how to explain his presence. He didn't want a scene, especially not here – he didn't want any more bad memories to heap onto those that already held him captive. He rolled down the window.

'Theo! Oh my God! Theo, it *is* you! I don't believe it!' she called out with something closer to delight than distress, her fingers lying flat against her chest.

'Hello, you.' He beamed, studying her. 'I didn't want you to think…' He ran out of words, not sure what he was apologising for. The image of her on the bus was still crisp in his mind; the way she had implored him with her eyes to stay away.

This was different, felt different. She looked well and wasn't tense in the way she'd seemed then. She stared at him, seemingly at a loss for words. He climbed slowly from the car, aware of his slightly crumpled suit and the mud clinging to the soles of his shoes.

'So which is it – hell or high water?' she asked slowly, her hands on her hips.

'What?' He was confused and embarrassed that he hadn't picked up the thread.

'I seem to remember you saying that those were the only two things that would ever drag you back here to Vaizey.'

She took a step towards him, her face now only inches from his, as if this was the most natural thing in the world and this was exactly the right distance to have between them. But whereas once he might have held his ground, drinking in every bit of her, today he took a step backwards.

'Yes, I probably did say that.' He smiled and shoved his hands in his pockets. 'If you must know, I've been fishing and I'm about to gatecrash a funeral, if you can believe that.'

'Oh I believe it.' She grinned.

'And what about you?' He jerked his head towards the school, expecting Angus to pop up from somewhere at any moment. He decided that he would shake Angus's hand firmly, smile, and meet his eye – getting to know Wilson really had been helpful in laying his school ghosts to rest.

'Just dropping off.'

'Where's Angus?' he asked, looking over her shoulder towards the quad.

'How should I know? On a golf course probably.' She shrugged. 'Did you think we were still together?'

His gut lurched. 'Are you not?'

'No, not for a while. But it works – we share the kids' care and we are quite good friends now, better friends in fact than we ever were when we were married.'

'So that's good?'

'Yes, it's good!' She laughed again. 'Angus is... with a new partner and happy.' She nodded and gave a thin smile. 'So it's all good!' A flicker of nerves seemed to have disturbed her casual demeanour. 'So you're off to a funeral?'

'Yes. Mr Porter's, actually, who used to be the groundsman here.'

'Oh, I remember him! He had a lovely crinkly smile.'

Theo was happy that she remembered this about him. He pictured Mr Porter standing not far from where they were now, with a wheelbarrow full of compost.

'I must admit, I never had you down as the huntin' and fishin' type! What did you catch?'

'Nothing.' He raised his hands and let them fall as he looked skywards. 'Absolutely nothing. I actually went for the stillness, the quiet.'

'Stillness and quiet – that sounds like bliss. Sometimes I can hardly hear myself think.' Theo noted the creasing of her brow. 'Actually, that's not fair, I think I keep busy to stop from thinking.' She bit her bottom lip and he got the impression that she rarely confessed to this.

'Kitty, I've spent the last few years overthinking and it turns out it wasn't actually very good for me.' He nodded.

'Well, good for you, Theodore Montgomery.' Kitty leant a little further in, her voice now barely more than a whisper. 'It is *so* good to see you.'

'It's good to see you too.'

'Are *you* still married, Theo?' Her enquiry was casual.

'Yes, Anna's great – greater.' He looked at the ground, flustered.

'"Great – greater"? Gosh, you really didn't pay attention in Mr Reeves's class, did you! That is terrible English!' She threw back her head and laughed.

He laughed too, glad of the joviality, which erased any nervousness.

There was a beat of awkward silence as both of them allowed their façades to slip.

'That letter I sent...' she began, taking a deep breath.

Theo nodded. What could he say?

'It was a very difficult time for me.' She shoved her hands in her pockets and held his gaze.

'It became a very difficult time for me too,' he acknowledged, quietly.

'I never in a million years imagined... after that one time...' She pulled a face as if the words were physically painful. 'I was about to get married... There was so much going on in my head.' She tapped her forehead.

'You don't need to explain. I've spent a lot of hours thinking it through and I get it. I totally see why you didn't want anything to do with me, didn't want me in our... your child's life. Why would you? I'm hardly good father material. I had nothing to offer.' *Weirdo...*

'Oh my God, Theo, is that what you thought?' Tears filled her eyes.

He nodded.

Kitty shook her head, her mouth twisted as if she was trying to stop herself from crying. 'No! No, it wasn't that at all. I've never hidden the truth from Sophie – or Angus. Quite the opposite. You, Theodore, are the kindest, sweetest, gentlest friend I ever had. You are smart and funny and any child would be lucky to have you in their life, so lucky. It was never about you! It was only ever about me. I couldn't see any further than what I was going through. I robbed you.'

An inexplicable feeling of weightlessness came over Theo. He exhaled and leant back on the car, fearing that if he didn't, he just might fall. 'But… But then on the bus…' He faltered.

Kitty shook her head. 'Angus and I were falling apart, I was pregnant with Oliver, and little Soph…' She smiled up at him. 'It would have been too much for Soph right then, and too much for me.' She sniffed. 'I am so sorry, Theo. I was young and stupid and frightened when I wrote to you, and if I could—'

'Mum! Mum, have you got my hockey stick?'

Kitty whipped her head round and smiled through her tears at the confident girl striding towards them.

'Why are you crying?' Sophie wrinkled her nose with embarrassment.

'I'm not.' Kitty swiped away her tears and pulled her daughter towards her. She took her face inside her hands and kissed her nose. 'Sophie, this man… This is…' Emotion stopped the words from forming.

Theo stepped forward and held out his hand.

The young girl with the clear skin, dark curly hair and brown eyes placed her hand confidently in his palm. 'Hello.' She smiled. 'I'm Sophie. Sophie Montgomery Thompson.'

*

Theo didn't often feel the need to give thanks, but as he parked the car and looked up towards the heavens, he closed his eyes. 'My name! She has my name! My daughter, my little girl, Sophie – what a wonderful, wonderful, thing!'

Gathering himself, he wondered if he had come to the right place. There were very few cars around and the beautiful moss-covered Norman church looked strangely quiet. He couldn't help but compare the scene to his father's funeral, when clusters of well-dressed mourners had stood outside the church in Barnes, dabbing at tears and shaking hands with gusto. He flattened his suit lapels and adjusted his tie before pushing on the heavy arched wooden door. There was only a handful of people inside. A couple of elderly folk were already in situ in the front pews and one or two others, men mainly, had taken seats further back. Theo only glanced at them, avoiding eye contact, feeling like an interloper on this sad day.

A keen-looking moon-faced vicar walked over and handed him a single-page order of service. Theo took it and nodded his thanks. As he gazed down at the black and white photograph of Mr Porter he felt a rush of emotion. He coughed to clear his throat and sat up straight, unable to take another look for fear of losing control in public, in front of strangers. The old man in the picture, 'the Fishing-Fly Guy', as Anna called him, looked thinner and very old, but his smile and the crinkle of kindness around his eyes were exactly the same. He was wearing a tweed cap and Theo pictured him raising the front and scratching his head, deep in thought, revealing the dark tan line across his brow.

Music began to play. Theo stood and smiled to hear the

faint strains of Elgar's 'Nimrod' coming from the speakers as the simple wooden coffin was wheeled up the aisle. The music was most fitting, Theo thought, as he recalled snippets of their conversation about Mr Porter's wartime service: '*We were all as scared and desperate as each other. And let me tell you, those that didn't make it home were mourned by their families just the same, goodies and baddies alike.*' For the second time that day, Theo's tears threatened.

The vicar followed the coffin to the altar, then stood in front of the grand brass lectern and spread his arms.

'Welcome, all, to St Barnabas on this sad day when we say goodbye to Cyrus. But I would like to remind you that it is also a happy day, as we celebrate his long life.'

Theo looked around and counted the congregation. There were only thirteen of them in total, and that bothered him. He wondered how different today might have been, how crowded the pews, if Mr Porter's wife, Merry, had lived and they'd gone on to have children, even grandchildren. He thought then of his own dad, who also never got to be called Grandpa, and again his whole being was filled with the image of Sophie.

The vicar continued. 'Cyrus Porter was a man who liked to garden.'

As Theo listened to him reading from his crib sheet, he thought how shabby that was – how hard would it have been to learn a few things by heart?

'He liked to garden and indeed won first prize three years running for his marrows in the village harvest festival competition. He had been a soldier in his youth and fought in France, before taking up the post of gardener at the prestigious Vaizey College, a much revered establishment in our county.'

Theo felt a flash of heat on his skin and, as if powered by something bigger than him, he stood and shuffled to the end of the pew. He walked steadily down the aisle, aware that all eyes were on him as his shoes, now wiped clean, clip-clopped on the tiled floor. He approached the lectern, looking first at the vicar and then at the elderly men and women in the front pew.

'It wasn't France.' He leant in.

'I'm sorry?' the vicar asked with a tense, fixed smile.

'Mr Porter fought his war in Italy. That would have mattered to him. It would have mattered a lot.'

'I'm so sorry.' The vicar coloured. 'I can only go on the information I've been given.' He held up the flimsy sheet of paper that for Theo only added insult to injury.

'Might I?' He nodded at the lectern.

The vicar looked towards an old woman in the front pew, who looked bemused but nonetheless gave a slow nod.

Theo took the vicar's place and gripped the side of the brass stand.

'My name is Theodore Montgomery. Mr Porter was the groundsman at Vaizey College and that's where I met him.' He cursed the tightening of his throat and coughed before resuming. 'He was so much more than that, however, to a young boy who needed a friend, who needed an ally and an escape. He taught me...' Theo was only vaguely aware of the tears that now coursed down his cheeks. 'He taught me more about life than anyone else, before or since. His voice has lived in my head since I was a boy, giving me advice long after I lost contact with him.' At this he felt a stab of pain as sharp as it had been on that day he'd found the crooked cottage empty. He bowed his head and wiped his face with the back of his hand, seeing himself as a fourteen-year-old falling to his knees and howling. '*My friend! I'm sorry!*'

'He was so much more than the groundsman of Vaizey College, so much more than a man who grew prize marrows.' He paused again to regain what composure he could, but his eyes flamed and his tears spilled.

He reached for his suit lapel and turned it over to reveal the small gold pin decorated with a fishing fly of green and blue feathers above a square red bead.

'He was like a father to me.'

He gripped the sides of the lectern as the breath stuttered in his throat and the tsunami of emotion that had been swelling inside him for so long now found its release. The hush in the church was broken by the creak of a pew near the back. A portly man in his late fifties stood and walked forward until he reached Theo's side. He turned over his lapel to reveal a similar fishing fly and shook Theo's hand before turning to the assembled mourners and speaking through a mouth contorted with emotion.

'He was like a father to me too.'

And then a third man came forward; his fishing fly sat proudly on his shirt. 'He was like a father to me,' he offered in a rich Middle Eastern accent.

Then up came a fourth, a fifth, a sixth and a seventh, all of them standing in a line behind the coffin of the man who had scooped them up when they had needed him the most and cared for them when kindness had been in short supply. Their collective tears turned to laughter as they stood shoulder to shoulder, the now grown-up sons of very, very busy people.

Each had thought they were the only one.

'Seemingly Cyrus was a most wonderful man!' The vicar stood next to them, giving words to the air of celebration that now filled the church. 'How very lucky you all were to have him guide you when you were at your most vulnerable.'

'Yes.' Theo nodded, still unable to stem his sadness. 'Very lucky.'

It no longer mattered that there were only thirteen people present. The love those thirteen felt for Mr Porter could have filled a cathedral built for a thousand mourners.

Later, as he threw dirt into the freshly dug hole that had received his dear friend, Theo felt a strange sense of elation.

'Mr Montgomery?' a voice called from the church path as he was making his way back to the car.

'Yes?' He turned to stare at the elderly woman from the front pew, who was supported by a nurse on one side.

'I'm Nelda, Merry's sister,' she explained in a rasping voice. 'Cyrus was my brother-in-law.'

'Yes, of course. Hello!' He shook her hand warmly; the skin was paper thin and cool beneath his touch. 'I'm sorry if I…' He pointed towards the church, feeling a little awkward now, in the daylight, that he had taken centre stage without invitation.

'No, don't be sorry.' She shook her head and smiled at him. 'Cyrus would have been so very proud, touched, I know. I have something for you. He didn't leave any instructions, but my son found an envelope in a box and it has your name on it. Truth be told, I wouldn't have known where to begin if you hadn't shown up today – I would probably have discarded it. But that's by the by, because here you are.'

'Yes, here I am.' He smiled. 'Where is it, the envelope?'

'Back at his house. Only five minutes' drive.'

Theo followed Nelda's Ford along the winding lanes until they came to the village of Marlstonbury. Having left the nurse in the pub, he and Nelda made their way slowly across the village green, Nelda holding onto his arm.

'I'm glad the rain held off. It's turned out nice after all.' She waved her stick towards the sky.

'Yes, it has. Is your son here today?'

'No, he had to go back to Glasgow – that's where he lives now. So far away. I do miss him.'

He thought of Spud.

'Here we are, at Cyrus's house.' She pointed ahead and there, next to a paddock, sat a small cottage, not quite crooked but not far off. 'Not quite sure what we'll do with it – sell it, I suppose.' Nelda pulled out a key from her handbag and opened the front door.

Theo stepped into the narrow hallway. The peculiar aroma – of earth, smoke, oil and wood – instantly took him back to the day when, at seven years old, a cottage like this had provided him with a refuge, a home.

'Do you know, I once slept in the little house Mr Porter lived in at Vaizey College. It was in the grounds of the school and it was very much like this. I felt safe and cosy and I remember thinking how lovely it must be to wake up like that every single day of your life. I was about fourteen.'

'Did you not have parents?' she asked matter-of-factly.

'I did, yes, but they were… they were very busy people.'

She gave a nod of understanding.

'How did Merry die? If you don't mind me asking.'

Nelda inhaled sharply, as if the event was still fresh or at least still hurt as much as ever.

'It was a terrible thing for us all. She was my older sister and she was an adventurer. It's a sad story. She was a newly qualified nurse and got caught in a bombing raid on Liverpool during the war. She was injured but didn't die. My family were of course overjoyed that she'd survived, but we didn't understand just how badly she'd been damaged. She was very quiet, stoic and I like to think she hung on to see Cyrus home safe, but she was never properly well again and she died three weeks after he came home from Italy. I was always glad they'd had that short time together.'

'I'm sorry.'

'Long, long time ago. Another world.' She patted his arm before wandering into the adjoining sitting room.

He let his eyes scan the shelves crammed with books, recognising many of the dusty knick-knacks and ornaments that sat in a row on the mantelpiece. He looked through to the tiny kitchen and there on top of the cupboard sat the green enamel kettle. He again cursed the tears that gathered.

'Here we are then.' Nelda held out her hand. In it lay a cream-coloured envelope with his name inscribed on the front in handwriting he recognised.

'Thank you,' he whispered.

Nelda bent forward and held him in a loose hug. 'He would have been so happy to hear what you said today. And who knows, maybe he did?'

Theo smiled and considered this.

He abandoned his car in Muckleford just as the sun broke though the clouds and set off along the bridleway, climbing steadily. The track opened up and he trod the incline with his hands in his pockets until eventually, with his breath coming in short bursts, he reached Jackman's Cross. His chest heaved and the cool wind stung his skin. The view was every bit as breathtaking as he remembered from his walk there with Mr Porter. He let his eyes rove the horizon, taking in the spires of distant churches and the glorious swathe of green fields. Tucking his mac beneath his legs, he sat down on the damp earth of the hill and reached into his pocket for his letter.

The envelope opened with ease, the old glue having yellowed and turned quite brittle. Carefully, he extracted a lined sheet of A4 paper, torn from a gummed pad. The top line read:

The World through the Eyes of a Blackbird
by Theodore Montgomery.

Oh my God! My homework assignment!

Theo paused and took a deep breath, exhaling slowly before holding the paper up to his face and reading it. He devoured the first two paragraphs with a tremble to his lip and a clamp around his heart. But it was the final few lines of the third paragraph that really made him smile. His tears fell as the wind lifted his hair and his spirits.

As I make my way over fields and lakes, marvelling at the changing landscape below me, I realise that what I learn year on year is what makes me stronger. With strength comes confidence and with confidence comes the ability to be the master of my life, to own my happiness and to make the changes necessary to be the best I can be. And that is why I sing! I sing loudly! Letting the world know that I might be small in the scheme of things, I might be just a bird, but what do I bring to the world? I bring this, my own unique song.

Theo sat for some minutes with tears in his eyes until he felt able to do what he'd been wanting to do for a very long time. He lifted his phone from his pocket and with a sense that time was chasing him, he dialled the number for home.

'Hello?'

'Anna?'

'Theo! Oh my God, I've been so worried about you. Radio silence is never good! Are you okay?'

'I'm...' The strength of his emotions made speech almost impossible. 'I'm more than okay,' he managed.

'Well, that's good to hear.' Her relief was palpable. 'I... I found your note in the study. Your list – your mum told me where to find it and I love it!'

He could hear the joy in her voice and it warmed him. 'You did?'

'I did! I really did. You alphabetised me! You did my game.'

'I tried.' He laughed. 'It was a long time ago, but I wanted so badly to get it right. I wanted you to know how much I loved you, how much I love you.'

'Oh, Theo, it's perfect. It...' There was a hesitation and Theo thought he heard a sob. 'It... couldn't have been written by anyone but you, Theo. Only you know me that well.'

It was Theo's turn now to try and mask his sobs.

'I've missed you so much, Theo, and it seems such a waste, all this... being apart.' She sniffed down the line. 'I love the things you wrote about me. They've made me happy.' The sound of another sob. 'H for happy...'

'I want to make you H for happy, Anna. I really do.'

There was a pause, then Anna changed tack. 'Are you outside somewhere?' she asked.

'Yes, I'm on the top of a hill looking at the whole wide world.'

'Are you drunk?' she asked. 'You sound... different. More... emotional. Has something happened?'

'I'm not drunk, no, but I do feel as if a mist has lifted. That's the only way I can describe it. I went fishing and then I went to Mr Porter's funeral, and I even visited Vaizey College, and something strange has happened to me... I feel like I can see clearly for the first time.'

'In what way?'

Her tone was heartbreakingly hopeful, and he pictured her clutching the phone to her ear, wondering what on earth he was going to say next.

'I met Sophie. I met her, Anna, properly met her – totally by chance – and she is incredible. And I want you to meet Sophie. I want to grow up, Anna. I want the responsibility of being the best husband I can possibly be. I'm not going to let the past shape me, not any more. Someone...' He swallowed. 'Someone whose opinion I valued above all others—'

'Let me guess – Mr Porter, the Fishing-Fly Guy?'

'Yes!' He laughed. 'The Fishing-Fly Guy. He's just told me that I need to be the master of my own life, to take charge, be confident and watch the changes. I need to cut away the shadows of my childhood.'

'Oh my God, he is right, Theo, he is absolutely right, and you can do it, *we* can do it! I have Shania and the twins here and, oh, Theo, seeing those two new lives begin to blossom, it's such a pleasure and a privilege. You will fall for them just as I have,

I know you will. Your Fishing-Fly Guy is absolutely right, my love – the universe is a marvel.'

'Yes, it is, and I want us to discover it together, my Anna. My love. I'm coming home. I'm coming home to make a plan. We should try and be parents, Anna, just like you've always said we should. No ifs or buts. There are kids that need guidance, kids like you and kids like me. We will try our very hardest and one way or another we will make our family. I'm going to be a dad, and you are going to be the best mum ever.'

'Theo…' she managed. 'My Theo.'

'I'll be there as soon as I can. I'm coming home.' He spoke quickly. 'I am sorry, so sorry, that I held back, that I didn't give you all of me, but I will make it up to you, I promise. We have time – we have all the time in the world. Mr Porter was eighty when he died – that means we aren't even halfway through! My Anna, we're going to live the best life!'

His energy was infectious. 'My Theodore, you have no idea how happy I am right now. Drive safely. I love you!'

'I love you too.'

'And I will be waiting for you, right here. Griff and me.'

Theo placed his phone back in his pocket and looked out towards the hedgerows, where blackbirds, dunnocks and wrens were busy feeding their young and keeping their nests nice and cosy, doing all they needed for their little families to flourish.

He stood and reached for the keys in his pocket.

'I'm coming home, Anna! I'm coming home.'

Epilogue

2002

'There you are! Thank goodness. I was about to send Griff out with a little barrel of brandy around his neck to come and find you!' Anna shouted as Theo walked through the front door.

He watched her disappear from view, scooting across the tiled floor in her socks, heading towards the fridge while holding a dish laden with some goodies she had no doubt been prepping for most of the afternoon.

Griff barked his approval at Theo's homecoming and, as ever, it made him smile. His faithful friend.

'Where on earth have you been?' she called.

'I've been walking along the river.' His voice was calm, steady.

'I don't blame you, escaping the madhouse.' She smiled. 'You're nervous,' she whispered.

'I really am. I went out mainly to call Spud, but he just said I needed to pull up my big-boy pants and get on with it.'

She laughed. 'Wise advice.'

Walking slowly into the kitchen, he felt his heart swell with love at the sight of the Easter table, beautifully set with sparkling glassware and polished silver cutlery. The radio was burbling away in the background and the sumptuous smell of roast lamb wafted from the range. Anna was going to so much trouble.

She pulled the blue linen dishcloth from where it hung on the range door and wiped her dainty hands on it. 'You don't have to be nervous, Theo. It's all going to be fine, I promise. You are surrounded by people who love you.' She stood on tiptoe and kissed his mouth.

'Anna...'

'Yes, love?' She scooted in the opposite direction, off to fetch a small spoon from the cutlery drawer.

'Thank you.'

'For what?' She looked up at him with a wrinkle at the top of her nose.

'For making it easy. For being you.'

She beamed, batting away the compliment. 'I'd do anything for you. For us.'

'We need kitchen paper in here!' came the shout from the sitting room.

Anna grabbed the roll and walked briskly in response to Shania's call. It was a sight of near chaos that greeted her. Joshua and David, her twins, now boisterous toddlers, were running off the effects of several Easter eggs, chasing each other around the sofa. One or both had inadvertently knocked over Stella's rather large gin and tonic, which had been perched on a side table. Samuel, their dad, smiled awkwardly. 'Sorry, Anna.'

'Don't be daft! I love having them here. And, trust me, when you four are all back in St Lucia in a few days' time, I will be longing for the sound of them running around, trashing our home!'

Shania laughed and smiled at her friend, knowing it was the truth.

'In a few days, you say? Well, there we are,' Stella shouted, her expression indicating that the exit of these little human wrecking balls couldn't come soon enough.

'I was just telling Shania that the sooner she gets these kids hooked on TV, the more life she'll get back.' Melissa pointed at Nicholas and Isabel as if to prove her point. Both lay on their tums with legs kicked up, chins on upturned palms, staring at the TV screen.

'I'm doing my level best to keep them away from the TV.' Shania sighed.

'Well, good luck with that!' Standing in front of the fireplace, Gerard, Melissa's husband, raised his wine glass in a show of support. 'Although I guess if I lived in an island paradise, I might find things to do other than watch rugby on TV.'

It was Samuel's turn to laugh. Theo thought he looked smug, happy, and this feeling he understood only too well. 'Come and see us any time – you know that. We love having guests.'

'Do I have to bring this lot or can I come alone?' Gerard ducked, trying to avoid the cushion expertly hurled by his wife.

Shania looked up at Anna and Theo and smiled broadly. 'All these joys await you, you lucky things! Any more news from the adoption agency?'

Theo glanced at Anna and winked at her. 'Well… we've officially passed the "suitable parents" test, apparently, so the next step will be when the agency calls us with a possible match.' He grinned. 'We've asked to adopt two kids – siblings, if possible. We might even get twins, like you guys! So we'll be wanting lots of tips, that's for sure.'

'Oi oi! There's a cab just pulled up!' Sylvie shouted from the chair by the window, a position she liked to occupy, being perfect for watching the comings and goings of the street. As usual she had her slippers on her feet and a mug of tea in her hands and was ready with a running commentary.

Theo looked at Anna, noting the almost imperceptible nod of her head. *I've got this...* He gripped her hand and the two walked into the hallway and threw open the front door.

'Aaaagh!' Anna screamed and ran down the path to meet her cousin Jordan, who looked immaculate in his navy Crombie and with a soft grey cashmere scarf knotted at his neck. 'Goldpie!' She jumped into his embrace and he twirled her around with his arms clamped around her.

'I love you so much!' he yelled to the sky.

Levi, his partner, shook his head with barely disguised embarrassment and walked towards Theo with his hand outstretched. 'How you doing, Theo?' he offered sedately.

'Good, good, Levi. It's great to see you.' He took Levi's hand into both of his.

'Where is he?' Jordan shouted as he plopped Anna onto the floor.

Theo braced himself as Jordan ran at him, almost knocking him sideways, and wrapped him in a tight hug. 'Have you missed me?' Jordan squeaked.

'More than I can say.' Theo screwed his face up as Jordan planted a kiss on his cheek before releasing him.

'Are Lisa and Micky here?' he enquired after Anna's half siblings.

'Not yet, they're having lunch with their mum and then coming over later. Don't worry, you'll see them. Be warned, Kaylee is hoping for a singing lesson!' Anna grimaced.

'Bless her, it would be my pleasure. Are the babies here?' Jordan clapped.

'They are, but they're not babies any more – they're three and running around like loons after too much sugar.'

'Oh goody!' Jordan trilled. 'That is *exactly* how I plan on spending today!'

Theo ushered the new arrivals into the sitting room and Anna followed with a cold bottle of champagne and two glasses.

'Everyone!' Theo called the room to attention. 'Most of you already know, but this is Jordan and Levi!'

Sylvie dragged her attention away from the window. 'Oh, the Americans! Aren't you two a couple of erm… a couple of…' She clicked her fingers as if the word evaded her.

It seemed to Theo that the room held its collective breath, wondering what the word might be and considering when it would be appropriate to jump in.

'Actors!' Sylvie shouted.

'Yes!'

'Actors!

'We act!'

'Actors!'

Laughter rippled around the room.

'Not that well known, I would suggest, if my son finds it necessary to tell us their names. I don't think Humphrey Bogart or Robert Redford would have to be similarly introduced!' Stella downed what was left of her G&T.

Anna was just opening her mouth to reply when the front doorbell rang.

'Oh my God!' She put her hand over her mouth and pulled up her shoulders. Theo's heart sang to see her joyful anticipation.

Untying her pinny, she threw it over the back of a chair and ran her fingers through her hair.

'Come on – together.' He reached for her hand and the two of them walked slowly down the hallway, side by side.

Theo opened the door.

There was a split second of silence as they all allowed the enormity of the moment to sink in.

It was Kitty who made the first move, as she walked in. 'Hello, Theo! Good to see you. And Anna, so lovely to meet you.'

Theo watched as the two women held each other in a brief but sincere embrace. He felt nothing but relief.

'You too.' Anna smiled. 'I feel as if I know you already, I really do.'

'Same.' Kitty nodded.

The two women turned and stood next to Theo and all three stared at the teenage girl hovering nervously on the doorstep.

'And you must be Sophie.' Anna, his beloved Anna, took the girl's hand and guided her into their home.

Sophie nodded, embarrassed, awkward and a little overcome.

'This is quite a day for you, for us all,' Anna offered with her customary kindness, and Theo felt another rush of love for her.

'Hello, Sophie.' He smiled at the beautiful girl and felt as if he was dreaming. *Here she was, in their house!* He had to curb his instinct to rush ahead, give her a key!

'Hi...' Sophie hesitated. 'I don't really know what to call you.' She looked over to her mum.

'Whatever you're comfy with, darling.' Kitty winked at her girl.

It was permission of sorts and Theo was thankful. 'Theo is fine,' he managed, his voice full of emotion.

'Or Dad-Theo,' Anna suggested without embarrassment. 'I know you already have a proper dad – Angus – but as someone who grew up with no one I could call Dad, I can only imagine how wonderful it might be to be able to say that to two people.'

Sophie beamed at Anna. 'Yes, you're right.' She looked at Theo. 'Hi, Dad-Theo.'

'Hello, Sophie,' he repeated, just for the sheer joy of being able to address her by name.

Anna placed her hands on Kitty and Sophie's backs and ushered them towards the sitting room. 'Now, be warned, the house is bursting at the seams and we are an eclectic bunch, but everyone is very much looking forward to meeting you.'

'I'm looking forward to meeting them.' Sophie spoke with confidence. 'And I'm used to eclectic bunches. My family – my... my other family – we're all really weird.'

'Then I think you're going to fit in just fine.' Anna laughed.

Theo gulped down the tears that gathered and gazed at the girl who looked a lot like him. His tears, however, were for his wife, his beautiful Anna, who had given him the biggest gift in the world.

She made him feel like an ordinary man and not in the slightest bit weird; the kind of man, in fact, who was capable of being a dad.